Maverick
by Joan Hohl

Praise for Joan Hohl

"A compelling storyteller who weaves her tales with verve, passion and style."
—*New York Times* bestselling author
Nora Roberts

"Joan Hohl is a top gun!"
—*New York Times* bestselling author
Catherine Coulter

"Joan Hohl writes romance that goes straight to the heart."
—*New York Times* bestselling author
Jayne Ann Krentz

"Writers come and writers go. Few have the staying power, the enthusiastic following of Joan Hohl. That's talent!"
—*USA TODAY* bestselling author
Kasey Michaels

The Playboy's Passionate Pursuit
by Emilie Rose

ᗡᏳᎧᏱ

"I want my five minutes."

Toby's words stopped Amelia in her tracks.
Adrenaline raced through her veins, flushing
her skin and quickening her breath. She'd
foolishly wagered with Toby because she'd
believed winning was a sure thing. She'd been
wrong.

He stopped behind her, close but not touching
"What's my penance?" she asked.

"Eager, sugar?"

He nuzzled her temple, pressing his face to
hers. Soft lips teased the shell of her ear. The
nip of his teeth on her earlobe startled a gasp
from her. Toby's breath teased the sensitive
skin beneath her right ear and his chest
moulded her back. Sparks scattered through
her bloodstream.

"Toby, this is not a good idea." She couldn't
give in to him. Not now.

"You agreed. Five minutes. Of whatever I
want."

Available in July 2008
from Mills & Boon® Desire™

Married to His Business
by Elizabeth Bevarly
&
Six-Month Mistress
by Katherine Garbera

ᗡᏇᏇᏇᏇ

Maverick
by Joan Hohl
&
The Playboy's Passionate Pursuit
by Emilie Rose

ᗡᏇᏇᏇᏇ

The Executive's Vengeful Seduction
by Maxine Sullivan
&
Rich Man's Revenge
by Tessa Radley

Maverick
JOAN HOHL

The Playboy's Passionate Pursuit
EMILIE ROSE

MILLS & BOON®
Pure reading pleasure™

*First published in Great Britain 2008
by Harlequin Mills & Boon Limited,
Eton House, 18-24 Paradise Road, Richmond, Surrey TW9 1SR*

The publisher acknowledges the copyright holders of the individual works as follows:

Maverick © Joan Hohl 2007
The Playboy's Passionate Pursuit
© Emilie Rose Cunningham 2007

ISBN: 978 0 263 85907 2

51-0708

*Printed and bound in Spain
by Litografia Rosés S.A., Barcelona*

MAVERICK
by
Joan Hohl

Dear Reader,

Hi once again, friends. Yes, yes, I know. It's been a long time since my last book, some of you may think much too long. I hope! Well, as I am human and not a machine, parts wear out, I run low on fuel and at times need some TLC. Hey! Maybe I am a machine. A machine who needed a part removed recently. I'm recovering, but each passing year adds another to the score, and, sad as I am to admit it, my score is getting pretty high and I'm slowing down.

As you have likely noticed from the back cover, our hero in the story is, yet again, one of the Wolfe family, or Wolfe pack if you will! Any reader who has read any of my BIG, BAD WOLFE series knows the Wolfes are strong, honest men devoted to their profession – the law.

But Tanner is the maverick of the family. He follows his own rules. Tanner is a bounty hunter, and he does very well at it, thank you. Still, he has never broken the law, nor killed a man. And he always works alone.

Until the lovely Brianna knocks on his door…

Thanks for your loyalty all these years. I truly appreciate it.

Best,

Joan Hohl

JOAN HOHL

is a *New York Times* bestselling author of dozens of books. She has received numerous awards for her work, including the Romance Writers of America Golden Medallion Award. In addition to contemporary romance, this prolific author also writes historical and time travel romances. Joan lives in eastern Pennsylvania with her husband and family.

For Melissa Jeglinski

For all the patience and understanding
she has shown me.

Thanks, Kid!

One

All things considered, she was a traffic stopper.

Tanner raised a questioning eyebrow at the breathtaking woman standing beyond the threshold of the apartment door he had just opened at the buzz of the doorbell.

"Mr. Wolfe?"

A tingle attacked the base of Tanner's spine. Her voice had the effect of warm honey trickling down the length of his back. Her eyes were the color of brandy, her hair a rich, deep, glossy burgundy wine. Combined, they warmed him as if he'd imbibed the drinks themselves.

"Yes." He was rather proud of the steady, almost bored sound of his voice, when bored was the last thing he was feeling. Hot, yes. Bored, no. He lifted one brow. She stood there, all five foot nine or so, slim and classically beautiful, dressed casually but expensively.

One deep, dark eyebrow arched, mirroring his action, as she asked, "May I come in?"

The tingle he felt grew into a sizzle. Damn, it had been a long time since a woman had had such a strong effect on him at first meeting. Come to think about it, no woman had ever had this strong an effect on him.

"Do you have a name?" He injected a droll note into his voice.

"Brianna Stewart," she answered, extending a slim-fingered hand to him. "Now, may I come in?"

Curious—about the woman's courage in entering the apartment of a stranger and about several other things—he took her hand, repressed a shiver, then nodded and stepped back, swinging the door wide as he did so.

"Thank you." Head high, spine straight as an arrow, she walked past him into the neat-as-a-pin living room, her stride relaxed, easy. The late-morning sun's rays slanting through the wide window struck fiery lights off her slightly-redder-than-auburn hair.

"What can I do for you, Ms. Stewart?" he asked. Other than sweep you up and carry you to my bedroom. Telling himself to grow up, he repressed the errant thought.

"May I sit down?" She made a graceful move of one hand to indicate his favorite plush leather recliner.

"Yeah, sure." What else could he say? "Would you like a cup of coffee?" He wasn't about to impart the information that it was the first pot he'd brewed since rolling out of the sack a half hour before she rang his chimes, so to speak. Hell, his hair was still damp from his shower.

"I'd like that, yes, thank you." She smiled.

He suppressed a groan. As slight and polite as her smile had been, it dazzled his senses. What in blazes was wrong with him? he chided himself. She was just another woman. Okay, another gorgeous woman. Wasn't she?

"You're welcome. It'll only take a minute." Avoiding his mental question and telling himself to pull it together, Tanner escaped into the kitchen. Well, he had hoped to escape.

She followed him into the room. "I hope you don't mind, but we can talk in here just as well."

That's easy for you to say. Keeping the thought to himself, where it belonged, Tanner said, "No, I don't mind. Have a seat." He flicked a hand at the retro yellow-and-white chrome-and-Formica kitchen set. "Would you like something with your coffee…some cookies, a muffin, a scone?" Me?

Knock it off, Wolfe.

Sliding onto a plastic-covered chair, she started to shake her head but hesitated, saying, "What kind of scones do you have?"

"Blueberry," he said, removing two diner-type mugs from a wall cabinet.

"Yes, I would. Thank you again." She smiled as if amused at herself. "Blueberry is my favorite."

Damned if her full-blast smile didn't cause a ripple along his nervous system. Lord, the woman was lethal. There was no way he'd admit to her that blueberry was his favorite, too. Even though it was likely obvious, as that was what he had to offer. "Want it warmed?"

"Yes, please." She dazzled him with another smile.

Tanner grabbed two scones into paper napkins, shoved them into the micro and pressed the buttons for twelve seconds. He set the steaming mugs on the table while the micro hummed. The timer beeped while he was setting a carton of milk, a sugar bowl and two spoons on the table.

"Want butter or jam on that?" he asked, going to retrieve the pastries.

She shook her head, swirling the smooth red mass around her shoulders. On the spot, Tanner decided he loved red hair. It was a bit of a surprise, as he had always thought he preferred blondes…even though he didn't consider himself much of a gentleman.

Settling his six foot four inch frame opposite her, he bluntly got to the point. "Okay, now, what brings you to Durango, and what can I do for you?" he said, certain she wanted something from him. The question was, what?

"I want you to find a man for me," she said, her voice calm, almost serene.

What's wrong with *me?* Tanner didn't give

voice to that thought, either. He knew what she meant. "Why?"

Her voice went hard. "Because he needs to be found."

He smiled—almost. "Why, and by whom?"

Her eyes went as hard as her tone. "By my sister, my father, my mother, me and the law."

Now they were getting somewhere. "The law?" Right up his alley. "For what?"

She drew a deep breath, as if to contain a long-simmering anger. "For the rape and murder of one young woman and the attempted rape of another."

"Who sent you to me?"

Brianna raised her eyebrows. "You are a very well-known bounty hunter with an excellent reputation."

"Uh-huh." This time he did smile, wryly, repeating, "Who sent you to me?"

"Your cousins."

He gave her a bored look. "Honey, I have a lot of cousins. Give me some names."

She exhaled a weary-sounding, much-put-upon sigh. "Matt and Lisa."

"Ah, the Amazon twins." He smiled fondly at the memory of his six-foot, gorgeous, only female cousins, the former cop, Matilda, called Matt, and the legal eagle, Lisa. His smile vanished as quickly. "How do you know them?"

"Lisa's my lawyer. She introduced me to Matt," she explained. "But I already knew your mother. She was my history professor in college."

The fond smile hovered once more, while his eyebrows rose in question. "You're from Sprucewood?" It was his hometown in Pennsylvania, before he'd moved out west to Colorado. His mother, the history fanatic, taught the subject at Sprucewood College. His father was chief of the Sprucewood Police.

"No." She shook her head before clarifying. "Not really. I'm from the, er, suburbs."

Tanner wondered about the slight hesitation but let it pass for the moment. "And the man you want found is Jay Minnich. Right?" Before she could respond, he said, "Are you the attempted-rape victim?"

"No." She set her hair rippling again with a sharp shake of her head. "My younger sister, Danielle. The young woman he murdered was Dani's best friend."

"So I read." Tanner nodded.

"Will you find him for us?" Her soft voice held a tinge of pleading. "There's a bounty," she quickly added.

"I know—ten grand." His tone was dismissive, as though ten thousand dollars was nothing. "Posted by your father, the founder and president of Sprucewood Bank."

She frowned at his tone but responded mildly. "Yes, but my father has raised the bounty."

"When?" Surely Tanner would have heard about the bounty being raised if it had been announced. It hadn't.

"Now."

"Say again?" He felt he had somehow missed something.

A small, slightly superior smile touched her soft mouth. "Let me explain."

"Explain away," he invited, raising his mug to his lips and staring intently at her over the rim.

"Dani is an emotional wreck." Her voice was low, sad. "Ever since the…awful events, she has withdrawn into herself. She's terrified that terrible man will come back, find her and kill her, as she was the one who identified him. She won't go out of the house…ever." She paused to sigh before continuing. "In fact, she seldom leaves her bedroom, which she keeps locked at all times. Even her family members have to identify ourselves before she'll open the door. She locks it again after we enter."

"That's too bad," Tanner said sincerely. "It's a horrible experience for any woman to go through, especially a woman her age." Having read everything about the case, Tanner knew the girl was not long out of her teens. And he knew, as well, the woman seated opposite him was a few years older.

"Yes." Brianna paused a minute, then went on. "Although we feel hopeful the law will eventually find this monster, for Dani's peace of mind we want him found and incarcerated as soon as possible. That's why my father entrusted me with finding the best bounty hunter and offering a higher bounty."

From information he had gleaned here and there, Tanner suspected the felon was holed up somewhere in the Rocky Mountains, a big territory to scour. Although recently there had been a rumor the man had been spotted in and around Mesa Verde and the San Juan mountain range. That was still a lot of ground to cover. Tanner had previously considered hunting down the man, but he had been bone-tired from his last hunt. Still, he could always use the cash. But then, who couldn't?

"How much higher?" he finally asked, a thread of skepticism in his voice.

Her soft voice hardened. "A million dollars."

A cool mil was worth a man's time needed to comb through that rugged terrain, however tired, Tanner decided. The thought of a million bucks was enough to reenergize a man. If that made him ruthless, tough. Nice guys seldom wound up catching the badasses. Hell, even cops had to be ruthless at times. He should know; there were enough of them in his family.

"Well?" A mixture of anxiety and impatience strained her voice and expression. "Will you accept the job?"

"Yeah," he said in flat tones. "I'll go scour the mountains for him."

"Good." She exhaled the breath he couldn't help noticing she was holding. "I'm going with you."

For a moment Tanner was on the verge of exploding, showering her with heated refusals. Instead he let loose a roar of ridiculing laughter.

"I don't think so," he said when his laughter subsided. "I'm not babysitting a rich man's daughter in stilettos as she traipses around those mountains."

Tapping the toe of one stiletto-clad foot, Brianna smiled serenely. "Mr. Wolfe, I don't need a babysitter, thank you. I can take care of myself."

"Yeah, right," he mocked her. "In a fine restaurant or an upscale dress shop. Go home to Daddy, baby," he advised. "I hunt alone."

"I don't think so," she shot back at him. "This time there'll be two hunters in the mountains."

Tanner laughed again.

He should've kept his mouth shut.

Brianna sat ramrod straight across from Tanner Wolfe, her coffee and scone cooling, her gaze meeting his stare for glaring stare. There was no way he'd keep her from going hunting with him. Not when her sister's life and happiness depended on capturing her offender.

Brianna wasn't about to sit idly by and leave that to someone else. She had to take action, be a part of the hunt. It was the way she had been raised and the way she lived her life. One put family above all else. Besides, back in Pennsylvania, at the university, that was the way she ran her research library. Always in charge.

It didn't matter that this wasn't as routine as finding obscure facts for a student's thesis or a pro-

fessor's lecture. This was a life-or-death situation—
and it could very well be her own death.

But she was doing it for Dani.

She gave Tanner her iciest stare and waited for
his reply.

"I said no, Ms. Stewart." His eyes had narrowed
to glittering dark stones. "I won't be responsible for
anyone else. I always hunt alone."

"Why?" Deliberately, with a show of noncha-
lance, she raised her mug and took a deep swallow.
"I would think two hunters would be better than one."

"Why? Because you're a woman, that's why."

A woman indeed. Brianna fought back a sneer.
The man's arrogant, superior tone was getting to
her. "I've heard there are women bounty hunters."

"There are," he said, raising his own mug and
draining it. "But they're tough, not sleek and
pampered daddy's darlings." His smile was no
longer gentle. "Even so, I won't hunt with any one
of them, either."

Now Brianna was getting more than annoyed. She
set down the mug to keep from flinging it at his thick
head. She detested a condescending male attitude.
She drew a deep breath before educating him.

"Mr. Wolfe, I don't know about women bounty
hunters, but this 'daddy's darling' knows how to
take care of herself. My father, an avid hunter,
began teaching me about firearms when I was
twelve. I've followed him up one mountain and
down another. I've trekked beside him in Africa.

And, although I hunt with a camera, I'm an expert shot with both a rifle and a handgun."

"I'm impressed."

He sounded bored.

Damn him, Bri thought, gritting her teeth to keep from screaming at him. "I'm not finished," she said, her voice tight. "I've also had training in the martial arts and Krav Maga. I know how to defend myself."

"I'm glad to hear it." He didn't sound at all glad; his voice carried a thread of impatience. "A woman should be trained to protect herself. But that changes nothing. I still hunt alone."

He was a Wolfe, all right, spelled *wolf,* pure alpha male, self-contained and confident. That was certain despite his appearance.

Not that there was anything wrong with the way he looked. It was just that he didn't seem to fit the rest of the Wolfe clan.

Her friends Lisa and Matt were twins, blonde and gorgeous. Bri had never met their parents, but she had met their father's brother, the Sprucewood chief of police, and she had seen pictures of several of the other Wolfes, uncles and cousins. They were all tall, blond and handsome. She had not seen a picture of this particular Wolfe cousin.

Tanner Wolfe was different from the rest. For one thing, he didn't have the same blond hair as the others. While he was every inch as tall as the rest of his family, that's where the resemblance ended.

The other Wolfe males, while handsome, looked the role of tough law-enforcement officers.

The only descriptive word for this Wolfe that had flashed through her mind when he'd opened the door was *saint*. Tanner Wolfe had the face of a saint, with soft brown eyes and a gentle, if possibly deceptive, smile. His hair was wavy and shoulder-length, light brown with red-gold highlights, very clean and shiny.

When she'd first seen him, he had literally taken her breath away. Her immediate thought was that she had rung the wrong doorbell. This saintly-looking soft-eyed man could not be a tough bounty hunter.

But he was. In spades.

Tanner Wolfe was believed by many to be one of the very best criminal hunters in the business.

Incredible.

"Did you fall asleep?"

His softly voiced question drew Bri from introspection. Blinking, feeling foolish, she naturally bristled.

"No, of course not," she denied too strongly, but she sure wasn't about to tell him she'd been doing an inventory of his attractive male attributes. Nor that she'd felt an immediate physical attraction to him.

"Then what were you doing?" Amusement now tinged his soft voice, irritating Bri enough to blurt out the truth—or at least the partial truth.

"I was wondering how someone who looks as nice as you could be so intractable."

"Intractable?" He laughed.

The sound did funny things to her insides, making them kind of quiver. She didn't like the sensation.

"Yes, intractable," she said. "You know, you're being unreasonable by refusing to let me go with you."

"Unreasonable?" He was no longer laughing. In fact, he scowled at her. "Tracking a man is hard, dangerous work."

Bri heaved an impatient sigh. "So is tracking a wild boar or a rogue tiger. But I've tracked both. I'm not a fool, Mr. Wolfe. I'm fully aware of the danger."

"In that case, run along home to Daddy and let me do what I get paid to do."

"No." Sliding back her chair, Bri stood up. "Let's just forget it. I'll find another hunter, one who will allow me to go with him."

"No." Tanner literally sprang out of his chair. "I'm telling you it's not safe."

"And I'm telling you I can take care of myself, possibly even help you." Bri raised her chin, tilting it at a defiant angle. "And I'm telling you I am going—with you or without you. It's up to you, Mr. Wolfe."

"You really are a spoiled brat, aren't you?" he said, his soft voice sounding edgy with frustration and anger. His eyes and mouth were hard. The saintly appearance was gone now, replaced by the hunter.

"No," she calmly denied. "I'm really not. What I am is confident of my abilities and determined to help catch this monster." She drew a deep breath, steeling herself for the blast of fury she expected him to hurl at her. "I'll say it once more—I am going, either with you or with another hunter."

He didn't speak for long seconds, staring at her with narrowed eyes, as if warning her to be careful. His look was absolutely deadly.

Gritting her teeth, Bri managed to hold his gaze, her pulse racing, her heart thumping. She felt like running but stood firm, resolute.

Bri had never allowed any man to intimidate her. Damned if she'd back down from this one, even if he did scare the breath from her body. "A woman."

"What?" Although she had thought Tanner's stare couldn't possibly become any more fierce, it did. "What's that supposed to mean?"

Bri managed a halfway credible shrug. "I mean, I'll look up a woman hunter."

"You will not go after that killer with a woman hunter."

"I'll go with whom I please," she said, her voice calm, resigned.

Although his eyes flashed with anger, he exhaled a quiet sigh of concession. "Okay, you win. I'll take you with me. But I'll have one thing understood before we go any further with this."

"And that is?" Bri had a hard time containing her sense of victory, along with a thrill of excitement.

"I give the orders."

"But—"

"And you will follow them, at once and without protest or question."

Bri went stiff with outrage. Just who did this guy think he was? she railed in silent frustration. Unable to keep her feelings inside, she shot back, "I am not a child to be ordered around. Who do you think you are?"

"I'm the bounty hunter you want or you wouldn't have sought me out in the first place." He smiled, stirring all kinds of emotions inside her. His gaze skimmed her from head to toe, flooding her body with heat. "Just for the record, I'm well aware you're not a child. However, those are my demands."

Defeat was a bitter pill to swallow, but Bri knew she had little choice. She had deliberately sought him out, and not only on the advice of her friends or his cousins.

Bri was thorough in everything she did. She had done her research. She had pulled the information that not only was Tanner considered one of the best bounty hunters around, many believed him to be *the* best at finding his man in rough terrain like mountains.

"All right," she reluctantly agreed. She thought she should feel steam spewing from her ears; instead she felt…protected? She gave a mental shake of her head. No, Tanner Wolfe wasn't feeling protective of her; he was very likely feeling superior.

"Good." He flicked a hand at the table. "Have a seat. We've got a lot of plans to go over."

Wary but resigned, Bri slid onto the chair she had vacated moments before. She picked up the mug, took a sip, made a face and set it down again.

"That's gotta be cold." He grabbed the mug along with his own and turned away. "I'll get us refills." He raised his eyebrows. "What about your scone?"

Bri shook her head. "No, thank you. It's fine this way." Raising the pastry to her mouth, she took a bite. "It's very good."

"Whatever." Shrugging, he turned away.

Chewing another bite of the scone, she watched him, studying him from the rear. It was a very nice rear, narrow, firm and taut. His back and shoulders weren't bad, either, broad and muscular, not in a pumped-up way, but more lean and rangy.

Mugs refilled, Tanner returned to the table, giving her another chance to more closely examine the front of him. That was even better.

His flat, muscled chest veed to a slim waist. His legs were long, straight, his thighs nicely straining the denim of his jeans as he arranged his tall frame in the chair. He regarded her in calm, watchful silence.

Quiet and composed, his features appeared sculpted from marble, sharply delineated. His nose was straight, cheekbones high, jawline defined, square and hard, as if the sculptor had carved it lovingly. If it weren't for those soft eyes and that tender smile, he'd look like a statue. That tiny flare of excitement flashed inside her again. Why? The question hammered at her mind. Bri couldn't find the answer, and that seriously bothered her.

"What are you staring at?" His quiet voice jolted her out of her reverie.

Damn, once again he'd caught her brooding, staring. What in the world was the matter with her? she chastised herself. She had never been so strongly affected by any man. The closest she had ever come to feeling so drawn to a man had been a disaster, for he had proven to be a handsome, charming son of a bitch, a practiced user of young, susceptible women. At the time, she had been both.

"You," Bri admitted, but that was all she intended to admit. "I'm trying to figure you out."

He grinned. "How are you making out?"

"Not too well," she said, deliberately grinning back at him. "You're not easy to read."

"Don't feel bad," he said, growing serious. "I can't figure you out, either. You're sure not what you appear to be."

Bri raised her brows. "How do I appear to be?"

He studied her a moment. "My first impression of you was of a beautiful woman, very well dressed, well-bred and educated."

Despite her suspicion of easy compliments— the SOB had been extremely easy with them—Bri felt her cheeks grow warm, flushed not only by his

words but by the open admiration in his eyes. "I—
I don't know—"

Tanner silenced her with a quick shake of his
head. "Don't get all flustered. I doubt you'll be as
pleased with my opinion of how you're different
from my snap impression."

Bri raised her mug to her lips to sip at the hot
brew, looking relaxed, while in fact she was steeling
herself for whatever he said next. "Go on." How in
the world she had managed a cool tone, Bri hadn't
a clue.

"I think you have been spoiled rotten," he said
with blunt honesty. "You want what you want,
when you want it. I read you as self-centered, self-
confident and too damned sure of yourself."

Why Tanner Wolfe's assessment of her personality should hurt her, she couldn't imagine, but hurt
it did, like the very devil. Odd, usually she wasn't
so sensitive to anyone else's opinions of her. Since
the episode with the silver-tongued weasel, she
thought she had grown a thick skin.

"Now you want to take a shot at me?"

"Of course," Bri said. "But first I'd like to know
how you managed to come to that conclusion in
such a short time with me."

"Easy." Tanner laughed. It sounded relaxed,
genuine. "I recognized the traits because they're
very similar to my own." He paused to laugh again.
"The only difference is I'm not beautiful."

Two

"You're spoiled?" She couldn't help laughing, thinking he was wrong on one point. He *was* beautiful, just in a different, masculine way.

"Sure," he answered, laughing with her. "I have great parents. While instilling morals, values, ethics, good behavior and good housekeeping skills into their sons, they also spoiled the hell out of us. In a good way," he quickly added, grinning.

"You have two brothers, both older than you, right?" she asked, although she knew the answer.

"Yeah." He nodded. "Justin's the oldest, now thirty-two. Then Jeffrey, thirty. And lastly, yours truly, twenty-nine." He grinned again. "There's also a slew of cousins."

"So I've heard." She grinned back at him.

"How old are you?"

Well, no one would ever accuse him of being hesitant. The thought brought a smile to her lips. "I'm twenty-seven."

"You're too young to risk your life traipsing around in the mountains, looking for a killer."

Bri rolled her eyes while heaving a sigh. "I believe we've already plowed that field, Mr. Wolfe. I'm going, period."

"I know, but I had to try one more time." His sigh was heavier than hers. "And the name's Tanner. It would get pretty tiresome hearing Mr. Wolfe over and over for who the hell knows how long."

"Okay…Tanner," she agreed. "My friends call me Bri."

"That's too bad." He smiled at her startled look. "I like Brianna better. It's a lovely name and fits you perfectly. Like you, it's classy."

Bri grew warm with pleasure. He thought she was beautiful and classy? Though many men before him had called her beautiful, his compliment left her speechless for a long moment. Finally she found her voice, if rather weak and a bit breathless.

"Thank you," she murmured, feeling herself grow warmer. "That was very nice of you." Oh, gag me, she thought, disgusted with the inanity of her response.

"You're welcome." Tanner's lips twitched, betraying his urge to grin.

She didn't blame him. She joined him, laughing easily at herself. "Pretty lame, huh?"

He shook his head. "No, surprising. I would have thought you'd be used to compliments."

"Well, yes," she said. "But—"

"But what?" His eyes gleamed with a teasing light.

"Oh, let's just forget it," she said, certainly not for a moment about to admit he flustered her simply because she felt a physical attraction to him. A strong attraction.

"Why?"

"What do you mean, *why?*" She frowned. "Because it's getting silly, that's why."

"Too bad." He sighed. "I thought it was just getting interesting."

Bri rolled her eyes. This man is impossible. Gorgeous, sexy as hell, but impossible. "I think it's time to get down to the business at hand."

He gave another, deeper sigh. Boy, this guy was some actor, Bri thought, struggling against the urge to laugh, amazed at how much she was enjoying their banter, not to mention his company, his appeal. No, let's not go there again, she told herself. As they were going to be spending a lot of time together, it would be in her best interest to avoid thinking about his appeal.

"Are you sulking?" she asked after several long moments—moments in which she had thought about nothing but him.

He smiled. "I never sulk. Children sulk. And, just

on the odd chance you hadn't noticed, I'm a man, not a child."

"Oh, I've noticed," she said, thinking she had noticed too damn much.

He smiled again. "Oh, I've noticed you, too."

His smile was an invitation to sheer temptation. Pull it together, Bri told herself, fighting to control her rapid heartbeat and leaping pulse. You've had one go-round with a sweet-talkin', overconfident type. That encounter was one too many.

But Tanner was an attractive, sexy man. And she was every bit as susceptible as any other normal woman. Why did the devil have to look so angelic?

Tanner smiled—a devilish, suggestive and too damned appealing smile.

Now Bri not only felt warm, she felt hot all over. And tingly. And funny inside. Stop it, she told herself. As if *that* helped.

"Uh…um…business," she said, stumbling a bit over her words—something she had never done. "I really think it's time to get down to business."

"Too bad." Tanner shook his head, looking or trying to look sad. His gleaming eyes gave him away. "But, if you insist, we'll get down to the nitty-gritty."

"I do. And that is?"

"Set a day to leave and gather the supplies needed for this hunt."

"I can leave tomorrow."

"I haven't told you yet everything we'll need to

take with us," he said. "So how can you be ready by tomorrow?"

She shot him an impatient look. "If you'll recall, I did tell you I have been hunting since I was a kid. I know how and what to pack."

"Okay, kid," he said, heavy on the *kid.* "But I think I'll do a list, just to be on the safe side, make sure we're on the same page, so to speak." Getting up, he walked to the counter and pulled open a cabinet drawer. He took out a pencil and a pad of paper, then hesitated, turning his head to glance at her. "More coffee?"

"No, thank you." Bri shook her head and shot a glance at her watch. "How long is this going to take?"

His lifted one brow. "Why? Are you in a hurry?"

"No, but the only thing I did was check in to the hotel and get my room card. I left my stuff with the bell captain and came right here."

"How did you know I'd be here?"

"Lisa told me." She smiled, maybe a bit smugly. "She spoke to your mother last night, who told Lisa you had called and said you had just returned."

Tanner scowled.

Bri rushed to clarify her statement. "Your mother knew I was coming here to try to hire you." She drew a breath and went on more normally. "She told Lisa she would let her know as soon as she heard from you."

"Women." He heaved a sigh and shook his head.

She bristled at his dismissive tone. "What's wrong with women?"

Tanner slid a wry look at her. "Most of the time, like children, they should be seen and not heard."

Stunned, Bri was speechless for a moment. Though sorely tempted to explode all over him, she forced herself to remain calm, icy calm. "Mr. Wolfe, that is the stupidest, most sexist remark I've ever heard. What century are you living in?"

"Honey, I'm right here and now," he said, every bit as calm and icy. "I may not be politically correct, but I'm honest. I'm a women jabber. Simple as that."

"Forget it."

"Gladly. Now…"

"No," she shook her head, sliding her chair back and rising. "I mean forget about finding that poor excuse for a man. I'll hire someone else." Before the last word was out of her mouth, she turned to leave. "Or hunt him myself."

"No, you won't." His voice was sharp with command. "I'm going, with or without you," he repeated her earlier ultimatum back to her. "Now, Brianna, sit down and let's get down to business."

Bri hesitated, telling herself that if she had any sense or pride, she would tell Tanner Wolfe to go to hell, walk out of there and look up another hunter. Her sense must have deserted her, for she sighed and swallowed what was left of her pride. In the final analysis, she was determined Minnich would be caught and she wanted the best mountain hunter. So, still glaring at Tanner, she reseated herself.

"Smart girl." He offered a slight smile. She

refused the offer. Instead he shrugged. "Okay, let's get it done."

Smart girl. Yeah, right. She had caved to the caveman, dammit. She soothed her tattered composure by reminding herself Dani's well-being was worth her pride.

"Guns."

Bri blinked herself out of her musings. "What?"

"You said you had your supplies," he said patiently. "What kind of weapons do you have?"

"Oh." Bri felt flustered and foolish. Telling herself to get with it, keep up with him, prove she was a smart girl, she replied, "I've got a .270 rifle with a three-by-nine scope and a .357 hunting revolver." She arched her brows at his sudden intent expression. "What do you pack?"

"A .30-06 and a 7mm rifle with the same scope, and a .44 mag." He looked impressed. "And you really do pack some heavy-duty heat."

Not as much as you do, she thought, referring not to his weapons but to his body. "I told you I knew what I was doing," she said, working at not sounding too smug or too breathless. "Anything else?"

His lips twitched, evidently amused by her. "Clothes, backpack, sleeping bag?"

"Yes." Now her lips twitched. "All of the above."

He smiled. "Wanna tell me about them? Just a hint?" His smile grew into a grin.

Bri gave a mock sigh, fighting the smile tickling the corners of her mouth. Darn him, why did he have to be so attractive? "I have clothes suitable for mountain terrain, including a ski jacket neatly packed in my backpack, along with other necessities. My sleeping bag is the best available and waterproof. I lay it on a nearly weightless ground sheet. Now are there any other questions?"

"As a matter of fact, there are," he said. "What about food? Have you thought of that?"

This time she gave him a droll look. "Of course I have, but I didn't bring much with me. I figured we could get what we needed here in Durango."

He nodded. "You figured correctly." He pushed the chair back and stood. "Let's get lunch. We'll take my truck."

"Wait a minute," she protested while standing and following him from the kitchen. "Who said anything about lunch?"

"I just did." He shot a glance at the big red-rimmed clock on one wall. "It's nearly one. I'm hungry for something more substantive than a scone. Aren't you?"

"Well, yes," she admitted reluctantly, because she was feeling too attracted to the arrogant Neanderthal. "Why not take separate vehicles?"

Tanner paused, holding open the door for her. "You know your way around Durango?"

She had never even been to Durango, Colorado, before. "Well, no, but—" She was about to mention the restaurant in her hotel, but that's as far as she got before he cut her off.

"That's what I thought. We'll take my truck."

Bri had no intention of doing so. She shook her head. "I want to go to the hotel and freshen up a bit. Give me directions. I'll meet you at the restaurant in a half hour."

The restaurant Tanner had directed her to was done in Western decor, not honky-tonk but with style and ambience. Now, in early afternoon, there were few patrons, so the place was quiet.

"This is very nice," she said to Tanner, seating herself in the chair the host held for her. She smiled at the man. "Thank you."

"Wait till you've tasted the food," Tanner said.

She looked over the long list of dishes offered on the menu. Her glance halted at shrimp and pasta in a light herb dressing. On the spot, she dumped the idea of her normal luncheon salad.

She placed her order when the waitress came, then looked up at Tanner. She felt certain he would order red meat, like a rare steak. He surprised her. A talent he seemingly had in abundance.

"I'll have the pasta, as well, but with chicken."

The server no sooner turned away when a young woman came to an abrupt stop at their table. She was blond, petite and more than pretty. Her big blue eyes sparkled with surprised pleasure. Her teeth gleamed in a brilliant yet sensuous smile.

"Tanner, honey!" Miss Sunshine exclaimed,

moving into his arms when Tanner stood. "I haven't seen you in ages. What have you been up to?"

For some inexplicable reason, everything about the young woman annoyed Bri, from her cooing voice to the possessive way her arms curled around his neck. For a few seconds Bri was even more annoyed at the way Tanner smiled down at the small woman clinging to him. Her annoyance fled with his drawled response.

"Well, Candy, I'm up to the same six feet four inches I was at the last time I saw you…'ages' ago. What has it been—all of a week or two?"

Somehow Bri contained the laughter bubbling up inside her at his reply. And her name! *Candy.* It certainly fit, all right. She was arm candy for hungry males.

The thought sobered Bri. Was Tanner one of the hungry males? She was so startled, so bothered by the very idea of Tanner being that predictable, she almost missed him setting the woman from him and turning to her. She quickly rose.

"Brianna, I'd like you to meet Candy Saunders. She's from back east, too—"

"The Hamptons," Candy was quick to arrogantly insert, rudely cutting Tanner off. All sweetness and light were gone, her eyes and smile calculating as she swept a dismissive glance over Bri.

Looking bored, Tanner rolled his eyes at Bri, a wry smile twitching the corners of his mouth.

"Candy of the Hamptons, meet Brianna Stewart of Pennsylvania."

Candy gave a delicate sniff, obviously not impressed. "How nice. Are you visiting someone here in Durango?" She arched one perfect bleached eyebrow. "One of Tanner's friends, perhaps?"

Bri didn't know whether to laugh or slug the overbearing woman. She did neither, of course. Instead she answered drily, "No, I'm not visiting. I have business with Mr. Wolfe."

"Really?" Both eyebrows went up.

"Yeah, really," Tanner said, now sounding as bored as he looked. "If you'll excuse us?" He indicated a table toward the back. "I think your friend is getting impatient for you to join him."

Candy turned back to him, instantly changing to Miss Sunshine again. "Yes, of course, darlin'," she cooed, raising a small hand to lightly drag her dagger nails down his face. "Toodles," she said, drawing her hand away and wiggling her scarlet-tipped fingers at him. "Call me." Without so much as a glance at Bri, she sashayed away.

"Toodles?" Battling another bubble of laughter sparked by the drama queen, Bri resumed her seat just as the server approached the table with their meals.

"That's Candy," he said, shrugging.

Yes, Bri mused, but did he like candy? Mentally dismissing the oddly disturbing idea, she asked, "A good friend of yours?" The question was out before she could stop herself. Dammit, she didn't give a rip either way…did she?

Tanner saved her from her self-condemnation. "No." He shook his head, setting his long waves rippling, brushing his shoulders. "She's a bit of an airhead, I'm afraid, and calls every man 'darlin'' in that cloyingly sweet voice." He shrugged. "But she can be polite and even amusing at times."

"I see." Bri hid a frown of dissatisfaction by lowering her head to inhale the aroma wafting from the steaming plate the server set in front of her.

The food was delicious. The conversation, which didn't include candy of any sort, ranged from favorite foods to favorite movies to general likes and dislikes. Bri relaxed, let her guard down.

It was a mistake she rarely made.

On leaving the restaurant, feeling mellow—too mellow—she soon realized she had been led down the conversational garden path, so to speak.

"Where are you staying?" Tanner asked as they headed for their vehicles.

"The Strater Hotel. It's lovely."

"Yeah, a landmark, built in 1887." His tone held a tiny note of the proud resident. "You know, Will Rogers stayed there. And Louis L'Amour wrote several of his Western novels while he was staying there."

"He must have stayed a while," she said, smiling at his instructive tone. "Or written very fast."

He grinned.

Bri felt something inside go all squishy. Why did he have to have such a sexy grin? She swallowed a sigh of self-disgust—or was it longing?—and was relieved when they came to her rental SUV. "This one's mine."

"I'm right behind you." He moved his head, indicating the much larger, kick-ass SUV. "I've got some calls to make before I go for the food supplies and some loose ends to tie up tomorrow. Suppose I pick you up the day after tomorrow? I want to get an early start. Is five okay with you?"

In that instant Bri became wary of his intentions. "You *will* be here, won't you?"

At once, his pleasant expression changed, his features growing taut. "Didn't I just say I will?" His voice carried both anger and insult.

"Yes." Bri was not about to apologize. "But I want to be certain you won't take a flit on me."

"A flit…" He shook his head. "What are you getting at? Do you believe—" As he paused, she pounced.

"That you're going to take off on your own, leave me cooling my heels here in Durango?" she finished for him. "Oh, yeah, Mr. Wolfe, that's exactly what I think you might try. I guess I should have listened to your cousins. They warned me you were a loner, a maverick who went his own way alone." He started to speak, but she charged on. "And that's what you intend to do to me, isn't it?"

"Okay, I admit I prefer to do my hunting alone,

as I always have. But I had agreed to your going with me, so why in hell did you get the idea that I was planning to take off without you?" Now Tanner sounded angry, and his features had hardened, turning the saint into the bounty hunter.

Bri wasn't impressed by either his voice or the hard look of him. At least she worked to appear unimpressed. In truth, she was shaken, trembling inside. But that was because she was just as angry.

"Oh, couldn't be because you now seem eager to get rid of me while you get your stuff together, now could it?" She didn't wait for him to ditch the stunned, speechless look, but continued, "It might even have worked except for one minor detail. You forgot that I'm carrying the check."

"I didn't forget a damned thing."

Whoa. If she had thought he was angry before, she was now seeing real anger. More like fury. And furious, Tanner Wolfe was downright frightening.

"Good, because even if I'd have bought into your softening-up routine in the restaurant—" he again opened his mouth to interrupt but she held up her hand, keeping him still while she rushed breathlessly on "—and you skipped off on your own and brought in that bastard, you wouldn't have gotten anything but the original ten thousand bounty."

"Finished?" His cold tone was chilling.

The tremor inside Bri turned into an icy shiver she was hard-pressed to hide from him. "Yes." How she had managed so calm a tone amazed her.

"Feel better for having your little rant?" There was something new and dangerous in his voice that froze the icy shiver solid.

Bri stiffened her spine and raised her chin to a defiant angle. "I was not ranting."

"Coulda fooled me," he drawled. "And there was no softening-up in the restaurant. I guess I'm not too bright, because I thought we were having a nice time getting to know each other." He gave her a quizzical look. "What made you think I was setting you up, anyway?"

How did one explain a feeling, a sudden on-slaught of intuition? she asked herself. A hard lesson learned from another man who'd been a pro at stringing along women?

"I'm not quite sure myself," she admitted. "When we were talking, I relaxed, and the next minute I began to feel suspicious." She told herself the sudden feeling had nothing to do with how he had allowed that man-eater Candy to step into his embrace.

At the back of her mind, another unsettling suspicion niggled at her. The suspicion that he might have been in a hurry to send her packing so he could go back to the restaurant to indulge in some after-dinner candy. *Then* he would collect his stuff and head into the mountains without her.

Bri brushed the suspicion off, not about to recognize it. There was no way she would voice it to Tanner. His heavy sigh dissolved her uncomfortable reverie.

"Do you want to spend the next two nights with me?"

Yes, she thought at once. "No," she said in firm denial of her first response.

"Then I suppose you'll have to trust me." He smiled quite like a chess player who had his opponent checkmated. "That is, if you still want to go with me."

"You know I want to go with you," she snapped, angry at him, at herself for stepping so blindly into his game of strategy. "As long as you remember who holds the purse strings."

Tanner shook his head as if in pity for her. "I don't forget details, Brianna, even when they are recited by a spoiled little rich girl."

Bri simmered over his parting shot at her the rest of the day and all through the next, all the while she wandered around, checking out the shops closest to the hotel.

She'd show him what a spoiled little rich girl could do.

Three

Damned if she wasn't wearing killer heels.

Tanner stared in amazement as he brought the SUV to a stop in front of her hotel. It was early, still dark, not so much as a hint of gray on the eastern horizon. But standing in the well-lit entranceway of the hotel, leaning indolently against the brass handrail, he spotted the incongruous heels at once.

At any other time, the so-called shoes—consisting of two narrow straps across her toes and ribbons wound around her ankles, paper-thin soles and those slim, long, spiked heels—would have looked sexy. Worn with jeans and a field jacket over a green camp shirt, they looked ludicrous…and sexy.

Brianna stood there waiting for him, her gear piled next to her left leg, the strap handle of a rifle carrier in her right hand by her side. To his chagrin, her gorgeous mass of auburn hair was tucked away inside a New York Yankees baseball cap. He felt plain, ordinary and underdressed in black jeans, a black leather jacket and sturdy boots. He also had pulled his hair away from his face, tied it with a leather thong at his nape.

Stepping from the SUV, Tanner circled around the back to open the trunk lid. The hotel doorman stashed the gear next to Tanner's. Before he could dip into a pocket to tip the man, Brianna handed him a couple bills and uttered a soft, "Thank you."

"Good morning," Tanner said to her.

"Mmm," she hummed in reply, turning away to get into the front passenger seat.

It would appear she was still ticked off at him. Tanner sighed and slid behind the wheel. Mentally shrugging, he drove away from the hotel, heading out of Durango.

"I love your shoes," he drawled. "I can just imagine you tromping around rough mountainous terrain in them."

She laughed. "I'd hoped you'd appreciate them."

"Oh, I do. They're spectacular, and the color is perfect. Glittery gold straps go great with jeans, field jackets and caps."

"I thought so." She laughed again when he flashed her a grin. "I'm sorry to have to disappoint you, but I won't be wearing them to tromp around any rough terrain. I do have hiking boots with me."

"Aw, gee, that's too bad," he said. "I was looking forward to watching you try to keep up with me." Now the quick look he sent her was glittery with teasing. "Then again, I'll likely still be watching you try to keep up with me."

"In your dreams," Brianna shot back. "What you'll likely be watching is my back."

Tanner couldn't help himself; he roared with laughter. She was so damned sure of herself, so boldly feisty. He also couldn't help but admire her. On the spot, he decided it was probably because she reminded him of himself.

"We'll see," he said, still chuckling.

"Yes, I guess we will." She grew quiet, gazing out through the windshield and side window at the landscape as it changed from mountainous to flatter, barren desert.

"Where are we going?" she asked.

"Not far from Mesa Verde."

"Mesa Verde? I thought you said our quarry was headed deep into the San Juan Mountains."

"What I said was I had picked up a rumor that he was heading there." He spared her a brief glance. "Before I go tearing into the mountains, I want to check out the rumor for myself."

"And who are you going to check out these rumors with—the ghosts of the Indians who lived there?" Her tone held more than a hint of sarcasm.

"Clever," he said, sighing. "Actually, I didn't say we were going to Mesa Verde itself. The rumor I'd picked up was that he had been spotted around Mesa Verde before hightailing it to the mountains. I'm headed for a town where the rumor came from."

"Oh, okay." Brianna was quiet for a moment— a short moment. "I wouldn't mind stopping in Mesa Verde."

Stunned by her startling remark, Tanner nearly lost control of the vehicle. It went off the road, onto the rough shoulder, before he righted it.

"You want to do what? Have a look-see at Mesa Verde?"

"What's wrong with that?"

"Brianna," Tanner said between clenched teeth, "I thought we were out here to search for a rapist/killer, not go on a sightseeing jaunt."

"Well, of course we are," she said, abrading his irritation with her reasonable tone. "I meant someday I'd like to explore the cliff dwellings."

"I'm sorry." In truth, he wasn't at all sorry. "I thought you wanted me to stop today to go crawling around the ruins, and we have no time to waste."

"But you wasted all day yesterday," she protested.

Tanner was on the sharp edge of impatience. "Brianna, I told you I had a lot to do yesterday. Besides having to make some phone calls to tie up a few loose ends, I had to get our food supplies, which I paid for."

She sighed. "Okay, explanation accepted."

"Big of you," he drawled with a bite.

"I know," she said sweetly. "And, of course, I'll reimburse you for the supplies."

"Damned straight you will, honey." His voice had a hard edge he didn't like. Get a grip, Wolfe, he warned himself, before you find yourself without a mission…and the company of the gorgeous but irritating Brianna. As he fully expected, she retaliated.

"Don't go all predator on me. I'm not one of your prey," she shot back at him. "And don't call me 'honey.'"

Predator? She thought of him as a predator? Tanner frowned, not sure whether he wanted to laugh or curse a blue streak. Hell, predators killed their prey, sometimes ate it. He worked hard not to kill his, even the ones who deserved it. And he sure as hell didn't eat his prey, the mere thought revolting.

On second thought, he mused, gliding a quick glance over her body, he wouldn't mind taking a nip of Brianna's satiny-looking skin. The mere thought of tasting her was enough to stir his body. Get your mind back to business, Wolfe, he warned himself, where it's safe. This ultrasuperior, haughty, independent woman was not for tasting, not by him. Damned shame, too.

"I'll make a deal with you," he said, shifting in his seat to relieve an uncomfortable ache in that sensitive area. "You don't call me 'predator,' and I won't call you 'honey.' Deal?"

"Deal," she said, shaking the hand he held out to her.

"How about 'sweetheart'?" he asked, not missing a beat.

"Tanner Wolfe," Brianna cried sternly, before she gave way to laughter. "You're a…a…"

"Devil?" he asked, grinning in delight at having made her laugh instead of berating him.

She raised her hands in surrender. "I give up," she said. "You win—for now."

"Looks like a draw to me," he said as he slowed down. "Good timing, too. We're here."

"So I see," Brianna said, peering through the windshield as he drove into the town. "This is it?"

"Yeah, I know, not much to look at."

"A little larger than other towns I've driven through." She sat forward, as far as the seat belt allowed, to get a better look at the old town.

"Will we be here long enough for me to look for a coffee shop or diner? I need some caffeine."

He parked the SUV in front of a small café. "You want to go traipsing around in those?" He sent a pointed look at her shoes.

Brianna shook her head. "Of course not." She feigned shock. "I couldn't walk around in public in heels and this attire," she went on haughtily. "I'd never dream of committing such a fashion faux pas."

Was she serious? Tanner stared at her for a moment, then laughed.

Brianna laughed with him. "I suppose it is time to change, isn't it?" She flashed a megawatt smile.

Tanner felt something strange inside, a sensation unlike anything he had ever felt before. It was as if there was something coming alive, unfolding deep within him, a current of soft warmth. It was weird. He had experienced heated desire many, many times. But this feeling was different. And it was directly related to the woman seated next to him. He had to swallow, moisten his throat and lips before he even attempted to reply.

"Yes, I suppose it is." He sighed, not even caring if she heard him mutter, "I'm gonna miss 'em." Swinging open the door, he said in the most normal tone he could manage, "I shouldn't be long. Wait for me inside." Stepping out, he motioned to the place. "We might as well have lunch while we're here. Then we won't need to stop again." He raised a brow. "Okay?"

"Fine." She nodded, quickly calling after him as he slammed the door and started away, "I'll need to get in the back to get my boots."

He was lifting the trunk before she had finished. "Yeah, I know."

Releasing the seat belt, she turned to look at him. He grinned, lifting a Western hat and settling it on his head. "I needed this, too."

Bri felt her breath catch with his grin. Darn, what the devil was it about this man? What *something* did he have that no other man had ever possessed to make her heart race, her breath catch, her body go all warm and squishy? Her feelings were even more intense than they had been with— She cut her thoughts short, not even wanting to think that rotten man's name.

"Brianna?"

His voice brought her to her senses. She blinked. "What?" God, she hated the confused, disoriented sound of her own voice.

Tanner frowned. "Are you all right?"

"Yes, of course," she answered crisply. "Why wouldn't I be all right?"

"Beats the hell out of me." He shook his head, still frowning. "All of a sudden you seemed...I don't know...kinda lost or something."

Sure, Bri thought, it was the *something* that got to her. "I was, er, just thinking." Brilliant, Brianna, she chided herself.

"About?" He was frowning again.

About...about...jeez. "About maybe I should just go with you," she said, wincing inside at the inanity and wondering how she could extradite herself from him so she could think clearly.

Fortunately Tanner performed that all by himself with two succinct words. "Think again."

"Huh?" She smothered a groan.

"Brianna, I am not about to take you with me to talk to an informant. Somehow I feel said informant would very likely pretend he didn't even know me. Understand?"

"Yes…yes, of course," she said, feeling more ridiculous by the minute. Looking away from his curious expression, Bri undid the ties around her slim ankles, slipped out of the heels and tossed them into the backseat. "If you would please hand me my pack, I'll change and then go…get some coffee."

"Wouldn't it be easier if you told me where the boots are so I can hand them to you?"

Smart-ass. Bri gritted her teeth to keep from saying the word aloud. "There's a plastic bag attached to my backpack. They're in there."

"Now we're getting somewhere," he drawled, his lips twitching with a smile.

Bri felt her own lips tickle, then she gave way to the laughter bubbling up into her throat. She couldn't explain to herself why it was that when he laughed or smiled, she had to respond in kind.

The trunk lid slammed shut. A moment later he opened her door. "Your slippers, Cinderella." His eyes danced with silent laughter.

"Thank you." She took the sturdy boots from him. "And if you're expecting me to call you Prince Charming, you have a long wait ahead of you."

Tanner laughed out loud, tipped his hat respectfully at her and strolled away.

Now, she thought, *that* was charming. And disarming, thus dangerous to her peace of mind—never mind her libido. Brianna was not a child or a fool. She was a smart, well-educated woman. A woman with the appetites and desires of every healthy human, female or male. She was attracted to Tanner Wolfe, and he was attracted to her. It didn't take a mental giant to figure that out. Human nature would have its way.

Yeah, she mused, pulling on the socks she had jammed into the boots, she had to be careful, on her guard, against herself as well as him. The two of them were going to be spending a lot of time together, closely together, in the mountains.

She had been hurt badly before and was determined she wouldn't be again. She couldn't emotionally afford to get involved with Tanner Wolfe, bounty hunter.

Groaning softly at the very idea, she yanked on the boots, grabbed her shoulder bag and stepped out of the SUV.

Drawing a deep breath, she strode out, determined to put off her ruminations until later. But her stride soon turned into a meandering stroll, while her mind raced ahead with what-ifs.

Bri knew full well the possibilities, knew they narrowed down to one. Her imagination drew a vivid picture of herself and Tanner, their limbs entwined, their mouths fused, his body—

Hold it right there, she told herself, blinking to erase the too-explicit scene from her mind. She was breathing hard and fast. Suddenly aware, she glanced around her to see if anyone had noticed her flushed cheeks, her forehead damp with perspiration. If anyone did, she'd blame it on the noonday sun directly overhead. In her jacket, no wonder she was so uncomfortably warm.

Her breathing slowing but still uneven, Bri turned on her heel to practically run back to where Tanner had parked the SUV in front of the café.

Pulling herself together and shrugging out of her jacket, Bri entered the café, her throat parched. Whether her thirst came from the heat or from her thoughts, she didn't know; all she knew was she needed a cold drink to cool down her fevered mind.

She was seated in a booth, a large glass of ice water set next to a steaming cup of coffee in front of her, working at appearing cool, comfortable and slightly bored, when Tanner entered the café. His sharp gaze locating her at once, he strode to the booth and slid onto the bench across from her. Removing his hat, he set it on the bench next to him. "Hi."

His soft, almost intimate voice sent tingles dancing along her spine.

"Hi, yourself." How Bri had found her impersonal yet friendly tone she hadn't a clue.

"The coffee looks good," he said, indicating her cup with a swift movement of his head. "It's warming up outside."

"I noticed." Bri immediately decided that had to be the biggest understatement of her life. "That's why I asked for the ice water."

"Hmm…and I'm parched."

You're telling me? she thought, taking a quick sip to cool her drying throat.

"Hungry?" she asked, not able to think of anything else to say.

Tanner didn't respond for a few tense seconds, during which he slid a slow, intense look from her face to her waist. "Er, yeah."

He didn't have to say any more; Bri felt his exact meaning in every cell in her body. Oh, boy, she thought, watching his eyes darken as she thoughtlessly wet her dry lips with a glide of her tongue. Oh, yes, indeedy, she was in deep trouble.

"You?"

"What?" Try as she would, Bri couldn't control the slight tremor in her voice.

"I asked if you were hungry. Are you?"

"Yes." There was no way in hell she was going to run her gaze over him, no matter how much she wanted to do so. "And, as you said, we may as well eat now. I have menus." She handed one to him.

"Thanks." He smiled.

Damn him. Keeping the thought firmly inside her mind, where it belonged, she opened the menu and pretended to peruse the lunch specials even though she had already made her selection.

They didn't talk much or tarry during the meal, and within forty-five minutes of Bri having entered the café, they were back in the SUV and on the road.

Bri contained her patience until they were at last heading for the mountains.

"So what did you learn from your informant?" she asked when he remained silent.

He slanted a grin at her. "I thought you'd never ask. You surprised me by holding out for as long as you have."

"You have no idea how long I can hold out," she shot back at him, leaving it up to him to decide whether her response contained a double meaning.

He slanted a sideways, contemplative look at her, his eyes alight with devilment. "Is that a challenge?"

Bri raised her eyes and fluttered her eyelashes, her expression one of pure innocence. "Why, Mr. Wolfe," she said, her voice as close to a purr as she could make it, "a woman would have to be very brave to challenge you."

He gave a short bark of laughter. "Yeah, that's what I meant."

"You think I'm a brave woman?" Bri felt inordinately flattered even though she knew she was a brave woman. Her father had tested her, and she had passed his test of bravery and endurance. She had aced it, actually.

"Oh, yeah, you're brave," he said, sparing another glance at her. "You're brave and a bit reckless and, I'm afraid, very, very dangerous."

That last stopped her cold. She stared at him in astonishment. Her…dangerous? In what way? She had never deliberately harmed or intimidated anyone in her entire life.

"Dangerous to whom?" she asked, too bewildered by his remark to feel anything but puzzled.

Tanner sliced a smile at her that made her tingle all over. "I'd say you're dangerous to every male between the ages of fifteen and a hundred and fifteen."

Bri just couldn't hold back; she laughed.

"You don't think so, huh?"

"Of course I do," she said as her laughter subsided. "I'm sure every male out there between those ages is just trembling in fear of running into me. Get real, Wolfe," she said drolly. "I'm far from being dangerous to anyone of any age."

He slowed down a bit to give her a dry look. "Does that include the man we're on the hunt for?"

Bri stiffened. "That's different."

"In what way?"

"In the obvious way," she retorted, getting really rattled. "He's different. He's a killer."

"Yeah, he's a killer and a rapist," he agreed in an annoyingly reasonable tone. "But there are a lot of killers and rapists out there, and you're not on the hunt, packing heat, for them."

"No, I'm not," she snapped, getting seriously angry. "And that's because I'm not a hunter or a killer. But if we catch up to this...this monster, I will not hesitate a moment to use my weapon."

"Wait a minute." In an instant, Tanner practically stood on the brake, bringing the vehicle to a squealing, jarring stop. "You, me, neither one of us is going to shoot to kill him. Is that understood?"

He didn't wait for a response. "I'm warning you, Brianna, if you don't give me your word on this, I'll turn around, drive back to Durango and drop you at the Strater like you were on fire. I have never killed a man in my life and I'm not about to start now, and neither are you—not as long as you're with me. Have you got that?"

Bri didn't know whether to laugh or weep. She did neither; instead she calmly faced him. "I never so much as entertained the idea of killing the man, Tanner. I only meant I'd use my weapon to wing him, enough to bring him down. I don't want him dead. That's too easy."

He frowned. "Then what do you want?"

She hoped Tanner could actually see the icy determination on her tight lips. "I want to see him rot in prison for the rest of his life, living with his conscience—if he has one—and the memory of every woman he killed or hurt. I hope he lives to be one hundred and every day is spent in fear some other convict will decide to mete out his own brand of punishment."

Four

Tanner suppressed a shudder at the deadly, frigid tone of Brianna's voice, her cold expression. Wow, he thought, when this woman hates, she puts every part of herself into the lethal emotion. On the spot, he found himself hoping she never decided to turn that emotion on him.

"You still haven't told me what you learned from your informant."

The change in her was startling. Her tone had thawed to conversational, her expression, while not exactly warm, had relaxed somewhat. Swallowing a sigh of relief, Tanner put the SUV into gear and drove forward once more.

"He was seen leaving town two days ago. Apparently he's heading deep into the wildest section of the mountains. He left on horseback, leading a packhorse, and from the direction he was going, I suspect he's making his way to the Weminuche Wilderness."

Brianna frowned. "I vaguely recall having heard of it, but where and what is the Weminuche Wilderness?"

"The Weminuche is one of the largest designated wilderness areas in the country at somewhere around nine and a half thousand acres," he said, keeping his eyes on the inclining road. "While many tourists hike and bike in it, there are sections that are nearly inaccessible. It seems our man is heading in that direction."

"Well, if he is on horseback, leading a packhorse, I would think we could catch up to him in this SUV before he can reach one of those sections. Couldn't we?" She sounded satisfied with her deduction.

Tanner hated having to burst her confidence bubble, yet he had no choice. "No, we can't, Brianna. Even this vehicle can only go so far into the mountains. Later this afternoon, we'll stop for the night and go on by horseback in the morning."

She shot him a puzzled look. "But… How…I mean, where are we going to get horses out here?"

"I have a friend who owns a horse ranch tucked out of the way in a small valley." He shot her a grin before she had a chance to question him further. "We can spend tonight there."

By the quick glance he sent her, Tanner could tell by her expression she had questions, lots of questions, likely tripping over one another to see which one she could get out first. Within moments, she appeared to have sorted them out. She shot them out rapid-fire.

"How do you know your friend is there? How can you know we'll be welcome to spend the night? How can you be sure he'll have horses for hire? How—?" That's as far as he let her go.

"I know," he cut in, "because I know my friend. If he's not there when we arrive, he'll be out in the hills somewhere, and we'll wait until he returns."

"But—"

Tanner didn't hesitate to cut her off again. "Brianna, you'll have to trust me on this. We can't follow our man in this SUV. It can go a lot of places but not into the roughest terrain in the mountains."

"I understand that," she shot back impatiently. "But you just sprang this other person at me out of the blue. Who is he, other than your friend?"

"His name is Hawk," he began. Apparently she thought it was her turn to interrupt.

"What's his real name?"

"Hawk." He slanted a droll look at her. "His last name is McKenna. And, yes, he's a half-breed."

"I do not like that expression," Brianna said in a clipped, stern-teacher tone.

Tanner was hard put not to laugh. "Neither do I, but that's how Hawk refers to himself. He's not ashamed of his heritage. Matter of fact, he's proud to have both Scot and Apache blood in his veins." Now he laughed aloud, softly, almost as if to himself. "I think you'll find that Hawk is something else."

"And what might that something be?"

"Different," he said after a moment's silence. "He's one of a kind."

"One of a kind of what?" Her tone was clear warning she was getting edgy again.

Tanner shrugged. "One of a kind of man, of human being. I don't know how to explain it, he just is."

"Does he live alone?"

"Usually."

"Tanner..." There was a sharp note of impatience in her voice.

He laughed. "It's the truth, Brianna. Hawk is usually alone, but now and again he has his sister staying with him. Cat isn't as proud of her heritage."

She frowned. "Cat? Hawk and Cat?"

Tanner slid a quick grin at her. "Hawk is just that—Hawk. He's named after his maternal great-grandfather. Cat is short for Catriona, the Scot and Irish name for Catherine. She's named after her paternal great-great-grandmother."

"And she doesn't like being of mixed racial parentage," Brianna said, obviously choosing her words with care.

"No, she doesn't. So every so often she runs away from the world by hiding out with Hawk."

"Hiding out?" she nearly yelped. "Is he hiding out from the law?"

"No, Brianna, Hawk is not hiding from the law. He's not a criminal."

"Well, what is he, then? A hermit? Has he always lived away from society? How old is he?" She once again zapped the questions at him rapid-fire.

He shot the answers back at her in kind. "A man. No. Since he became an adult. I'm not sure—somewhere in his midthirties, I suppose."

"Odd," she murmured.

"Why?"

"Don't you think it's odd, a man deciding to live away from family, friends…women…at such a young age?"

Tanner shifted another glance at her. "I didn't say he was a cloistered monk, Brianna. When he's in the mood for company, he does see his family, friends." He paused deliberately, as she had. "And he does see women."

"You know—"

The SUV plowed over a natural speed bump, silencing her except for a startled, "Oh!"

"Sorry," he said, biting back laughter. "I told you it was rough—and it's going to get rougher." He couldn't hold back a slight grin. "A whole lot rougher."

She glanced around at the terrain, the narrow shoulders bordering the macadam road, and the thickening forest beyond. She frowned and shifted in her seat. "You said we'd stop at sunset. The sun's starting to track west now." She glanced around again. "Tanner…"

"There's a clearing up ahead," he said, anticipating her question as well as the need causing her suddenly restless shifting. He swept a hand in an encompassing movement. "We're in a national park area. Not only is there a clearing, there are restroom facilities."

Brianna sighed in relief. "I'm glad to hear it." She smiled. "I wasn't thrilled with the idea of asking you to stop while I made a dash into the bushes."

He laughed. "I know what you mean. I'm experiencing the, er, same pressure."

"Don't you dare make me laugh, Tanner Wolfe," she said. "I would rather not embarrass myself, thank you."

"Well, you're in luck, Brianna Stewart," he assured her. "The clearing is just beyond the bend up ahead."

"Here we are," he said moments later, pulling the vehicle into a spacious clearing by the side of the road. Along one side of the area, just beyond a posted sign reading Restrooms, was a good-size building. They headed toward it quickly.

Within minutes, they were back on the road. An hour and a half later, Tanner made a quick turn.

"What exactly— Oh!" she said, startled by the jostling of the SUV as he drove off the paved road onto a dirt, stone-strewn track undeserving of the name *road*. "Where are you going?" Bri demanded, glancing at the forest, which seemed to be closing in on them.

"To Hawk's place." He shot a flashing glance at her frown. "What? You expected Hawk to be living smack-dab in the middle of a superhighway?"

Bri's frown turned into a scowl. "No, of course not," she said, one hand gripping the edge of the seat, the other clinging to the dash in an attempt to keep from being flung back and forth within the confines of the seat belt like a rag doll.

"Just hang on," Tanner said, his grip solid on the steering wheel. "It's gonna get worse before it gets better."

"I…d-didn't…think it c-could get any worse," she finished in a rush.

"Ah, honey, you're in for a bouncy surprise."

She sighed, ignored the cramping in her fingers and glared at him. "I told you not to call me 'honey.'"

Tanner laughed all the way down the track to the valley that spread away from it at the bottom. Tucked on the leeward side of the mountain was a one-story ranch house much like the ones seen in Western movies.

Hawk's place was hardly the small, run-down outfit Bri had been expecting to find. In the waning afternoon light she could see several rail-fenced corrals, all containing horses, their coats gleaming in the slanted sunlight. But the ranch was the least of the surprises in store for her.

Bri was so distracted by looking around the property she never noticed Hawk McKenna standing in the shadows of the wraparound porch until he stepped out into the light. At his side stood the biggest dog she had ever seen. More like a pony.

Her startled gaze watched man and animal as they sauntered toward the vehicle Tanner pulled to a stop.

Hawk was not quite as tall as Tanner, but slimmer, rangier. Though older, McKenna was every bit as handsome as Tanner, if in a different, somewhat rougher way.

Where the younger man's appearance was sculpted, Hawk's features had a harshly rough-hewn look. His hair was even longer but as clean and well kept as Tanner's. Most startling of all, it was the same shade of brown and, in the golden glow of slanting sun rays, shot with streaks as dark-red as Bri's own.

Tanner got out of the truck and the two men hugged like long-lost brothers. The dog, not barking or whining, just stood beside his master as if waiting for his turn to greet the company.

As soon as the men were done hugging and slapping each other on the back, the animal moved to Tanner. When he greeted the dog, it jumped up, front paws on his shoulders, standing almost as tall as Tanner.

"Hey, Boyo. No kisses, not on my face," Tanner

said, laughing as he twisted his head to avoid the excited dog's eager reception. "Yeah, the hand's okay." Still laughing, he ruffled the dog's coat.

Boyo, Bri thought. What kind of name was that for such a large dog? He was massive, formidable, his silvery-gray coat marked by small streaks of black. Fortunately the dog appeared friendly or she wouldn't have considered stepping foot from the safety of the SUV.

Tanner's sudden appearance at her door broke into her concentration on the animal.

"Brianna, are you getting out?" He grinned, pulled her door open. "Or are your fingers locked on the seat and dash?"

Startled from her inspection of the dog, Bri gave him a dry look and a blatant lie. "I'm afraid to move, since I feel as if every bone in my body was disjointed during the ride down here."

"I thought maybe you were terrified by the sight of Boyo."

"That, too," she admitted. "But I see he's friendly." She frowned. "What kind of name is Boyo for an animal his size?"

"It's Irish for *boy,*" he explained, laughing again. "Come on, Hawk will protect you."

Lord, Bri loved the sound of his laughter. Steeling herself against her feelings, she took the hand he held out to her.

His hand wasn't soft, his nails weren't manicured as were the hands of her father and most of the other men she knew. His broad, long fingers were used to work, hardened and rough.

An image flashed before her with sudden clarity. His rough hands caressing her body, gripping her bottom to draw him closer as he crushed his mouth to hers.

A tremor shot through her.

"Are you cold, Brianna?" Tanner frowned, placing the other hand at her waist to steady her as she jumped to the ground.

"No…" Bri took a quick breath, stalling for time to come up with a reasonable excuse. "I'm hungry." Was that reasonable enough? "It's been a long time since lunch, don't forget. Aren't you hungry?" She stretched and took a few steps, easing the stiffness in her back from sitting so long and being jarred on the drive into the valley.

"Plenty to eat in the house," Hawk said.

"Come on, Bri. Come meet Hawk." Tanner gently took her by the arm to lead her around the SUV toward his friend. "And Boyo."

Hawk McKenna had a solid handshake and a winning smile. For some inexplicable reason, she instantly both liked and trusted him. Something inside told her this was a good man. Something about him reminded her of Tanner.

Wait a minute. Tanner…good? Trustworthy? She had to admit her mental jury was still out on that verdict.

Boyo stood by his master, his long, black-tipped

tail swishing back and forth, his body trembling in eagerness to greet her.

Bri tentatively reached out a hand to the animal to sniff.

"You may touch him," Hawk said, his deep voice edged with amusement. "He won't bite you."

She touched the dog's muzzle and was promptly rewarded by a swipe of his tongue. Laughing, Bri caressed his head, scratched him under his wide jaw and ran her hand over his back. The rough, wiry feel of his coat against her palm surprised her; he had looked so sleek and smooth.

"You have a nice spread here, Mr. McKenna," she said, glancing up at him, her compliment sincere.

"Thank you." He smiled at her before sweeping the property with an appreciative look. "It's home."

He led them to the house, Boyo in step on the far side of him.

"Welcome," Hawk said as he pushed the door open, stepping back and sweeping his arm in invitation.

Boyo trotted into the kitchen, and within moments they could hear him lapping up water.

"Thank you." Bri smiled at him as she stepped into what was obviously the living room. She glanced around her at the sparse yet homey decor.

"This is very nice," she said, turning to smile at Hawk. "Navajo?" she asked, indicating a beautifully woven blanket hanging on one wall.

"Yeah," Hawk answered. "A gift from a friend."

"It's lovely." Bri smiled, moving forward for a closer look. "You have nice friends. That blanket must be worth a small fortune."

"It is. And I do." Hawk nodded and glanced at Tanner. "And Wolfe, there, is the friend." He smiled, slow and easy. "Wanna tell Ms. Stewart what you paid for the blanket, Tanner?"

"No." Tanner shook his head but smiled back. "He earned it, Brianna," he explained. "He helped me track a man, a real badass, two years ago. The jerk was a multiple killer with a big bounty on his head." He shot a dry look at Hawk. "I wanted to share the bounty with him. He said no but that he'd accept a particular blanket. You see—"

"Wolfe," Hawk said, a warning in his tone.

"You don't scare me, ole son, so save your breath." Tanner grinned at him.

Hawk narrowed his eyes. Tanner's grin widened.

Fearing that any second they'd be at each other, fists flying, Bri held a hand in the air in the signal to halt. "Don't start anything here, you two. This house is too beautiful to wreck it in a free-for-all." Her voice was soft but stern. "If you're going to beat up on each other, take it outside."

Tanner and Hawk stared at each other a moment, then roared with laughter.

Bri placed her hands on her hips, glared at the two of them and tapped one booted foot on the hardwood floor. "I do hope you're not laughing at me." Though pleasant, her voice held a sting.

"Wouldn't dream of it, ma'am." Hawk was obviously fighting to contain a grin.

"Never gave it a thought, *ma'am.*" Tanner didn't bother to hold back a grin. He laughed out loud.

"O-kay. I've had enough of your silliness." Bri was having difficulty maintaining the laughter rising in her throat. "I need a bathroom first, a proper bath and something to eat. Oh, and my pack."

Hawk slanted a sober look at Tanner. "She always this bossy?"

Tanner nodded, sighing. "'Fraid so. It's enough to drive a simple man to distraction."

Bri rolled her eyes and opened her mouth to blast the two of them. She wasn't fast enough.

"Yeah." Tanner gave a slow head shake. "I just don't know what to do with her."

Bri was torn between amusement and annoyance. She was silent just long enough for Hawk to get in another shot.

"Oh, buddy, I'd know what to do with her." Teasing laughter danced in his dark eyes.

"Well, yeah, but—"

That's as far as she let Tanner get. "But you're going to be too busy getting my gear from the SUV. Right?" Her tone held a definite warning.

"Er, yeah, right, I'm on it." Softly chuckling, Tanner turned and strode out the door.

"And I'm gonna finish supper." Hawk headed for the kitchen, clearly visible in the open floor plan, flicking a hand toward a hallway on the far side of the living room. "Bathroom's the second door to the left."

"Thank you." Bri headed for the hallway, hearing Hawk ask Boyo if he was hungry, too.

She was washing her hands, grimacing at her appearance in the mirror, when a soft knock sounded on the door.

"I've brought your pack, Brianna. Should I leave it here, outside the door?"

"No." She opened said door as he finished speaking. "I'll take it. Thank you." She rewarded him with her most brilliant smile, took the pack and then closed the door in his face.

"Whoa," Tanner murmured on an exhaled breath, thinking Brianna had the most beautiful and arousing smile he had ever had aimed at him. His jeans were suddenly tight, chafing him in a delicate part of his body.

The sound of the shower reached him through the door. Tanner imagined her standing under the tingling spray, naked and wet, the water sluicing down her slim body. Not only did his jeans get tighter, his chest grew tight, too.

Damn, get away from the door, Wolfe, before you explode and embarrass yourself by having to listen to McKenna laugh his ass off.

Drawing deep breaths and telling himself he could control his own body, his automatic reactions to a beautiful woman, Tanner gathered up the gear at his feet and headed to the bedrooms. He opened the door just enough to place Brianna's gear inside the room Hawk had designated as hers, the one Cat stayed in when she visited. From there he went to his room, the one he always used when he stayed at Hawk's place.

By the time Tanner nonchalantly strolled into the kitchen, he, aided by a cold shower, had worked his mind over matter…at least enough that it didn't show.

"Your lady friend is something, Wolfe," Hawk said, leveling a hard look at Tanner. "But why in hell did you bring her along on a hunt?"

"I didn't have a choice," he began, but apparently Hawk wasn't hearing him.

"Are you trying to get that beautiful creature killed?" Hawk demanded.

Tanner sighed. "I told you, I didn't have a—"

"Choice," Brianna finished for him in a decisive tone. "I played the trump card."

"Yeah," Tanner muttered, turning to look at her. Brianna stood in the entrance to the kitchen area, her still-wet hair hanging straight down her back, her face free of makeup, but glowing from her shower.

"What trump card?" Hawk frowned, glancing between his two guests, who continued to stare at each other.

"Money," they answered in unison.

Hawk arched his dark brows. "I like money," he

said, his voice laconic. "Though not enough to endanger a beautiful woman—or any woman, for that matter—by taking her along on a manhunt for a killer." His gaze narrowed on Tanner. "How much money are we talking about?"

Tanner switched his steely stare to Hawk. "An impressive amount of money."

Hawk smiled—well, almost—and turned his narrowed gaze on Brianna. "How much?" It wasn't a question so much as an order.

"A million dollars."

Tanner admired her cool composure. Not many people, men or women, could withstand that particular piercing look from Hawk. In the next few minutes, Brianna ratcheted up his admiration for her even further.

Hawk whistled. "That's a lot of dollars."

Flashing her traffic-stopping smile, she nodded in agreement. "Yes, it is." The smile fled, replaced by a haughty expression. "I take it you disapprove."

"I don't disapprove of the money," Hawk said with a quick shake of his head. "But I do disapprove of Tanner taking along a woman."

"Yet there are women bounty hunters," she retorted. "Are there not?"

"She used that same argument on me," Tanner inserted, just to remind them he was still there.

Hawk flicked a look at him.

Brianna ignored him.

"I don't approve of women bounty hunters, either. It's too dangerous for a woman."

"Indeed." Brianna's voice was icy.

"Yeah, indeed." Hawk matched her tone.

Tanner grinned, not that either one of them noticed. They were too busy trying to stare each other down. This should be interesting, he mused, settling down in a kitchen chair to watch the battle of wills.

No one knew better than he that Hawk was nothing if not tenacious. On the other hand, Tanner had personal knowledge of how stubborn Brianna could be. Yes, indeedy, he thought, controlling an urge to laugh, this should prove very interesting.

Brianna sighed as if sorely tried. "As I pointed out to your friend, I have had excellent training. I am well equipped to take care of myself."

With that, she had lobbed the ball into Hawk's court. Tanner waited for the return volley.

Hawk slammed it back at her. "I don't give a f—" He caught himself up short before finishing with, "freaking damn how well you've been trained. You don't belong in the mountains, tracking a criminal."

Whoa. Tanner stared at his friend in surprise. Hawk was losing his cool, and that didn't happen often. Tanner decided it was time to referee this match.

"Okay, boys and girls," he said, pushing himself from the chair to step between the two combatants. "Take a break. It's time for a truce."

"But, dammit, Tanner, it's just not safe!"

"Save your breath, ole buddy," Tanner said,

shaking his head. "I went through all that with her, chapter and verse." He shot a quick glance at her face, her expression one of detachment. "It's like talking to a brick wall."

"How charming, so complimentary," Brianna coolly inserted. "But can we drop the subject now? I'm so hungry I could eat a…brick wall, maybe." A smile teased her lips and danced in her bright eyes.

"Told you so," Tanner said with a grin, chiding Hawk.

Hawk heaved a deep sigh. "I give up."

"Good." She rewarded him with a charming smile. Too soon.

"On one condition," Hawk went on, challenge hard on his voice.

Bri narrowed her eyes. "What condition?"

Tanner frowned, wondering what Hawk was up to now.

"You take Boyo with you."

"But…" she began in protest.

"Good idea, Hawk," Tanner said, deciding it was time to end this match. "Brianna, Boyo is a good hunter. You know, the Irish wolfhounds were bred to hunt and bring down wolves and elk."

"Wolves?" She shifted her gaze to the dog, who had cocked his head at the sound of his name. "Well, he certainly looks big enough and strong enough for it. But he doesn't seem natured to do that. He's as friendly as a puppy."

"Of course he is," Hawk agreed. "Here he's a big, sloppy sweetheart. Matter of fact, most wolfhounds are simply house pets these days. But take him out hunting, turn him loose on a scent, and he reverts to breed and can be one mean son of a—" Again, he caught himself from cursing. "He can be rough."

"But…" she began.

Tanner smothered laughter to interrupt her. "You may as well give in, Brianna. Hawk can be as stubborn as you, maybe even more so."

"Oh, all right. We'll take Boyo…but only if I get food—pronto."

Hawk slid a look at Brianna, a smile twitching the corners of his mouth. "Man, you're tough. But you win. Food's ready. Let's eat."

Tanner lost it and let loose the laughter he had been holding back.

Hawk followed in kind.

Brianna looked from one to the other before her laughter blended with theirs. She was first to regain control. "Okay, you clowns, what's for supper?" She gave a dainty sniff. "Whatever it is, it smells wonderful."

Hawk sobered except for a lingering chuckle. "It's chili. Hope you like it spicy."

"Love it," she said.

Tanner wasn't surprised. He'd figured Brianna Stewart wouldn't have it any other way.

Five

Bri sighed with contentment as she dabbed her lips with a napkin. The chili was delicious. And spicy. She had hungrily finished off two bowlfuls, along with several slices of Hawk's homemade corn bread.

"That was a wonderful meal," she said to her host. "Thank you."

"You're welcome." Apparently pleased with her response, Hawk pushed back his chair and stood. "Are you ready for coffee and dessert now?" He glanced from Bri to Tanner.

"Coffee," Bri answered without hesitation. "But I couldn't eat another bite."

"Just coffee for me, too," Tanner said.

When they had finished their coffee, Bri stood up and began clearing the table.

"You don't have to help," Hawk said.

"I know. But I want to do it." She shooed him away with a hand. "You two go relax or something."

"You win. I don't often get out of kitchen duty." Hawk led the way outside to let Tanner choose the horses for the hunt.

At the door, Tanner paused to tell Bri how to find the room where he had stashed her gear. No sooner had he shut the door behind him when Hawk lit into him.

"Are you out of your mind?" he demanded, striding for the stables.

Tanner sighed. "Don't start, McKenna. I had my fill arguing with Brianna back in Durango. I'm not in the mood to argue with you."

Hawk snorted. "In the mood or not, you're getting an argument. Dammit, Wolfe—"

That's as far as he got before Tanner cut him off. "Yeah, dammit. Hell, double dammit. What else was I supposed to do?"

Reaching the stable, Hawk yanked the door open and flicked on the lights to illuminate the dim interior. "How about making it clear you wouldn't bring her. End of argument. Period."

"I tried that." Tanner gave his best friend a fierce scowl. "Didn't work. She told me if I refused, I should forget it, she'd find herself another hunter." He exhaled in a bid to ease the tension riding him.

"And you didn't want to give up a big payoff?"

"Are you nuts?" Now Tanner was getting angry. "Hawk, you know me better than that. And you know as well as I do there are bounty hunters out there that will agree to any conditions, even to allowing a woman to hunt with them, if the price is right."

Now Hawk sighed. "I know. But I don't like this at all. Brianna is a beautiful woman. A nice woman." He strode inside. "I'd hate like hell to see her hurt."

"Don't feel like the Lone Ranger. I feel the same way." His mouth curved into a wry smile. "That's why I'm not taking her along."

Hawk narrowed his eyes suspiciously. "Aah, are you saying what I think you're saying?"

"You got it, ole buddy." He grinned. "I'm leaving her here, in your capable hands."

"But what the hell's the difference if you leave her in Durango or here with me?"

"Hawk, you're not thinking," Tanner chided him. "If I'd have left her in Durango, she'd have either contacted another hunter or set out on her own." He shuddered. "I don't even want to think about that. Out here, with you, she's stuck. All she can do is ask you to drive her back to Durango."

"Where she will promptly look up and hire another hunter," Hawk pointed out.

"I know, but by then I'll be way ahead of the pack, so to speak."

Hawk shook his head as if in frustration. "And when you bring him in and hand him over to the law, you know damn well she will likely hand you a check for the original ten grand posted."

"I know." Tanner nodded. "And I don't care. Hawk, it's no longer the money. It's Brianna and her safety." He paused before continuing. "I'm attracted to her. Very attracted. It was there from the minute I opened my door and saw her standing there."

A small smile tugged at Hawk's lips. "That's understandable. Brianna's gorgeous and sexy as hell."

"Tell me about it." Tanner shook his head. "She had no sooner walked into my place and I wanted to swing her up into my arms and…well, never mind. I'm sure you can figure it out for yourself."

"Sure." Hawk nodded. "I've been there."

"I have, too, but not like this," Tanner admitted. "This is stronger than—" He broke off. "The point is, I couldn't leave her in Durango and I can't take her with me. This Minnich creep is a killer. He's killed at least one woman, and the law suspects there's more. If anything happened to her, if he got a chance to harm her in any way, I swear I'd go berserk." He shuddered at the very idea of Brianna injured. "Hawk, I can't take her with me. I can't take that chance."

Hawk nodded. "There's the hunter I know and love like a brother. You had me a tad worried that you had slipped a cog."

Tanner laughed. "Not to worry. Now let's look at horses."

Hawk paused at the second stall inside the stable. "We're going to have to play it cool, you know?"

"Yeah." Tanner nodded. "We can't take a chance of her getting suspicious. Leave the lights on in here when we leave. I'll bring her out to show her the horses we've chosen."

"Show her the mare." Hawk indicated the chocolate-brown horse in the third stall. "She would be the logical choice for a woman."

In no time, Brianna had the kitchen spotless and went in search of her room, musing on the idea that Boyo obviously liked her, for he padded after her.

Finding the room easily, Bri stepped inside, and immediately wondered if Hawk had frequent visits from lady friends. The bedroom had definite feminine touches, including a vanity table and bench, the surface littered with an array of skin-care products, makeup and a silver-backed comb-and-brush set.

Along the back wall was a queen-size bed, set between two windows through which the last rays of sunlight shone. Crossing the room, Bri drew back a sheer curtain panel to stare out at the vista. A huge meadow spread out from the side of the house and along the foothills of the mountain. She was puzzled for a moment by a large, flat, whitish circle on the ground a good distance from the house.

Then realization dawned. The white circle was a helicopter pad, right there on the edge of the meadow.

How convenient, she thought, smiling as she turned away from the window. A chopper would come in very handy when snow blocked the roadways in the dead of winter.

She had to smile. Boyo had made himself comfortable and lay stretched out on the foot of the bed as if it were his right to do so. Deciding it probably was, she walked back across the room, sitting down at the vanity to gaze into the mirror. Her hair, drying now, twirled into its natural waves. Her face appeared pale and dull. Bri was considering whether to retrieve her makeup case when she heard the front door open, close again and Tanner call to her.

"Brianna, Hawk's making a fresh pot of coffee. Do you want some?"

Sliding off the bench, she went to the door and called back, "Yes, I'll be right there." Glancing at the dog, she said, "You coming?" Boyo lifted his large head to give her a soulful look, then his head plopped back onto the mattress.

Guess not. A soft smile on her lips, she glanced again in the mirror, shrugged and left the room, thinking the hell with the hair and makeup. If Tanner and Hawk didn't like her bare face and unruly waves, they could just get over it.

"I like your hair down like that," Tanner said as she strolled into the kitchen. He grinned. "All kinda wild and loose around your face."

Bri gave him a droll look. "Thank you." Might

as well admit to the truth, she thought, smiling back at him. "I didn't bother to brush it."

"You didn't need to bother," Hawk said, placing two steaming mugs on the table. Crossing to the countertop to retrieve the third, he tossed over his shoulder, "You're among friends."

"I would hope so, as it's two to one here." She calmly glanced from Hawk to Tanner. "Not that those are bad odds, you understand, or that I couldn't handle the two of you. But it could get ugly."

Silence for a moment. Then both men broke up with laughter.

"I like this gal's style, Wolfe," Hawk said between lingering chuckles. "She might even be able to handle you, maverick that you are."

"I wouldn't bet the ranch on it, ole buddy," Tanner advised in a slow drawl.

Could she handle him? Bri asked herself hours later as she lay in the wide bed, staring at the diffuse moonlight shimmering on the ceiling through the sheer curtains. That same question had played games with her mind throughout the rest of the evening.

As soon as they had finished their coffee, Tanner had taken her to the stables to show her the horses Hawk had chosen for their use. Tanner's mount was a big roan with a shiny dark-red coat. For Brianna he had picked a brown mare, smaller than the roan but with a sweet temperament. The minute Brianna stretched out her palm, the mare poked her head over the gate on the stall.

Pleased with Hawk's selections, Bri introduced herself to the horses, talking softly to each as she stroked their noses and long necks in turn.

"I noticed from the bedroom window that Hawk has a helipad in the back pasture," she said later as they walked back to the house. "Does he own and fly his own personal helicopter?"

"No. He has the pad because he's alone out here most of the time. Although Hawk is a careful man by nature, accidents can always happen—to humans and animals. He installed the pad for convenience and for a quicker medical rescue response if needed." He tossed her a grin. "But, though he has lived here for a long time, he put in the pad only after Cat began using the ranch for a vacation getaway when she needed some space to be herself, breathe fresh air, roam free on the grounds."

"I see," Bri said, but then shook her head. "No, I guess I don't see. I can understand her wanting to visit her brother, but you said before she uses Hawk's place for a hideout. From what?"

"From the city, the crowds, the polluted air. Also from the jerks who get their kicks by making cracks about her heritage."

Anger flashed through her like a bolt of lightning. "I detest that sort of thing."

"Hey, don't attack me," Tanner said in a calming tone. "I feel the same way. But, like it or not, I'm afraid there are still some Neanderthals screwing up society. Men like the animal who attacked your sister and raped and killed her friend."

"I know." Bri nodded, exhaling to release the anger. "I have to deal with the crude type occasionally in the library."

"You work in a library?"

"Yes. I'm a research librarian at the University of Pennsylvania."

"The men come on to you, make suggestive remarks?" His voice carried an edgy note.

Confused by the sudden sharpness of his tone, she gave him a quick glance. His expression was bland, but his eyes were cold. Now what was biting him?

"Well?" he prompted, his voice now as cold as his eyes. "What did the crude jerks say to you?"

"Oh, the usual." She shrugged. "You know, juvenile things like, 'Oh, I've found the ice-queen types are always the hottest.'"

"Wonderful." His lip curled. "How smooth. How very debonair." He shook his head. "That line should have all the women falling on their backs for him. Stupid kids."

Bri shot a droll look at him. "That particular line came from one of the professors."

Tanner stared at her a moment, then laughed. "Some men never grow up, do they, no matter how smart and well-educated they are."

"So it seems," Bri agreed with him, smiling as they strolled toward the house.

When they reached the porch, he came to a stop, turning to face her, grasping her shoulders. "I guess I'm no smarter than the others."

"What do you mean?" Her voice began to fade and her breathing grew erratic, strained, as he lowered his head to hers.

"Fool that I am," he murmured, his lips barely a half inch from hers, "I'm going to kiss you, Brianna."

"Yes…please…" Her voice was swallowed up inside his mouth.

Incredible. His mouth claiming hers was absolutely incredible. And exciting. His tongue slid inside, sweeping every nook, tangling with her own.

Bri curled her arms around his taut neck, moving her body closer to him, against him. His arms circled her waist, drawing her closer still. Something seemed to sizzle through every cell of her being as he ground into her, making her all too aware of his erection.

Good heavens! She had never been kissed like this. At the time she had believed Mr. Smooth and Charming had been good, but he was a novice compared to the man she was now clinging to as tightly as ivy clings to a brick wall.

She wanted to cry out in protest when he lifted his head. She swallowed to keep it inside. "That was some kiss," she said, striving for normal, attaining something similar to a croak.

"Yeah, it felt like more." Releasing her, he stepped back, shaking his head. "But I'm not that much of a fool…I hope."

Bri didn't know whether to feel insulted or flattered. She felt confused. Who wouldn't be when a man called himself a fool for kissing her? Numb, she allowed him to lead her into the house.

From then on he was all business—except for the occasional brush of his arm or his hand against her. Bri had reached a point in her life where she believed there were no accidents. She knew his touches were deliberate.

But why? That was the question nagging at her tired and befuddled mind. Nevertheless, she and Tanner went through their gear, deciding, along with the occasional suggestion from Hawk and nose nudge from Boyo, what they should take.

Bri was relieved to learn they were taking a pack animal, which allowed her to take a few items more than the absolute essentials. One of those items was a bag of dark chocolate Hershey's Kisses she had stashed in an inner pocket of her backpack.

"You can't have any," she murmured to the curious dog sniffing at the pack. She ruffled his wiry coat, lowering her head to whisper, "They can make you very sick, and that would make me very, very sad."

The gear packed and ready for an early departure, Bri had excused herself and gone to her room, Boyo at her side. Once in the room, the dog again stretched out on the foot of the bed. Yawning, Bri curled under the plump comforter, as the night had grown much cooler.

Though it had been a long day, she couldn't go to sleep. Her mind was restless, repeating the same thoughts over and over.

Could she handle Tanner Wolfe?

Did she want to?

Damned straight, she wanted to.

Tanner couldn't sleep. Even with his eyes squeezed shut, an image of Brianna shimmered before him, teasing his mind, tormenting his libido. That kiss, that blazing, scorching kiss. Would he ever get the memory of it out of his mind, his senses?

"Damn," he muttered, tossing aside the comforter to allow the chill night air to cool his overheated body. "Stop reacting like a damn fool nineteen-year-old kid," he grumbled, shifting position. "You've got a job to do. Get your mind off the woman and onto controlling your imagination and your hormones. There's a lot of money at stake here...if she even pays you more than the original ten thousand posted."

That last animal-like growl silenced him. Money?

He hadn't really given a thought to the money since explaining his situation to Hawk. When had the money become secondary? *Secondary?* Tanner's now-overactive mind repeated. Secondary to what?

"Brianna." He whispered her name like a prayer. Brianna. Her name echoed inside his head like a mantra. She was the most unlikely woman. A gun-toting librarian. A woman of privilege who knew how to shoot and ride and track. Not at all the type he normally consorted with, he reminded himself, let alone fell for.

Jesus. When had she become so important to him? Not simply her safety but her, the woman? The woman he wanted more than he had ever wanted any woman before.

In that instant he knew without a doubt he would spend the rest of his life hunting down that killer, if necessary. Not for the money, Tanner thought, deciding then and there not to accept any, but for Brianna, for her peace of mind.

He would do it even at the loss of his own peace of mind…not to mention his sanity.

Tanner knew Brianna would not be there when he returned to Durango. He knew, as well, that she would never want to see him again.

Still, he ached for her, ached to be with her in the most intimate way a man could be with a woman. Tanner pulled the comforter around his body, which was both shivering and burning for Brianna.

Damn. What was the matter with him?

Tanner snorted. As if he didn't know. Still, he wouldn't admit it, not even to himself.

Six

A light tap and a murmured "Brianna" woke Bri. Frowning, her eyes barely open, she wondered why Hawk and not Tanner had come to wake her.

"I'm awake," she muttered, raking her fingers through sleep-tangled hair. Other than a small night-light plugged into a wall socket, the room was dark, and she reached to the nightstand to switch on the light.

"Coffee's fresh and hot."

"Give me a couple of minutes." Yawning, she tossed the cover back, grinning as Boyo lifted his large head, alert and apparently ready for anything.

"Hi, fella," she said, ruffling his hair. "Go back to sleep, you don't have to get up yet."

Obviously Boyo wasn't about to do any such thing as go to sleep. After stretching his legs, he jumped from the bed and padded to the door, waiting patiently until Bri opened it for him.

The hallway was well lighted, as was the living room beyond. Smiling, she wondered if Hawk had turned on every light in the house. That is, until she opened the bathroom door.

The bright sunlight filling the room jolted her like a shock. What the heck time was it? she asked herself, frowning as she entered the room. Hadn't Tanner said he wanted to get an early start?

Puzzled, she nevertheless took a quick shower and ran back to the bedroom to look at the clock she hadn't bothered to glance at before. The digital numbers flashed *8:45.* Stunned, she pulled the heavy blackout drapes over the sheers aside, staring in disbelief at the blaze of sunlight pouring through the window.

Suspicion tickling the back of her mind, Bri quickly dressed, braided her hair and left the room, following the aroma of fresh coffee.

Hawk stood by the stove. Boyo had his nose buried in his food bowl. There was no sign of Tanner or the gear he had set by the door last night.

The tickle of suspicion expanded into certainty. "Where's Tanner?" Her voice was cold, her stance stiff, her eyes narrowed.

"He's gone…left about five," he answered, warm compassion meeting her icy stare.

"Gone?" she repeated, voice rising an octave. "He left without me? That son of a—"

"Now, Brianna," Hawk cut her off in a soft, calming tone. "Come have a cup of coffee and some breakfast and I'll explain everything to you."

Annoyance curdled her tone. "Don't speak to me as if I were a child, Hawk."

"I'm not," he said, still soothingly calm. "I'm speaking to you as if you were an intelligent, mature adult. Now, please, come and sit down."

Still stiff with outrage at the deceiving rat Tanner, she nevertheless moved into the kitchen and sat down at the table. What else could she do? Rant and rave? She could do that sitting down over coffee.

Mere moments after her bottom hit the chair seat, Hawk set a plate of bacon, scrambled eggs and toast in front of her, followed by a steaming mug of coffee.

She sat there looking at the food, only sipping her coffee. She was way too angry to eat.

"I know you're angry," Hawk said, taking a seat across from her, "and I suppose you have every right to be. But not eating isn't going to solve a thing. Tell you what—you eat a little something, and I'll explain Tanner's reasons for leaving without you."

"I already know his so-called reasons. He doesn't want me, any woman or any*one* else hunting with him…the rat." Her voice dropped to a deeper, arrogant tone, mimicking Tanner's. "'Like it or not, I hunt alone.'"

"Yep, that's Tanner," Hawk agreed, surprising her. "Well, now that we agree on that, suppose you attack your breakfast."

Bri rolled her eyes. She drew a breath to tell him what to do with his breakfast, but in so doing got a whiff of the food, and her stomach growled. She gave in immediately.

To her surprise, Bri finished every morsel on her plate and every drop of coffee. Without being asked, Hawk refilled her mug.

"Thank you. Breakfast was delicious," she said, taking a careful sip of the hot brew. "Now I'm ready to hear Tanner's reasons for stranding me here."

Hawk smiled. "First of all, Brianna, you're not stranded. Second, he actually didn't deceive you."

Bri's back went ramrod stiff. "What do you mean? He deserted me when he said he would take me with him."

"And he did, in his way," Hawk countered. "He took you out of Durango and brought you here."

"That's not funny." She was getting steamed all over again. Suddenly her delicious breakfast lay heavy in her stomach. "He didn't say he'd bring me here, dammit! He said he'd take me along hunting with him."

Hawk was shaking his head. "He couldn't, Brianna."

"That's ridiculous." She glared at him. "He selected horses. Showed me the mare I was to ride. Stashed my gear next to his own by the door.

And now you tell me he couldn't take me. Why the hell not?"

Bri realized she was on the edge of losing it. She paused to breathe, calm herself down.

"He told me he could not—would not—expose you to the danger of possibly facing a killer."

"And I told him I can take care of myself, and Tanner knows it."

"I'm sure he does." Hawk nodded. "But then, I'm also sure it makes no difference to him." He gave her a gentle look. "Although I know Tanner's feelings about hunting alone, there is more to it in this instance."

"What?" Bri frowned. "What other reason, other than his pure, arrogant bullheadedness?"

Hawk sighed. "Your safety is important to him, Brianna. Very important."

Bri felt a tiny flare deep inside. Could Hawk possibly mean that Tanner cared for her? Oh, she was aware of the physical attraction between them. All too aware. But could he feel something stronger than that?

The mere idea, the thought alone, caused excitement to dance along her nerve endings. Then she came to her senses, telling herself to grow up and face reality. Tanner didn't care for her. He treated her the way he would any woman who wanted to hunt a killer.

But it was a lovely thought…for a moment.

Sighing softly, she lowered her head so Hawk

couldn't see the disappointment mirrored in her eyes.

"Okay," he said, sliding his chair back and standing. "I'll get these dishes cleared away and then I'll drive you back to Durango."

Bri snapped her head up. "I'm not going back to Durango," she said with quiet determination.

"You want to wait here for Tanner to return?" He hurried on before she could reply. "Not that I mind, you understand, but—"

"No, Hawk, I'm going after him."

"Alone?" Hawk stared at her. "Brianna, you should know it's never smart or safe to hunt alone." He shook his head. "This man is a killer."

Bri blinked, shook her head. "No, no, I'm not going after Minnich. I'm going after Tanner."

"It's just as dangerous."

"I'll be careful," she assured him.

"What if you get lost?"

Bri gave him a long look. "I do know how to blaze a trail, Hawk."

"But—"

"No buts," she said, shaking her head again. "I am going. Will you give me the use of a horse? I'll pay you the going rate."

"No." Flat, final.

Nothing could have made her reveal the hurt his refusal gave her. "Okay, I'll trek." She moved to rise, but Hawk held up a hand.

"You don't understand. I meant I won't accept

payment for the horse," he explained. "You can take any one you like."

Bri blinked against a rush of grateful tears. "Thank you, Hawk."

"You'll also need a pack animal."

"No, thank you. Another animal would slow me down. I want to catch up with Tanner before he catches up to Minnich." She started to leave the kitchen, but Hawk stopped her.

"Brianna, you'll need supplies and food. You can't go tracking Tanner without them."

"I've got trail mix and beef jerky in my pack." This time she did smile, keeping the chocolate to herself. "My father taught me early on to always carry some with me, just in case."

"You'll need more than that." He sighed. "I'll pack some food and water into saddlebags as soon as I finish up here." He raised his eyebrows. "Do you have all your stuff together?"

"All but the last-minute things," she said, once again heading out of the kitchen. "It'll take only a few minutes to get them."

Fully aware of the passing of time—time in which Tanner got farther away from the ranch—Bri quickly gathered her toiletries. Then she made up the bed and strode back down the hall.

Hawk wasn't there. For a moment Bri stood still, afraid she had been abandoned again. But common sense prevailed. Boyo sat by her backpack, glancing from the door to her and back to the door,

obviously waiting for his master to return. She
waited with him.

A few minutes later, Hawk walked back inside.
"I saddled the mare Tanner showed you last night.
Okay?"

"Yes." She smiled. "She's a sweetie."

"I'll get the saddlebags ready." He went into
the kitchen.

Bri knelt down to say goodbye to the dog.
"You're a sweetie, too," she murmured.

"I want you to take the sweetie with you,"
Hawk said, helping her to rise. "And no arguments," he went on as she opened her mouth to do
just that. "As I said last night, he'll protect you to
the death. And I've given him Tanner's scent." He
smiled. "Boyo will find him, and you won't need
to blaze a trail. In case he doesn't find him, he'll
find his way home."

Circling her arms around Hawk, Bri gave him a
big hug. "Thanks for everything," she said, stepping
back to smile up at him.

Hawk's high-boned cheeks wore a flush of
pleasure and embarrassment. "No—thank you,
Brianna. You're one to ride the river with."

Aware of the old Western saying, compliment-
ing her grit and suitability, Bri grinned. "Anytime,
Hawk. Just give me a call and I'm there."

"I'll keep that in mind," he said, stepping around
to open the door for her.

The mare Bri had decided to call Chocolate

stood waiting, the reins draped over the rail near the porch. Hawk had fastened the saddlebags in place.

"That should keep you till you catch up with Tanner…or until you're forced to give up the hunt for him and return here."

"That's not going to happen, Hawk. I fully intend to find Mr. Tanner Wolfe, big, bad hunter." Circling around to the left side of the animal, Bri shoved her boot into the stirrup, grasped the saddle pommel and swung herself up and over the mare, settling into the well-worn seat. Leaning forward, she stroked the mare's neck.

"Well, I see you know your way around horses," Hawk drawled, grinning back at her.

"I should. I've been around them since I was a kid, riding, grooming and, yes, even mucking stalls."

He laughed. "I don't think you'll have to do that on this trip." Then he sobered. "Reminds me— there's a sack of oats in the one bag, to supplement whatever grazing she can find, and food for Boyo."

Now Bri felt her cheeks flush with chagrin. "Thank you. I should have thought of their feed."

Hawk failed in covering a grin. "That's okay. You were a mite upset."

"No, I was a lot upset," Bri said, owning up to her anger. Gathering the reins, she thanked her host again. "I appreciate both your hospitality and your help."

"You're welcome." He tipped his hat. "Now time's a-wastin'," he chided, giving a light smack to the mare's rump. "Go, Boyo. Find Tanner."

The dog shot ahead of the horse to lead the way, beginning to weave back and forth, searching out Tanner's scent.

With a final wave to Hawk, Bri set the horse at a trot, following Boyo's lead. He quickly found the scent and settled into a lope. Keeping him in sight, Bri loped along behind him.

The day was long. Despite the bright sunshine, in the higher elevations the air was cool. It was a beautiful day to ride, but Bri wasn't riding for pleasure. She was on the hunt for two men. With any luck at all, she'd find Tanner first. Bri still felt angry but also eager, anxious and a bit scared, as well.

She had trekked the plains and jungles, the savannas and all types of mountains. Through it all, she had never felt the deep expectation and thrill of the hunt her father and his hunting buddies savored. After a while, she'd decided that one mountain looked pretty much like another, some smaller, some higher.

But this mountain, this hunt, were different. She had never hunted alone. Not going out alone was the first tenet her father had drummed into her.

Now she was on her own, trailing a dog, her sole companion. Boyo was following the scent a small distance from a stream. Made sense; Tanner and Minnich would need water.

Having eaten a solid breakfast, Bri kept going until past midafternoon. By then, she was glad to dismount and stretch. After rubbing down Chocolate, she dropped a handful of oats near a patch of grass. Next it was Boyo's turn. She scratched his head and under his long jaw and then put out the dried food Hawk had provided for him.

It was only then Bri took care of her needs. Digging into the backpack she had dropped to the ground, she pulled out a hand towel and headed toward the sound of the stream.

The rushing water foamed white around the bigger stones in the streambed. Clutching the limb of a pine tree, she lowered herself to her knees at the edge of the bank.

The water was as cold as the snow it had been at the higher elevations. Scooping handfuls, Bri cleaned her hands, rinsed her mouth and doused her face. The frigid splash took away her breath but refreshed her just the same. Drying her hands and face, she walked back to the animals and to what would be her makeshift camp for the night. The sun was lowering, and she had things to do before full sunset.

Entering the small clearing, Bri dragged a piece of a dead, dry log closer to the spot she had chosen for a fire. After gathering stones and placing them in a ring shape, she foraged for some kindling, which she ignited with a match. Once the twigs took flame, she fed the fire till the dry log began to burn.

Her growling stomach reminded her it was dinnertime. She searched the saddlebag to see what

Hawk had packed for her and found two bottles of water, peanut butter crackers, two apples, a sleeve of cheddar cheese and another of smoked ham.

Not too shabby, Bri thought, smiling. In fact, it was all nutritious as well as appealing. Silently thanking Hawk, she dragged a short log closer to the fire and sat down to eat.

Not knowing how long the food—or the hunt— would last, Bri ate sparingly, enjoying every bite. She allowed herself three pieces of chocolate for dessert.

Because the sun was quickly sinking, the shadows lengthening, she readied her sleeping bag a short way from the fire. By the time darkness fell, the air had turned decidedly cooler, so she'd shrugged into her jacket.

Wrapping her arms around her middle, she was assailed by a sudden feeling of loneliness. Another emotion overtook her, too. A yearning for Tanner. For his kiss.

Damn him, why had a simple kiss wound her up so tightly? Maybe because it was more—much, much more—than a simple kiss, she reluctantly acknowledged. His kiss was everything, the sun, the moon, the universe.

The rustle and howl of the night creatures interrupted her thoughts, and Bri realized it was now full darkness. She needed to sleep, to restore her energy for the hunt. After pulling off her boots and jacket, she crawled fully dressed into the sleeping bag, Boyo's impressive length stretched out beside her.

But sleep did not come. She lay awake for hours, watching the fire die down, while another fire roared inside her. The fire ignited by memories of Tanner and his kiss. She groaned and squeezed her eyes shut.

Even as sleep finally claimed her, she could taste Tanner's lips on her mouth.

Seven

A sound woke her before dawn. Shifting up onto one elbow, Bri glance around for the cause of the sound. It was Boyo, snuffling around on the ground.

"Hungry, boy?" she asked, grabbing her jacket before tossing back the bag's cover. Shivering, she pulled on the jacket, then retrieved Boyo's food and the oats for Chocolate. While the animals ate, she munched on a pack of peanut butter crackers between sips of water.

Within a half hour, Bri had everything together, Chocolate saddled and was on her way, once again trailing Boyo.

She made a brief stop around noon to give the animals as well as herself a break. Less than an hour later she was back on the trail. For the first part of their trek, they were following the stream upward. But slowly during the afternoon the ground leveled onto a fairly smooth plain. She let the horse pick her way through the trees and low brush while staying within sight of Boyo.

It was rough going. Once again, Bri stopped just past midafternoon. She was stiff and achy from being in the saddle so long. It felt wonderful just moving around on two legs.

After feeding the animals, Bri noticed Boyo beginning to roam. Certain he wouldn't go far, she visited the bushes for personal business, then strolled toward the stream to wash up.

Her foot caught on a root protruding from the grassy patch edging the low slope to the stream and she stumbled. When she regained her balance and glanced up, what she saw stopped her dead in her tracks. A man stood on the other side of the stream. He had changed his hair color and was wearing glasses, but Bri recognized him at once. Jay Minnich. In his hand he held a rifle hanging next to his thigh. And he was looking straight at her.

Even at that distance she could see the sick intent in his eyes. She took two steps back. He took three steps into the water, raising the rifle to his shoulder.

Bri froze. A lump of fear closed her throat, preventing her from crying out, although who she would have cried for she didn't know.

Yes, she did.

For Tanner. Where was he now, miles and miles away?

Barely breathing, Bri took another careful step back. His finger curled around the trigger. Shutting her eyes tight, she steeled herself for the impact of a bullet slamming into her body.

In that instant, not a bullet but another body slammed into her, knocking the breath completely out of her and sending the two of them to the ground. Her eyes flew open as the report from the rifle rang out and the zinging sound of a bullet whizzed overhead, a few feet above their bodies.

Tanner. She could have wept with relief, but her glance caught sight of his outstretched arm, a pistol grasped in his hand. He fired a shot, so close it sounded like a cannon blast to Bri. He gave a stern command to Boyo to stay.

Then he was up and splashing through the water. He halted about halfway across the stream to call Boyo to him. The big dog leaped into the water, crossing to the other side with Tanner. Bri could see him talk and motion to the dog, and as if in perfect understanding, Boyo sniffed the ground for a few minutes, then came to a quivering stop, head high, looking forward.

Bri knew Boyo had caught the scent of the man. Together, man and dog splashed back to her.

"He's gone," Tanner said, reaching a hand to her to help her stand. He lit into her the minute she was upright. "What in hell do you think you're doing?" He didn't give her time to reply but yelled on. "Are you trying to get yourself killed?"

Bri wet her dust-dry lips, almost as frightened of him as she had been of Minnich. "I was trying to catch up to you."

"Yeah, well, it's a damn good thing Boyo found me." He heaved a heavy exhale. "If he hadn't…" He trailed off, shuddering at the mere thought of the possible consequences.

"I won't say I'm sorry," she said, angling her chin in defiance. "I mean about tracking after you."

He sighed again. "I never expected you to." He turned away. "Let's go."

She hesitated. "Go where?"

"To my camp, of course, before it gets pitch-dark." He raised an arrogant-looking brow. "Or would you rather spend the night here?"

"No." She shook her head and made tracks to follow him when he strode away.

As Bri hadn't really unpacked anything but the food for the animals, very little time was required to get her gear together. She was in the saddle, trailing Tanner, as the sun slid toward the horizon.

His camp was surprisingly close to where she herself had stopped. Tanner had it set up, a fire going in a stone-ringed pit. A three-man domed sleeper tent was set up to one side. A log much like the one Bri had found the night before had been rolled near to the warmth of the fire.

"Home away from home," she said softly, sure he wouldn't hear her. He did.

"Yeah," he drawled a bit sarcastically. "Only we're not on vacation. You shouldn't be here at all."

"But I am, so deal with it," she retorted every bit as sarcastically. "As I told you I would be. You can't say I didn't give you an option."

"Okay, let's forget it. You're here and that's that." He turned to the fire pit. "Could you use a cup of coffee?"

"Oh, yes." She sighed. "I'd love one. But I have to wash up before it gets dark."

"I'll have the coffee and supper ready when you get back."

"Thank you." She made a beeline for the stream, energized by the promise of hot coffee and food.

After two days on the trail she felt so uncomfortable she stripped to the buff and rinsed herself all over, sorry she hadn't brought her shower wash with her. Freezing but refreshed, she rubbed herself dry and quickly dressed, unfortunately in her same clothes. She practically ran back to the camp to warm herself by the fire.

Tanner was nowhere in sight when she entered the campsite.

"Ah, there you are," he said, ducking his head as he exited the tent. "Hungry?"

"Starving," Bri admitted, hearing a low rumble in her stomach at the mention of food. "What can I do to help?"

"Not a thing," he answered, moving to the fire to stir a pot set on one of the flatter rocks. "Everything's under control."

"So I see." Bri glanced around the site. "How did you get it together so quickly?"

Tanner looked up. "I had started it when Boyo dashed into camp, to clamp his teeth onto my shirt and tug at me to follow him. Somehow I knew he was urging me on to find you." He actually smiled at her.

"Hmm," Bri murmured vaguely, her attention centered on the fluttery sensation his smile caused inside her more than on his explanation.

"How does soup sound for supper?"

"What?" Bri blinked herself out of bemusement. "Oh, soup, yes, that sounds good. What kind?"

"Vegetable. Hawk sent it along. It's dried but good. I've had it on other hunts. It shouldn't take much longer to get hot."

"You said something about coffee?" she reminded him.

"Yeah, there's some left in the thermos. Help yourself."

Bri wet her lips in anticipation, thrilling to the way Tanner's gaze followed her tongue. "Thanks." The last word came out in a dry croak that had more to do with Tanner's hot-eyed gaze than thirst.

He stood very still for a moment, staring into her eyes, then moved abruptly, striding for the gear to dig out the thermos when he realized she had no idea where it was. Pouring out a small stream of the coffee into the metal lid cup, he set it on the flat rock next to the soup pan. "Only take a minute."

The dry sound of his voice made Bri feel a little less vulnerable. Apparently she wasn't the only one affected by their proximity.

It was twilight by the time they ate their soup with chunks of dry day-old bread. For dessert, Bri took out her stash of chocolate and counted out four pieces each, to Tanner's obvious amusement.

As night began to fall, tension was a living entity between them. Every nerve in Bri's body quivered in a mixture of expectation and trepidation.

"There's a little coffee left. Would you like it?" Tanner watched her over the rim of his cup.

"Yes, please," she answered, grateful for an excuse to prolong the time to turn in. "What about Minnich?" she asked. "Do you think he might have crossed the stream with the idea that we would do the same?" Before he could reply, she rushed on, "I'd think he knows we're looking for him. What do you think?"

Tanner handed her the hot coffee before answering. "I think you're right."

Taking a careful sip, Bri nodded, swallowed. "So, then, how do we proceed? Do we cross the stream?"

He gave a quick shake of his head. "No. That's what he'll think we will do. We'll find out whether or not he crossed." His voice was mild, his tone confident.

Bri wasn't that certain. "How?"

"Boyo's got his scent. If he's crossed the stream, the dog will pick up his trail. And if he doesn't cross, he'll still follow it, because he knows damn well he'll need water."

"Of course." Bri felt like a dullard. Hadn't she seen Boyo finding the scent? Her only excuse was that she was so tense, so shaky inside about the deepening night, she wasn't thinking clearly. She lingered over the quickly cooling drink, drawing out the inevitable for as long as she possibly could. But she could procrastinate only so long.

Tanner stood up. "It's getting late," he said, stretching his arms over his head, giving her a peek at the ripple of his shoulder and chest muscles displayed by his open jacket.

Bri shivered. It was time for them to crawl into the tent. Would he expect a replay of their first wild and lingering kiss of two nights ago?

Did she want that to happen again?

Yes.

No.

At the moment she was too scared to decide. She ached from wanting his kiss, wanting him. But he was becoming too important to her, his smile, his laughter, all of him too necessary.

Tanner spoke, jarring her out of her introspection. "I'll clear away here and take care of the fire. You crawl into the tent and get undressed. I'll be with you shortly."

Bri froze for an instant. Undressed? Now was the time to tell him she wouldn't…she couldn't…

"Brianna, don't freak on me." His voice was soft, soothing. "I give you my word I won't try anything you tell me you don't want."

"Yes, but—"

"Sweetheart, I have some control," he said, shaking his head at her suspicious expression. "All I intend to do is sleep."

"But you said get undressed." Skepticism colored her tone and shaded her eyes.

"Down to your underwear. You do have long underwear, don't you?

"Yes." Bri hesitated another moment, staring into his eyes. Seeing nothing but caring there, she gave in with a quick nod and slipped inside the tent.

The interior was dimly lit by a small battery-operated lantern. The tent was roomy, plenty big enough for the two of them. But her breath caught when she looked at the sleeping bags already laid out for them. Tanner had zipped them together into one large sleeping area.

Oh, jeez.

"Brianna, I'm not going to be asking for anything you're not willing to freely give. Not now, not ever," he called to her as if somehow he knew she stood there, stock-still, staring at the bags. "Deal?"

"Y-yes," she said, carefully laying her rifle and handgun along one side of the sleeping bag, as he had placed his weapons on the other side. Then she raised her hands to her blouse to begin unbuttoning it. It was sheer relief to get out of her trail-grimy clothes. Naked, she picked up the damp towel she had used to dry off at the stream and rubbed her body down once more. Now she felt much cleaner. Tossing the towel aside, she dug into her pack for her long underwear.

Bri was snuggled inside the surprisingly roomy and comfortable bed of sleeping bags when Tanner lifted the flap and stepped inside, ushering Boyo in after him. Murmuring, "Down, boy," he pulled the zipper around the opening, enclosing the three of them inside.

Bri lifted her head. "Boyo is going to sleep in here with us?" She recognized the relieved tone in her voice.

Tanner's smile told her he recognized it, as well. "Yeah, it's getting cold out there and will likely get a lot colder by morning." With that, he began to undress.

Brianna's eyes flew wide, and he laughed out loud. "Don't panic. I'm only stripping to my underwear, and it's long underwear."

"I have silk." The words slipped out without thought. Bri was appalled at herself. She had sounded like a snit, the spoiled brat he had called her.

This time Tanner roared with laughter. "Okay, big deal. So have I."

Embarrassed, Bri turned onto her side, away from him, groaning softly at the sheer warmth, comfort and sense of protection she was feeling. In the next instant, she stiffened when his body slipped in beside her in the makeshift bed.

"Relax, kid, I'm not going to attack you."

She laughed; she couldn't help it. He sounded oh so amused beneath his serious tones. "I'm glad to hear it. I wouldn't want to have to hurt you."

His laughter was drowned out by Boyo, who stood, whining.

"I think he needs to go out," Bri said.

"No kidding," he grumbled. Getting up, he shrugged into his jacket, pulled on his boots. "Okay, okay," he said to the dog. "I'm coming." Unzipping the flap, he let Boyo outside. Pausing at the opening, he said, "I may as well check on the mare while I'm out."

"Chocolate."

He turned to stare at her through the dim lantern light. "You want chocolate now?"

"No." Bri had to laugh this time. "The mare. I've temporarily given her the name Chocolate, as I never asked Hawk what her real name is."

"Oh." He dipped his head and exited the tent. She heard his chuckle as he walked away.

Tanner was gone for some ten or so minutes, during which Bri shimmied around inside the sleeping bags. Once again she turned onto her side, this time facing the side he'd been sleeping on.

When Tanner did return, he zipped up the opening and shrugged out of his jacket and boots.

After turning around in a circle several times,

Boyo settled down across the opening of the tent. If anyone tried to enter during the night, they were going to have to walk over the big dog to do so.

Bri smiled at the very idea of anyone getting past the wolfhound and living to tell about it, possibly even if that someone were a bear. Her thoughts scattered when Tanner, smiling with her, slid in next to her.

"Are you warm enough?"

She nodded. The bed warmed her skin, but Tanner's smile warmed her body inside and out. "What are you doing?" she blurted when he drew her close to him, cradling her in his arms.

"I just want to hold you, Brianna," he said, his breath fluttering over her forehead. "Comfortable?"

"Hmm," she murmured, snuggling closer, so close she could feel his chuckle before she heard it.

"Good. Sleepy?"

"Not really," Bri said, stifling a yawn. "I'm just happy to stretch out, be warm and relaxed and off the back of a horse for a while."

This time he laughed aloud. Bri loved the sound of his laughter. It seemed to surround her with a sense of warmth and security.

"So you're not as tough as you thought you were," Tanner said, teasing her.

"Yes, I am," Bri said, pulling her head back to glare at him. "It's simply that I haven't been on a horseback trek in some time. I can handle it. It's only a little stiffness."

"I never doubted it." Tanned did his best to look serious. The gleam in his eyes gave him away.

"Yeah, right." She scowled.

He laughed again, cupped her head to draw her face closer to his and planted a gentle kiss on her temple. "I really didn't doubt it, Brianna."

Bri melted. She loved the way he said her name. "Okay, you're forgiven." Her temple was tingling where his lips had touched.

"Thank you." Laughter danced along his voice. "Is that a blanket forgiveness, covering my having left Hawk's without you?"

She hesitated long moments, smothering the anger she had been nursing since she had discovered him gone. "I suppose so," she said, giving in, but only because she really wanted to do so.

"Grudging, but I'm grateful for it."

They were quiet a moment, his breath teasing her skin, sending tingles from her temple to every nerve ending in her body. Desperately hanging on to her desire to have him kiss her, maybe make love to her, Bri raked her mind for something to say to break the feeling of sensual intimacy curling around them, seemingly drawing them closer to the precipice of no return.

To defuse the volatile intimacy, she said, "Tell me about yourself, Tanner, your life." Her voice sounded ragged even to her own ears.

"Why do I have this sneaky suspicion you don't trust me?" His tone was drily amused.

"It—it's not that," she said. "I do trust you." Bri realized she truly did, that she would trust him with her life. Odd, she mused, after having known him such a short amount of time. But there it was. Then again, he had saved her life only hours ago.

"If it's not that," he said, "what is it?"

"Me." Bri's throat felt suddenly parched. "It's myself I don't trust, Tanner."

"I don't get it." He sounded more than a little confused. "You don't trust yourself about what?"

Once again Bri hesitated, unsure if she should explain her feelings. "You. I don't trust myself with you," she admitted, glancing up at him, her confidence bolstered by the fact that his face was in the shadows.

She could feel his body go completely still, feel the tautness in his arms around her. What must he be thinking? Had she unwittingly insulted him?

Frustration was sharp in his voice when he spoke. "Brianna, I told you, I won't—"

"No, Tanner, please listen. You don't understand," she said, burrowing closer to him. "I know *you* won't." She sighed. "The problem is I'm not sure *I* won't."

"I see." Enclosing her again in his arms, this time even more tightly, he kissed her ear, whispering, "You know something, Brianna? You're a little nuts."

No one had ever said anything like that to her before. Her reaction began with a giggle and grew from there to laughter that spilled out from deep inside. Burying her face in the curve of his neck, she laughed harder than she could recall having laughed in a very long time. Partly because she thought it funny and partly in sheer relief.

"You know something, Tanner?" she gasped through her dying laughter. "You're right."

His lips brushed her cheek. "That's okay, kid, because I'm a bit nuts, too."

Eight

She loved this man. The realization flashed through her mind like a sudden bolt of lightning.

Bri's insides seized. What was she thinking? Love? She couldn't have fallen in love this quickly. Could she? Abruptly her laughter died in her throat, but she kept her face pressed against his shoulder, inhaling the spicy, male scent of him.

"Amuse you, do I?" Tanner asked, laughter dancing on his own voice. "I really didn't think it was all that funny."

"Oh, Tanner, you have no idea." Bri had to pause to take a breath, collect herself, get her thoughts back in line. "That's one of the reasons I don't trust myself with you. You're so up-front and straightforward. So few people are today, it's refreshing to find someone who is." She was chattering, making it up as she rattled on, determinedly blanking all thoughts of Minnich and the L word from her mind. At least that's what she told herself.

"Despite your PC phrasing, why do I get the idea you're impugning my gender?"

Bri couldn't help it; she smiled. If he had been trying to sound offended, he had failed completely.

"I'll plead the Fifth," she said, shooting a quick look at him.

"Right now I wish I *had* a fifth."

At that, her laughter erupted. Even Boyo lifted his head at the happy sound of it.

Within seconds, Tanner joined her. The sound was music to Bri's ears.

"What exactly are we laughing at, do you know?" he asked as his laughter subsided.

"At ourselves, I think," she answered, drawing a deep, sobering breath. "It was fun, though, wasn't it?"

"Yeah." Tanner was quiet a moment, doing some deep breathing of his own. "What do you want to know?"

"What?" His sudden question threw her.

"You said before that you wanted to know more about me," he said. "So what do you want to know?"

"Everything." The word burst out before she could hold it back.

"Oh, is that all?" He lifted one shoulder in a half

shrug. "That should take no longer than…oh, five, six hours. Of course, if I remember correctly, we went over our respective favorite things at lunch in Durango. Didn't we?"

"Yes, I know, but I meant…well, other things."

"Like what?"

"Have you ever been in love?" Oh, damn, why was she having trouble with that darn *love* word? Nevertheless, she waited, not breathing, for his answer. If he would answer.

He didn't hesitate. "I thought I was once." His shoulder shrugged and she breathed again. "I was wrong. Have you?"

Bri wouldn't allow herself to be less candid than Tanner. She even took it a step further. "Once. I was wrong, too. He was a handsome, charming snake, a cheat and a user."

"Gee, could you be a bit more specific?" he said, his voice teasing.

"He was a rat," she said, deadly serious. "I came back to the dorm one night from the library to find him in bed with my roommate. I threw him out first. Then, without a shred of remorse, I used my father's influence to get her out of the room and into another dorm."

"You are tough."

"I was mad." Memory anger colored her voice. "At least I didn't do either one of them bodily injury."

"I'm glad to hear it," he said. "For an instant there I was afraid you were going to tell me you punched her out and took a skinning knife to him."

"Son of a gun," Bri deadpanned. "Why didn't I think of that at the time?"

Tanner let go of a smile right before he brushed his lips over her mouth. "Next question?"

His breath bathed her lips, stole her breath, tangled her thoughts.

"Did you fall asleep?" His lips were now at her ear again, teasing, tormenting.

"No." It was barely a croak.

"Are you out of questions?"

"No, I'm…thinking."

"Does it hurt?" His tone was solicitous.

She gave him a look.

He grinned, unrepentant. "We could discuss favorite holidays. Mine's Thanksgiving. The turkey and trimmings, you know. Anything else?"

"Well…" She hesitated a moment, then took the plunge. "I was wondering about Candy."

He frowned. "The dark chocolate you've been doling out like it was gold?" He licked his lips, stirring a wish inside Bri that it were her lips being laved. "I love it, the darker the better."

"No." Bri shook her head in an attempt to shake off the sudden need of his mouth and quickly asked, "Would you like some now?"

"No, thank you." He chuckled. "Was that one of your questions?"

"No, and I think you know it," she said, suspicion growing. "I mean Candy of the Hamptons."

"What about her?" She could almost hear his frown in his voice.

"She seemed…oh, I don't know, kind of possessive of you. Are you…?"

"I believe I answered that at the time, Brianna." Impatience rode his tone. "There is not now, nor has there ever been, anything personal between us."

"I'm sorry." Bri was quick to back off. "I know it's none of my business."

He sighed. "There is no business so far as Candy is concerned. I'm not interested in her the way you mean."

"Personally, sexually?" Bri asked boldly.

"No, sweetheart, I'm not. Wouldn't do me any good if I were. She's engaged to the man who was waiting for her in the restaurant. Besides, she's not my type. Too forward, too easy."

Bri frowned. "What does that mean?"

"What you think it means. She's been with too many men. Not that it's any of my business. But I'm a lot more particular than some other men."

Satisfaction swept through Bri like balm. "I think I knew that."

She knew he shook his head as if in puzzlement, not only because she felt the motion but also because the strands of his long hair brushed against her cheek and tickled her neck.

"If you knew, why ask?"

Bri scoured her mind for a reasonable or at least plausible answer. "Uh…I'm nosy?"

"And a lousy liar," he retorted. "You wanted to know because you didn't like her on sight and thought asking me how I felt about her would give you some idea about my character—or lack of same."

Smart-ass. Bri kept the instant thought inside her head, where it belonged. But, of course, he was right, so she supposed she might as well admit it.

"Yes," she confessed, not at all contrite.

"Sneaky, Brianna," he chided her, amusement lacing his tone. "Clever but sneaky."

"Obviously not too clever," she said wryly. "You were on to me at once."

"Okay, then I'm clever." He pulled her even closer to him.

"Yes, you are," she said, trying and failing to swallow a yawn.

"Sleepy?" he murmured.

"Yes," she answered, thinking it was pointless to deny what had to be apparent to him.

"Twenty Questions over for tonight?"

"I suppose." She sighed. "Except…what's your favorite color?"

"Well, it used to be blue, like in jeans," he answered. "But now it's auburn-red, like the gorgeous color of your hair."

Said hair quivered at the back of Bri's neck. "Thank you." Her voice quivered, too. She was losing ground here, and fast. Bri knew if she didn't call a halt now, she could happily whistle goodbye to her need for sleep for some time.

"What's yours?"

Huh? Bri frowned in the dimness. Oh, her favorite color! What the heck was it? Biding for time to remember what should be obvious to her, she stifled a fake yawn against his neck.

"Don't lose sleep over it." His voice was both soft and tender. "You may answer and resume your third degree of me on the trail tomorrow."

Bri heaved a deep sigh of relief.

He chuckled.

Bri sighed heavier, wishing he wouldn't do that. "Oh, did you have to mention that? I was trying to forget I would have to get back on the horse tomorrow."

"You'll do just fine and you know it."

"Yes." She yawned again and stopped fighting her heavy eyelids. "Good night, Tanner."

"Warm and comfortable?"

"Deliciously." Her voice was slurring.

He chuckled. "Then go to sleep."

"Okay." The next instant, Bri was out. She never heard him say good-night to her.

As he had two nights before at Hawk's place, Tanner lay awake for a long time after Brianna fell asleep, breathing in the smell of herbal shampoo in her hair, the elusive natural woman scent. It was a heady aroma, pure female, delicious. He'd love to taste her.

He drew another, deeper breath, trying to calm

his senses. All it accomplished was to arouse them and him even more.

He lost himself in the fantasy of the smooth softness of Brianna's skin as he moved his hands over her body. How he had wanted to caress her, kiss her, every inch of her, hold her close to his hard body.

He wanted her so badly, ached to be deep inside of her, become a part of her. Everything inside him clenched with need, and he pressed his lips together to contain the groan swelling his throat.

Damn. He needed to get away from her, if only for a few minutes. He needed to get out of the tent, into the air. Maybe the chill of night would cool his overheated body, his hungry thoughts.

Stealthily he slid from the makeshift bed. Hushing Boyo, he unzipped the door and slipped into the night.

The air was chilly but not cool enough. Tanner thought what he really needed was a cold shower. The stream. Without another thought, he grabbed a towel from one of the packs and was moving through the forest, along the path, following the sound of water. He hadn't gone very far when Boyo loped up to pace protectively alongside him.

"You should have stayed with Brianna, boy," he murmured. "I can take care of myself."

As if understanding Tanner's every word, the dog slowed to a near stop, cocking his large head to look up at him, waiting, watching.

"I'll be okay." Tanner's voice took on a hint of

command. "Go back, boy, make sure she's safe in the tent."

A second of hesitation, then the dog turned to trot back the way he had come.

Shaking his head in wonder of the animal's obvious intelligence, Tanner continued on to the creek. The water wasn't merely cool or even cold; it felt like melted ice, which was very close to what it actually was.

Pulling off his underwear, Tanner briskly waded into the stream. He caught his breath at the shock of the freezing water and, holding it inside him, he lay out flat to submerge his entire body.

He lasted all of a couple seconds before scrambling up and onto the bank. Scooping up the towel, he swiftly and roughly dried his shivering and thankfully no longer aroused body. Pulling on his underwear, he made his way back to the protection of the tent, the warmth of the bed...and the woman asleep in it.

Shivering almost violently, he slid between the layers of the sleeping bag, close to her warmth but not touching her until his underwear warmed and his body stopped shivering.

Sighing with relief and moving slowly so as not to wake her, he reached to the side to turn off the lamp but hesitated for just a few moments to gaze into her face. Smiling, he switched off the lamp.

Beautiful, beautiful, he thought, settling close to her again, her face nestled in the curve of his neck.

Awake, laughing, somber, Brianna was beautiful. Asleep, she was even more so. She was exquisite.

She sighed and her warm breath fluttered over his skin. Tanner felt a twist in his chest. What was it about this particular woman that could make him ache, not only with desire but with admiration, caring and an urgent need to protect?

He had known many women, some intimately, some as pals, friends. He had cared for them, each and every one of them. He had even begun to believe he was in love with one of them. Yet none had ever affected him with the depth of feelings and emotion as Brianna.

"What is it about you?" Tanner whispered. Once again that twist curled in his chest. The descriptive word hovered in his mind, waiting to be recognized.

Love.

Tanner froze, rejecting the very concept. Love? He hardly knew her. And he had never believed in the fairy tales of love at first sight and happily ever after. He wasn't sure he believed in love at all.

No, he wasn't in love with Brianna. He couldn't be. Not so quickly. Could he?

She made a murmuring sound—not a sigh but not an actual word, either—and snuggled closer to him. Was she cold? The thought had him drawing her tightly to his once again warm body.

Then she sighed. Her eyelids fluttered, and she softly kissed the side of his neck. Tanner stilled. Was she awake or nuzzling him in her sleep?

"Tanner…"

Her voice was soft but not sleepy.

"I'm here," he answered.

"Will you kiss me?"

Everything went still inside him. Would he? He was dying with wanting to kiss her, make love with her. "If that's what you want," he whispered against her ear.

"Yes…" She murmured the word on a sigh and lifted her head, offering her mouth to him.

He gratefully accepted, claiming her lips with his own. Her mouth was sheer heaven and made him burn like the fires of hell. Tanner deepened the kiss, wanting, needing, desperate for more of the sweet, erotic taste of her mouth.

Brianna returned his kiss with a hunger that scorched him. The heat spread through his body, making him hard. With the last of his common sense, Tanner told himself to end it at once, before it was too late. But he had tuned out reason, not paying a bit of attention. Instead his mouth delved deeper into hers, savoring the nectar that was exclusively Brianna's.

Getting desperate, Tanner shifted his hips to bring his body against hers, letting her feel his arousal, his desire to be one with her.

Instead of withdrawing, as he was certain she would, she tightened her arms around him and, clinging to his mouth, ground her hips against his, inflaming him more, burning his common sense to ashes.

"Brianna." His voice was raw, roughened by passion whirling out of control.

"Yes." That was all she said. That was all she needed to say. The needy arch of her hips into his said the rest.

"Are you sure?" He had to know now, before he went up in flames.

Brianna remained silent but answered by moving away from him. Tanner went cold, then immediately hot again as she sat up and pulled her top over her head, tossing it aside to land atop her weapons.

Tanner was tempted to laugh for an instant, thinking the most dangerous weapons were right there, in the form of her satiny skin, her beautiful breasts, her puckering nipples.

He sucked in a breath, aching to suck on her, taste the offering she made to him. He leaned forward to her, disappointment streaking through him when she moved away from him.

What the hell? The thought was a wisp, gone when he saw her wriggling out of her pants. His body throbbing with lust for her, he jackknifed upright and shucked out of his underwear.

At the same moment he slipped back into the sleeping bag, she opened her thighs in invitation. Tanner was not about to refuse. As he slid between her legs, thrilling to the silkiness of her skin, he captured one nipple and sucked it into his hungry mouth.

He thought he could feast on her forever, but he was wrong. It soon became obvious Brianna would not simply lie there like a sacrifice. She ran her hands all over his body, his chest, his back, his hips, his belly, his…

"*Brianna.*" His voice was ragged with strain. He exerted every ounce of control to hold back, just kissing her, caressing her, giving her the utmost enjoyment.

She was having none of his restraint. Releasing him, she drew him up and over her, seeking his mouth. "Don't wait, Tanner," she whispered against his lips. "I need you inside me now."

Happy to comply, he moved into position and thrust his tongue into her mouth at the same instant he slid his body into hers.

She gasped. For a moment he froze, afraid he had somehow hurt her, but she grasped his hips, digging her nails into his flesh and arching her hips as she pulled him deeper into her body.

Tanner went wild. Still hanging on to a shred of control, he began to move, slowly, then faster, deeper. She moaned, arching high into each successive thrust, driving him on yet holding back until, crying out, she soared over the edge of utter pleasure. Tension became nearly unbearable inside him. He gave one final thrust and he was there, soaring with her in the most incredible completion of his life.

Bri lay beside him, her heart racing, her breathing harsh, her body sated and depleted. Never, never had she experienced anything so mind-shattering, so earthshaking, so absolutely wonderful. She wanted to laugh and cry at the same time. It had been so very beautiful.

"Are you all right?" Tanner's voice was close to her ear, soft with concern. He lay beside her, his own breathing labored.

"Oh, Tanner," she answered between gasped breaths. "That was so…so…"

"Yes, it was," he murmured, kissing her earlobe. "It was even more than that."

She sighed with satisfaction. "Thank you."

"Me?" He sounded astounded. "I should be thanking you. Brianna, you are magnificent."

Turning her head, she brushed her lips over his, whispering, "Yeah, I am, ain't I?"

Tanner laughed. Then he was kissing her, her temple, her cheek, her chin and, finally, her lips. Her lips clinging to his, she drowned in his mouth.

Minutes later, curled against him, her head pillowed on his perspiration-slick chest, safe and secure in the cradle of Tanner's arms, Brianna fell asleep. All thoughts of tomorrow had been swept from her mind by the release of her tension from their lovemaking.

Tanner lay awake, his mind playing with the idea of him and Brianna being, staying together. No, he thought. Damn. There was no way he could be with her. When their hunt was over, she would go home to Pennsylvania, her quiet library, her upper-class friends. He, on the other hand, would be here. Or there. Or wherever he needed to go, hunting down criminals for money.

They had had great sex one time. No, he corrected, they had made love one time. But one time did not make a relationship.

Brianna was above him.

Tanner shook his head. That was wrong. Her father may have more money than his folks, but that didn't put her above him…not in any way other than where he placed her. In his mind he placed her if not on a pedestal then as the most important person in his life. And he knew, without doubt, if necessary he would lay down his life to protect her.

Why the hell did he bring her along instead of dragging her back to Hawk's place? Certainly not for the money. He had already decided not to take anything from her. In truth, he really didn't need the money—he liked it, but he didn't need it. He had earned plenty enough in his chosen occupation and he had invested the bulk of it wisely. While Tanner wasn't wealthy, he had a very comfortable nest egg.

But money didn't have anything to do with his situation concerning Brianna.

Although she was experienced in the hunt, it was this hunt and this hunt only she cared about, and with good reason. She had told him she no longer liked trekking, even with a camera. She had an altogether different lifestyle in the world of books and normal activities.

Tanner felt certain Brianna considered his lifestyle abnormal. So where did that leave them when the hunt was over? He knew the answer. It left her on the East Coast and him in Colorado or parts unknown.

Brianna moved closer to him, one long leg sliding over his thigh. Tanner's body hardened in response. Grimacing in discomfort, he drew a deep breath, exerting control. It wasn't easy, but he shifted back an inch, away from temptation. The need raging inside him subsided a little and he released a long sigh of relief.

He ordered his body, his emotions, to forget the ifs and might-have-beens and focus on the long day ahead.

His inner voice had one piece of advice. Go the hell to sleep.

Nine

The first pale light of predawn tinged the horizon when Tanner woke her.

"Brianna," he said softly. "It's time to roll out. You have enough time to dress and wash up before the coffee's ready."

"Mmm," she answered. Kind of.

Tanner chuckled. "Is that an 'okay' or a 'get lost'?"

The warm sound of his soft laughter tingled Bri into full wakefulness. She yawned before saying, "Okay, I'll be out in a few minutes."

She was true to her word…almost. It was a little more than a few minutes, more like eight or ten, and two of those minutes were used up simply getting her tired body out of the sleeping bag. Once she was upright, Bri pulled on jeans and a shirt over her long underwear and clean socks before pulling on her boots. By the time she finished, the soreness in her body from having sex after so long a time had eased to a mild ache.

After using her toiletries and pulling her hair back into a ponytail, she repacked her bag and carted it outside. She dropped it next to Tanner's, then made a dash for the bushes.

His soft chuckle followed after her. Trying her best to ignore a tingle in response to him, she concentrated on the urgent business at hand.

Finished, she cleaned her hands on a toss-away sanitary wipe, then followed the aroma of coffee back to camp.

She found Tanner squatting over the fire, preparing two cups of instant coffee. He held one up to her and she took it.

As he worked to put out the fire, his muscular thighs stretched the denim of his jeans, reminding her of how impressive they'd felt against her last night. When he looked up and she saw his face behind the curtain of his dark hair, she remembered how his eyes had looked down at her with passion. She promptly dropped her cup.

Boyo jumped up, barking at the sound of the tin cup hitting a rock. Taking up the charge, the horses whinnied and restlessly moved.

"Now look what you've done," Tanner said, standing. "You've gone and spooked the animals."

"S-sorry, I don't know what happened. I'm not usually clumsy." Nor did she usually get affected like that by a man.

Tanner handed Bri his own coffee and, after calming down Boyo, went to settle the horses.

Bri watched his easy gait, his tight rear, and once again felt unsteady. She had to force her eyes away from his body and onto the horses. From a sack he'd pulled out of the pack, he sprinkled some feed on the ground for the two horses. His diversion worked. The horses went immediately to their feed.

He was impressive with the animals. Gentle, firm when needed but always attentive, just as he'd been last night with Boyo in the tent.

And with her, said an inner voice.

She managed to ignore the images that thought conjured.

"We've got to eat and get going," Tanner told her when he returned to the fire. "I'm sure Minnich isn't out there lingering over breakfast." Before she could agree, he handed her an oatmeal bar.

She was so hungry she downed it before Tanner had the fire out.

When he got up and noticed her empty wrapper, he seemed surprised. "Would you like another one?"

Embarrassed, she looked up at him from underneath her lashes. "If we have enough."

Chewing his own bar, he retrieved another and gave it to her. "We've got to get packed now."

She followed his lead, picking up her coffee cup and loading her saddlebag on Chocolate.

"Here, I'll take that." Tanner came up beside her to heft the other pack she held. "It's heavy."

"I can handle it," she said, but the words got stuck in her throat when she turned and found his face mere inches from hers. He lingered there, and, too awestruck to move, Bri drew in the scent of him. He looked even better in the light of day than he had last night.

When she found her voice, she asked, "What are you doing?"

"Me?" Tanner replied. "You're the one who was batting those long eyelashes at me before. Are they fake?"

"Fake?" Bri nearly screeched but held back to not startle the animals again. "I'll have you know, Mr. Wolfe, I have never in my life worn fake eyelashes…or anything else."

Tanner's face split in a grin. "I know. You're the real thing," he drawled as he ran a slow, heated look over her body from head to toe, allowing his eyes to travel where his hands had gone last night.

The slow burn in Tanner's eyes gave Bri a hot flash. Steadying the uneven rhythm of her breathing, she croaked out, "Is there any water?"

Without stepping far from her, he pulled a bottle out of his saddlebag. She took it and gulped a mouthful. The cold water did nothing to calm her heated thoughts. Last night had been…everything. It was as if they'd suddenly become one…one body, one soul, one completed entity. Making love with Tanner had been the best experience of her life, and she couldn't wait to do it again and again….

She couldn't stifle the gasp that rose out of her throat. Oh, Lord, she was in big-time trouble.

"Are you okay?" concern shaded Tanner's voice.

"Yes…I'm sorry," she managed to say. "The breakfast bar must have gotten stuck in my throat." At his skeptical look, she turned away, going to retrieve another pack.

Within twenty minutes they had their mounts ready, the packhorses loaded and were on the move.

They rode single file along the narrow track. When the path widened enough for two, Bri rode up alongside him.

"I've been thinking," she said. "Suppose Minnich doesn't follow the stream but moves high into the mountains?" She'd forced herself to ignore Tanner and focus on the reason they were here.

"Unless he knows exactly where there is more water, he can't afford to do that. He has food, but eventually he'll run out of that. Now he can last a good while without food, foraging for edible early-spring plants and berries. But water?" He shook his head. "The way I see it, he'll likely stay with the stream." He sent a sidelong look at her. "Naturally I could be wrong. The melting snow is filling many small streams and creeks. If he knows his way around these mountains, he'll veer off. But I'm banking he doesn't know them that well."

Bri nodded her understanding. "But I know you enough by now to be fairly sure you thought he would stay on this course. You didn't hesitate, you deliberately chose this way. Why?"

"Because this way leads into the thickest section of the wilderness, the least traveled by tourists, hikers and backpackers. And because this stream is well marked on maps of the area."

"Makes sense. I should have known better than to even ask such a stupid question."

"No." Tanner shook his head, swinging the ponytail hanging out from under the wide brim of his hat. "You can ask anything you want, Brianna. There are no stupid questions, just sometimes stupid answers."

"Somehow I don't think you give many of them."

He smiled at her compliment. Already soft, Bri's insides went all squishy. She gathered the loose reins to drop back again, but his hand snaked out, covering hers.

"Stay and ride with me, Brianna," he said, keeping a light, disturbing hold on her hand. "We'll be stopping for a rest and a quick lunch soon."

Ridiculous as it seemed, with his hand lightly resting on hers, Bri had never before enjoyed riding so much, even with the ache in her rear end settling in once again.

From her position next to him Bri could now

clearly see Boyo, moving in a wide area back and forth ahead of them, his head moving from side to side, searching.

"Boyo is a worker, isn't he?"

"Boyo comes from a line of grand champion wolfhounds." He turned to grin at her. "But he loves to hunt."

"Hawk doesn't show him?" She tried really hard to ignore the effects of his grin. It didn't work.

"Hell, no." Tanner laughed. "Can you see Hawk traipsing around a show ring, leading Boyo?"

Bri frowned. "There's nothing wrong with showing dogs. They're beautiful."

"I know," he agreed, to her surprise. "I watch the competitions on Animal Planet. But think, Brianna—can you really picture Hawk all duded up at a dog show?"

Bri tried to imagine it and soon gave up the effort. She smiled. "Not really."

"Thought so."

"Where did Hawk get Boyo?"

"He was a gift from Hawk's father."

"Is his father still alive?"

"Alive and well and raising champion wolfhounds in Scotland where he lives." He chuckled. "He gave Hawk his pick of a litter and Hawk chose Boyo. His father was delighted because Boyo was the runt and he was certain he wouldn't show well, anyway. Turns out, Boyo was the pick of the litter, the largest and the best, and would have made a great champion."

"Way to go, Boyo," Bri called, stretching her back and neck to catch a glimpse of the constantly moving dog. She winced at the pain that attacked her shoulders.

As usual, Tanner didn't miss a thing. "Need a break?" he asked, moving his hand from hers to massage her tight shoulder.

Bri sighed for betraying herself to him. She felt like a greenhorn, a feeling she didn't appreciate. "Yes," she admitted, immediately adding, "I'm sorry if I'm holding you up."

He slanted a scowl at her. "You're not holding me up, Brianna. I could use a short break, too. And I'm hungry. That wasn't exactly a filling breakfast this morning." His scowl gave way to a teasing smile. "Also, I need a cup of coffee as much as you do."

She laughed at the same time she saw her vision blur. What was she getting all misty-eyed over? She derided herself. A rush of tears just because he was being so caring and thoughtful of her? She heaved a silent sigh.

And she had asked herself if she could handle him? Dumb question, she chided herself. But then, she hadn't expected to fall in love with him, either.

Foolish woman, Bri thought, bringing the horse to a halt in the small clearing he had chosen. Only a fool would blindly go along, falling in love with a maverick.

While Tanner unpacked the things for their

lunch, Bri tried to walk out the stiffness in her legs from being in the saddle for hours. When he returned, she left him to go to the stream to wash her hands, splash water on her face.

Once again she followed the scent of coffee back to camp. But how could she smell it when he hadn't built a fire? The answer was waiting for her at the edge of the small clearing where they had stopped. Tanner was holding a steaming cup, creamer added, for her. And there was no sign of a small fire.

"How did you make that?" she asked, glancing around the clearing.

"I made extra this morning and filled one of the thermoses," he said, taking a careful sip from the cup in his other hand.

Duh. "I should have figured that out for myself," she said, blowing gently on the liquid before taking a sip. He grinned. Bri felt the beginnings of that now-familiar melting sensation inside. Giving herself a mental shake, she grinned back at him. "What's for lunch?"

"Come see. It's all ready." He led the way to the clearing, where they feasted on premade peanut butter sandwiches, apples and, of course, some chocolate.

They were back on the trail in less than an hour.

Bri hadn't been back in the saddle very long before, out of the blue, she said, "I'm sorry."

At Tanner's invitation, she was still riding along-side him. Turning slightly in his saddle, he tilted his head to give her a puzzled look.

"About what?"

She hesitated, licked her lips, then blurted out, "I realize now I shouldn't have forced you to take me with you, nor followed you when you left me at Hawk's. I'm slowing you down and I know it."

"Brianna..." he began.

She rushed on. "I haven't been on a horseback hunt in ages. Hell, other than a jog in my father's fields every so often, I haven't been on horseback at all, at least not long enough to ache." She barely paused to draw breath, not giving him time to speak, before babbling on. "Now I'm beginning to ache all over, and, and..."

"And, as I said," he quickly inserted, "you're really nuts."

He smiled, so softly, so gently, she felt a twist in her chest. "First off," he continued, "you didn't force me into anything. Trust me, sweetheart, I don't force easily. Secondly, we couldn't go any faster without wearing out the horses, especially the one packing." He smiled again, only this time his smile was sheer temptation. "And third, but most importantly, after a bit of consideration, I knew I wanted you along."

For an instant Bri's heart appeared to stop. No, everything inside her seemed to stop. "But you said—"

Once again he cut her off. "I know what I said. I changed my mind." One dark brow lifted. "Did you think only women were allowed to do that?"

"No, of course not, but—"

"Wait." Tanner brought his mount to a halt and reached out to halt her horse. "Look at Boyo."

Bri swept her gaze around, almost missing the dog standing perfectly still in the underbrush. Even from the distance separating them she could see him quivering. Boyo spotted something and was ready to spring into action.

Ten

"Stay, boy." Tanner's low command told her he knew the dog was ready to bolt for whatever it was he saw.

"It couldn't be Minnich already, could it?" Bri asked quietly. "He took off yesterday, but you had to wait for me. Could we have caught up already?"

"Yeah, but he didn't know he was being followed until yesterday, and even then he might have thought we were just packers," he answered just as quietly. "Why would we have spooked him?"

"Because you fired at him?"

"Maybe. But on the other hand, he saw you, apparently alone…."

"I was," she cut in. "At least I thought I was."

"Right, and so did he. So, yeah, it could be him. He's deep in the wilds now, likely giving himself and the horses a rest. I'm gonna have to get closer."

"We're going to get closer?"

"We are." Moving to the packhorses, he removed his gun belt from one of the packs and strapped it around his waist. Digging back into the pack, he retrieved his pistol, checked it and settled it in the holster. She couldn't miss the pair of binoculars in a pouch on the left side of the belt. Walking back to his horse, he slid his rifle from the scabbard.

Bri turned to her horse to get her own rifle.

He frowned. "Do you really think you'll need that weapon?"

"I'm taking it." She allowed him a sweet smile. "But I'll leave the pistol here."

"Wonderful." Sighing, he moved slowly, silently forward.

Boyo paced beside him on the left, while Bri matched his steps on his right. They hadn't gone very far when Tanner and Boyo came to a halt. Bri stopped next to him.

Across the stream, some distance away, she could just make out a man standing on the other side. There was a small clearing near the bank, but the horses were tethered and a makeshift camp had been set up to the back, under cover of the tall pines, surrounded by brush.

Tanner took out the field glasses. He gazed through

them a few moments, then slid them back in the pouch. "It's Minnich," he murmured, sounding positive.

Then all hell broke out, everything seemingly happening at once.

A shot rang out and Tanner's hat went flying. In unison, they dropped to the ground. Tanner scooped up his hat and poked his finger through the hole in front. Bri vaguely heard him mutter, "Son of a bitch, I thought that only happened in the movies."

With a bone-chilling yowl, Boyo took off running, as Tanner and Bri raised their rifles to their shoulders.

Another shot rang out. Boyo let out a horrible-sounding yelp and flew into the air, then crashed to the ground. At the same time, two more shots rang out. With an outcry of pain, Minnich went down.

"I got the bastard." Tanner took off at a run toward the downed man, splashing through the stream.

"I got him," Bri yelled, also running, but she was not running through the water but to Boyo.

She went cold at her first sight of the dog. He was lying still, not whining. Breath eased from Bri as she saw his chest move. He was alive.

She dropped to her knees next to him, gently running her hands over his wiry-haired body. Her hand came away wet with blood when she touched his shoulder. "*Bastard*'s too mild a word for the lowlife," she mumbled, parting Boyo's fur to examine the wound.

She sighed with relief when she saw the bleeding was not profuse, indicating a major artery hadn't been hit. But had the shell gone through his body?

Even as the thought went through her mind, Bri was carefully sliding her hand beneath Boyo, feeling for a wet spot. There was none. The bullet was still inside somewhere.

She had to stop the bleeding. Not wanting to leave him even long enough to run back to the horses for the first-aid kit, Bri yanked her shirt from her waistband, popping buttons as she pulled it off.

Without a thought that she was sitting there with only her silk long undershirt on or the chill in the air, she began tearing the shirt into strips. Folding them into pads, she lay them on the wound, applying gentle pressure. She had just changed pads when Tanner loped up to her with the first-aid kit in hand.

Sliding around to give him access to the wound, Bri gently lifted the dog's head to her lap. "You're such a brave boy," she murmured, stroking Boyo's head as Tanner poured water over the pad before carefully removing it from the wound. The dog didn't so much as whimper as Tanner dried and cleaned the ugly gash. Bri continued to soothe the animal with soft praise. "You risked your life for us, Boyo. You're a genuine hero." She stroked his head and muzzle, and every time she got close to his mouth, his long tongue flicked out to lick her hand.

"Why, thank you for the kisses," she said,

watching Tanner as he applied an antibiotic cream to the wound before pressing a sterile pad against it. Taking out a roll of gauze, he wound it around Boyo's body, anchoring the pad. Then he took out a syringe, rubbed a spot on the animal's leg with a sterilized pad and carefully slid the needle into the leg.

Bri glanced up at Tanner in question.

"For pain," he said. "I didn't want to waste time before we stopped the bleeding," he explained. "He should rest easy now." He raised his brows. "You must be uncomfortable. Do you want me to move him?"

"No, no, I'm fine." It was a bald-faced lie. Bri was aching all over now, partly from tension, but there was no way she was letting him move the injured dog away from her.

Tanner smiled as if he'd known her answer before asking the question. "Okay. I've notified Hawk. He and a rescue helicopter will be here in a couple of hours."

Bri frowned. "How did you reach Hawk?"

He smiled again, teasingly. "It's called a cell/walkie-talkie phone."

She gave him a narrow-eyed look. Then suddenly she remembered. "Minnich. Did you get him?"

Tanner nodded. "Took a couple of bullets, but he's still alive. I carried him back to our horses. He's in a lot of pain, so I tied him up real tight. Make him suffer for what he's done."

Seemingly picking up on her inner turmoil, Boyo licked her hand as if comforting her. "Do you think he might be thirsty?" she asked, nodding down at the dog.

"Probably." Tanner nodded, handing her the thermos he had used to clean the wound. "There's still some water in here. He can't get up, but you can lift his head enough so he can lap up some of it."

Bri was already pouring the cool liquid into the small cup and slowly lifting his head. "Come on, Boyo, help me here. You've got to be thirsty after all you've been through." She barely noticed Tanner turning away.

"I'm going to check on Minnich," he said. "Then I'm going to tear down that excuse for a shelter he threw together."

What seemed like forever later, Bri was cradling Boyo in her arms, her head resting against his. She was still murmuring encouragement to him, every bone and muscle complaining in pain at the awkward position she was sitting in, when she heard the sound of the helicopter approaching. She'd have cheered, but she didn't have the energy.

Boyo had been dozing from the effects of the painkiller, but he opened his eyes and moved his head enough to look up at the sky, golden now with the setting sun.

"Yes, baby," she said, ruffling his wiry coat. "It's the boss. He's come to take you home." For the first time, Boyo whined, but it had a happy sound to it.

Bri watched as the copter came into sight, then stopped to hover overhead. She saw the line with the rescue basket attached, Hawk in a harness, clinging to the line as it slowly dropped to the ground. Tanner was waiting to catch it.

Between them, Tanner and Hawk lifted an unconscious Minnich into the basket and motioned to have it hauled up. Before it was off the ground, Hawk was striding to where Bri sat cradling his wounded pet.

"So, then, laddie, you took a bullet for my friends, did you?" Hawk said, the contrived Scottish burr failing to conceal the concern in his tone.

At the sound of Hawk's voice, Boyo's tail began thumping against the ground. Bri blinked against the mist stinging her eyes.

Hawk dropped to one knee as another basket was lowered from the copter. "Okay, fella," he said, sliding his arms under the dog. "Grit your teeth, 'cause I'm gonna lift you." Slowly, very carefully, he rose to his feet. Cradling Boyo in his arms like a child, he carried him to where Tanner waited.

Gritting her own teeth, grunting, swearing to herself, Bri pushed herself upright and, moving stiffly, followed at Hawk's heels. She saw Tanner remove a small cooler from the basket as Hawk approached.

After Boyo was settled into the blanket-padded basket, Hawk turned to Bri and drew her into his arms for a strong hug. "Thanks for taking care of him, Brianna," he said in a suspiciously choked voice.

She stepped back to look at him with worried eyes. "Will he be all right, do you think?"

He gave her a nod and a shaky smile. "He's a tough one. He'll live to see his pups."

"But…" she began, confused by his remark.

"Gotta go," he said, turning to shake Tanner's hand, then pull him into a quick hug. "Thanks, my friend."

"Anytime, buddy." Tanner stepped back. Hawk fastened himself into the harness and grabbed the line, and he and the basket disappeared inside the copter.

The hunt was over.

Bri watched until the rescue helicopter was out of sight. When she looked around the area, she saw Tanner had not only cleared away the makeshift camp but had set up their domed tent and brought the horses from where they had left them.

"I see you were busy while waiting for the helicopter," she said, feeling a twinge at having not helped him. "I'm sorry I wasn't any help…." she began.

He gave a sharp shake of his head. "I didn't need any help. Boyo did."

That quick, at just the mention of the dog's name, Bri got all misty-eyed again. Just as quickly she felt Tanner's arm around her, pulling her toward him in a comforting embrace.

"Don't worry, Bri. He'll be fine. He's one tough dog. Now…" He slanted her a grin and wiggled his brows at the cooler Hawk had brought. "Let's eat."

"Hawk brought us supper?"

He nodded. "I guess he figured we'd be tired of trail grub by now."

"And he was right. What did he bring?" she asked, suddenly ravenous.

Tanner began withdrawing items from the cooler. "Chili…French bread…and real brewed coffee."

Bri sighed. "Be still my heart."

"And he even packed desert," he said, pulling out brownies.

"Wonderful," she replied, her mouth nearly watering.

As evening was nearly upon them, chilling the air, Tanner built a small fire inside a ring of stones and they sat to eat.

"Getting chilly?" he asked, when he saw her shiver. Without waiting for her reply, he draped her jacket around her shoulders.

Sighing with gratitude from the warmth of the jacket and the fire, she smiled her thanks.

Everything tasted delicious, warming her inside as the fire and her jacket kept her warm outside. Bri silently thanked Hawk for everything, sighing in contentment over her second cup of coffee.

"Feel better now?"

"Much, thank you," she answered. She stared into the fire letting her mind wander back to the action earlier that day. "Tanner, Hawk said something about Boyo living to see his pups," she said. "What did he mean?"

"Just what he said. Hawk has a friend, a breeder

of wolfhounds, and every so often he'll agree to her plea for him to bring Boyo to impregnate one of the bitches she feels is champion-producing material. His pups are due any day now."

Bri smiled, the first one since they had sighted Minnich. "I bet they'll be beautiful."

"So far, they all have been, and some of them have become champions." He gave her an encouraging grin. "And I'm sure Hawk's right—Boyo will live to see his litter and many others."

Bri was quiet a moment, not sure she wanted to know or even cared, but she finally asked, "And Minnich?"

Tanner's features went hard. "Oh, he'll live to face a jury." He was silent a moment before he added, "And by the way, we *both* got him. I hit him in the thigh, you got him in the shoulder. Now forget him. He's not worth one more moment of your thoughts."

"Right." Bri nodded, swallowing against a sudden tightness in her throat, blinking against a sharp stinging in her eyes. "I'm beat. Let's get this stuff cleared away so I can turn in."

"Go," he ordered. "I'll do it." He arched a brow. "Would you like me to warm some water so you can have a—" he grinned "—cup bath?"

"Oh, that would be wonderful, Tanner. Thank you." She heaved herself up off the log.

He waved her away. "Go, get ready, I'll be with you in a few minutes."

She was waiting for him in the tent, stripped

naked except for a towel she had wrapped around her shivering body. Tanner stepped into the tent to hand her the bigmouthed thermos and cup.

"Take your time," he said, lifting the flap to leave her alone. "I'm going to clean up at the stream."

Although it was big for a thermos lid, bathing from it was more than a little difficult. Bri managed, at least enough to make her feel reasonably clean again. Though she was cold, she relished the feel of the water as the cupful sluiced down her body. She imagined it washing away not only the grime but the horror she had seen that day. The pain that she had endured while watching her sister suffer. It was over now, but somehow she couldn't get it out of her system.

When the thermos was empty, she dried and dressed in another pair of long johns and socks she'd stuffed into her pack. She had just exited the tent when Tanner came back to camp.

"Better?" He was close enough for his breath to ruffle her hair.

"Yes." She spoke true, to a point. Her body and clothes were clean, but she was tired and emotionally exhausted. Maybe that's why the dam burst.

Tears welled in her eyes. Bri could no longer hold them at bay, nor the sobs clawing at her throat.

Turning away from him, she ran into the tent, and scrambled under the cover. Unable to stem the tide, she wept like a heartbroken child.

"Hey, Brianna, what's this?" Concern deepening

his voice, Tanner crawled into the sleeping bag next to her, turning her into his arms. "Honey, it's over now," he murmured, drawing her protectively closer to him. "Why are you crying?"

"I was thinking of Dani—" she sobbed. "Now maybe she'll unlock her bedroom door and come join the family again for meals, start living again."

"I'm sure she will." Tanner stroked her hair as he tried to reassure her. "Maybe you and your parents can even talk her into seeking professional help."

Bri nodded, the tears clogging her throat and blocking her voice. In his arms she wept and wept, for what seemed an eternity.

When the emotional storm passed and her tears had subsided, Bri managed, "Thank you." She took Tanner's hankie and wiped her eyes and cheeks.

"You're welcome," he said.

She sighed. "Now I've got your shirt wet."

"It'll dry," he whispered near her ear, softly, almost affectionately. "Now go to sleep."

"One more thing." She tilted her head up. He drew back to stare at her face with those heart-meltingly gentle eyes. "Since the hunt's over, do we have to get up at the crack of dawn tomorrow morning?"

He laughed. "No, sweetheart, we don't. You may sleep in an hour or so longer. But we need enough time to eat and collect our personal gear. Hawk said there would be a helicopter arriving to pick us up around midmorning."

"But what about the horses?"

"Wrangler friends of Hawk's will be along to take care of the animals and bring them in."

"Oh, okay." She yawned, so bone-tired now that she'd let out her suppressed emotions.

Tanner lowered his head to softly press his mouth to hers in a sweet good-night kiss.

But, as it had the night before, the kiss deepened immediately, setting off a firestorm of passion between them. Suddenly Bri was wide-awake, grasping his hair to pull him closer to her, returning his kiss with everything in her.

When he could, Tanner said, "Brianna, you're tired. Are you sure you want—"

"Yes, I want," she said, running her hands over his shoulders, down his already heaving chest. "I want your kiss, your body, all of you."

"And I want you the same way," Tanner muttered in a half growl of need.

After some hurried shuffling around, their clothes were gone, heaped on the tent floor on either side of them. Tanner was kissing her, her lips, her face, her breasts and lower. He kissed at the juncture of her thighs, and she cried out with pleasure. Before her cry faded, he was inside her, increasing her pleasure to near screaming point. This time when they climaxed, they soared over the edge of ecstasy together.

"That was lovely," she murmured, curling against him. In the next moment she was sound asleep.

"*You* are lovely," Tanner whispered. Fully aware she couldn't hear him, he added, "And I love you."

＊ ＊ ＊

The helicopter dropped them off on the helipad at Hawk's place. Bri lugged her gear to the house, eagerly waiting while Tanner unlocked the door with the key Hawk had given him. Hawk had remained in town at the animal hospital with Boyo.

The minute she stepped inside, she dropped to the floor everything but her backpack and took off for the bathroom.

"What's the hurry?" Tanner called after her. "Don't you want some lunch?"

"No." Bri kept going so had to raise her voice. "I want to soak in a tub full of hot water for hours. *Then* I want some lunch."

Tanner was laughing. She could hear him through the door of the bedroom she had slept in before. She practically tore off her dirty clothing, grabbed the one clean set of bra and panties she had left and made a dash for the bathroom.

Bri didn't soak for hours. She remained in the water only until it got cold. Then she turned on the shower to rinse off before shampooing her hair.

Feeling wonderfully clean and refreshed, she returned to the bedroom, dressed and went in search of food. After a satisfying lunch, she hit the bed. It was beginning to get dark when a light tap on the door and Tanner's voice woke her.

"Brianna? I've rustled up some supper for us. Are you hungry?"

"Starving," she answered with the sudden realization. The exercise of hot sex and emotional upheaval must have activated her appetite. "Give me five minutes."

"Take ten." Laughter danced in his voice. "It will keep."

Nine minutes later, Bri entered the kitchen dressed in socks and the wrinkled but clean blue jeans and T-shirt she had put on after her bath. "What smells so good and spicy?"

"Pasta with marinara sauce." Tanner smiled. "I poured you a glass of Chianti. Help yourself to the pasta."

The meal was delicious, the Chianti the perfect complement to the pasta. The fresh-brewed coffee afterward was wonderful, and the slice of apple pie Tanner had found in the freezer and baked was just the right finisher.

"We'll leave first thing in the morning," Tanner said when they'd finished.

Bri was relieved he didn't suggest they start out that night, as she was still feeling tired and sleepy. It *had* been a long time since her last trek.

Together, they cleaned up the kitchen to the spotless condition Hawk kept it in, then shared a final glass of wine, exchanging mundane conversation until, rising and stretching, Tanner said he was ready to turn in. As Bri was every bit as ready, she washed their glasses and he dried them.

They were so tired they slept in separate beds that night.

Tanner woke her early the next morning. There was one difference, though. This time she was ready to get up, and most of the aches and stiffness were gone. They were on the road less than an hour later.

Bri was glad to be going back. At least that's what she told herself. In truth, though, with each passing mile she felt more and more deflated, depressed. It was probably the sudden release of the tension of the hunt, she reasoned. It had nothing at all to do with her leaving Tanner and very likely never seeing him again.

"You've been awful quiet," he said as they parked by the side of the road to rest and eat lunch. "Is something bothering you?"

"No." Bri shook her head. "I, uh, I've been thinking about going home."

"Oh." He was silent for a moment. "I guess you're anxious to see your sister and parents."

"Yes, of course, even though they'll have heard the news of his capture by know, I suppose."

"Yeah."

The conversation between them was less than scintillating, more like desultory. Bri had a stupid urge to cry, which didn't make a bit of sense. She was going home at last. She should be feeling elated, not darn near morose. Shouldn't she?

Their lunch finished, Tanner didn't start the SUV; he just sat there, gripping the wheel.

"I love you, you know." His voice was flat, stark with an astounding note of pain.

Bri stopped breathing. When she could take in air again, she raised her head to look at him in wonder. He was so beautiful it made her heart ache. "I love you, too, Tanner."

"It can't work." He looked and sounded sad, regretful.

Tears rushed to Bri's eyes. She had to swallow before attempting to speak. "Tanner, couldn't we find—"

He silenced her with a rough shake of his head. "No, Brianna, and you know it as well as I do. You belong back east, doing research in your quiet library. I belong out here, somewhere, wherever. I'm not going to change. I am what I do."

"Couldn't we work together?" she asked, a pleading note in her voice. "Was I such a drag on you?"

He gave her one of his gentle smiles. "No, love. I enjoyed having you along. But this was a short, fairly easy hunt. Most of them aren't. And you were aching by the time we caught him. Sometimes I'm gone weeks, not days. It simply couldn't work for us."

Tears rolled down her cheeks. "Tanner…"

"Brianna, don't. You're tearing me apart inside." He pulled her close, shutting his eyes against the pain. "I wish it could be different, but wishing won't change anything. This time with you has been wonderful, more than I probably deserve. But it's over. We live in two different worlds, and mine is too dangerous to risk hurting the woman I love."

Accepting his word as final, Bri remained still, miserable throughout the rest of the drive into Durango, with barely a word spoken between them. What more was there to say? It was late when Tanner pulled up to the Strater Hotel, where they were holding Bri's room for her.

Her throat was tight with emotion she refused to reveal to him. She grasped the door release and softly said, "Goodbye, Tanner. I'll have your check for a million dollars delivered to you tomorrow."

"I don't want it, Brianna. This one's on me."

She gave a quick shake of her head. "No. The bounty is yours. You earned it. Don't bother sending it back. Remember, my father is a banker. It would be easy for him to have it deposited into your account."

"Okay, you win."

Right. Bri wanted to weep. She didn't, though; she turned to the door. He stopped her by curling one big hand around her nape and turning her to him, claiming her mouth with his own. His kiss was deep and passionate and tasted of urgency, desperation. When he let her go, he moved back behind the wheel, his face once again carved in stone. "Goodbye, Brianna."

Bri almost stumbled out the door. Tanner's voice stopped her as her boots hit the pavement.

"Take care of yourself."

She couldn't look back at him. "You, too," she said over her shoulder and went striding for the entrance doors. As soon as she stepped inside, she heard his SUV drive away. Knowing he was taking her heart with him, she kept moving, not looking back.

Eleven

Bri was back in her own apartment two days, and the pain was still unbearable. It had seeped beneath her skin, soaking her insides, drowning her in misery. She had given in to tears again when Tanner called her.

"Hi, Brianna. How are you? And how was your flight back home?"

The sound of his voice, low, intimate, even asking such innocuous questions, set her pulse thumping. "I'm fine and so was the flight," she answered, telling herself to grow up, while trying to catch her breath. "How are you, Tanner?"

"Fine."

Bri frowned at the handset. Was that all he had to say?

"That's good," she replied. What else could she say, anyway? Make an ass of herself by admitting she missed him so much she ached? What good could come of that? He'd told her a relationship between them wouldn't work.

"How is Boyo?" she asked, knowing she should have thought of the dog at once.

"He'll be fine. He's still in the hospital, but they removed the bullet, so all he has to do now is heal. And here's more good news. His pups were born yesterday morning. Seven of them."

"Lucky number. I'd love to see them. Have you?"

"No, not yet." He paused. "How is Dani?"

"Better. At least she unlocks her bedroom door and joins our parents for meals. But she doesn't go out much, and never alone."

"It'll take time." Again he paused, as if having run out of things to say.

"I know," she said. "One good thing—she has agreed to get professional help."

"That's good." He paused again. "Uh, besides wanting to know how you were doing, I called to tell you I've accepted another job."

For a second, when he said *job,* hope flared that he was referring to a regular nine-to-five kind. She should have known better, she chided herself. "Another hunt." It was not a question but a statement.

"Yes, this time in the city." He went on before

she could ask. "An embezzler suspected of having gone to ground in a rough section of L.A."

"Do you know the city well?" Bri was already worrying, and he hadn't even left yet.

"Not like I know the mountains," he admitted, adding, "but I'll find him." There was not so much as a hint of false pride or bravado in his voice, just certainty.

"I know you will." Brianna drew a deep breath. "Will you try not to get yourself hurt while you're at it?"

He laughed. "I'll work on it."

She tried laughing with him, but she couldn't push one past the tightness in her throat. She didn't want him to hunt—at least not without her along to watch his back, and having hers caressed with wonderful building passion.

"Brianna?" Concern shaded his voice at her silence.

"Yes?"

"I thought you had hung up." There was another tight, strained pause, as if he were now having trouble finding words. "I, er, I'd better hang up. I'm leaving tomorrow and I still have to pack."

"Okay. Goodbye, Tanner. Stay safe." She wanted to hold him close, keep him safe. Foolish woman.

"I'll give it my best." He hesitated, then said softly, "I miss you, Brianna."

He disconnected before she could reply. It didn't matter; she wasn't sure she could speak, anyway, not without sobbing. She stood there holding the phone, unaware of the low buzz on the line or the tears rolling down her face.

Brianna.

Tanner stood stone-still, gripping the handset. He closed his eyes against the ache throbbing through him, the need, the emptiness. He had never felt anything like the longing he was feeling for her, her laughter, the teasing light in her eyes at times, like when she was doling out her precious dark chocolate.

Damn, he thought, being in love hurt so badly, throughout his entire body, his mind, his soul.

Sighing for what could never be, he cradled the handset, telling himself to stop mooning like a kid and get his ass in gear. He had a job to do. Yet, try as he did, Tanner couldn't shake the thought that he'd miss having Brianna working right there beside him.

The following weeks were a drag for Bri. Spring and the final exams at the university came and went, along with the majority of the students. Although there were always summer students, a lot fewer than usual roamed the campus library.

Bri was bored and restless and hungry with a hollow appetite that had nothing to do with food. When not at work in the library, she worked hard at staying busy. She turned down every invitation to go out with both her women friends and several men. There was only one man who interested her, and he was off hunting a criminal, putting his life in danger. She worked real hard not to think about that.

She spent most of her free time at her parents' house, with her sister. Though improved, Dani still kept close to home and was now dreading the day she would have to testify against Jay Minnich, who had been extradited from Colorado to Pennsylvania. And even though the man was behind bars and not likely to be going anywhere soon, Dani was still afraid to go out alone, if she went out at all.

The mild weather of spring melted into the hot days of summer. While attempting to keep Dani's spirits up, Bri felt as if she were being eaten alive inside with worry over Tanner, who hadn't called again. Was he safe? Was he deliberately not calling to indicate a final break-off of their— What?— friendship? Relationship?

She cried a lot and slept little in her bed each night. And it was in the middle of one of those weepy, sleepless nights when the phone rang, startling and scaring her.

Was something wrong with her parents? Dani? Before panic could set in, Bri grabbed the handset to stare at the lighted caller ID window. It was a cell phone number, one she didn't recognize. She hesitated before answering in a cautious tone.

"Hello?"

"Brianna?" His voice was low, muffled.

"Tanner?" A full range of emotions, primarily relief, flooded through her. "Is that you?"

"Yes," he murmured. "I'm sorry to wake you."

"Oh, that doesn't matter." She didn't tell him she never slept. "Where are you? Your voice sounds strange. Are you all right?"

"Yes, yes, don't worry," he whispered. "My voice sounds strange because I have my hand cupped around the phone so no one can hear me. I'm still in L.A., in a twenty-four-hour grungy, hole-in-the-wall diner."

"What in the world are you doing there?" Even as the words poured out of her mouth, Bri knew it was a stupid question.

"I'm sure as hell not enjoying myself," he muttered. "I'm working, remember?"

"Yes, of course," she said. "Are you getting anywhere with your hunt?"

"Yeah, I'm practically on this crook's ass," he answered with soft satisfaction. "But that isn't why I called. You'll be receiving a delivery sometime tomorrow. Since it's Saturday, I hope you'll be home."

"A delivery?" Bri frowned. "I'll stay home until it arrives, but what is it?"

"I don't have time to go into it now." His voice was lower, rushed. "There's a letter with it that will explain everything. I gotta go now."

"Okay, goodbye." She swallowed a need to protest. "Please take care."

"Always." His voice dropped to barely a whisper. "Goodbye, Brianna." There came a pause, making her think he had disconnected, then with a sigh he said, "I miss you, Brianna. I love you." A click. He was gone.

I love you.

Throughout what was left of the darkness, Bri held his words close, warming her heart, even as fear for his safety chilled every bone in her body. By first light she had made a decision. Like it or not—and Tanner very likely wouldn't like it—she was going back to Durango, to him, to be his partner in everything.

Tanner claimed to love her, and she knew she was in love with him. So his work was dangerous. Bri knew she could deal with the danger so long as she was beside him, watching his back.

Rising with the summer sun, Bri began getting her things together, as many of her things that would fit in her car. She could send for the rest later. She decided she would keep the apartment for visits home. No, her home would be wherever Tanner was. She'd keep the place for visits to her parents and Dani.

By late morning her small living room was littered with suitcases, hunting gear and bags full of things she couldn't fit into her cases. Gazing around her, Bri was wondering how she had ever collected so much stuff when the doorbell rang.

The delivery Tanner had told her to expect. In her flurry of activity, she had completely forgotten. She went to the door, opened it and stood, stunned, staring at the uniformed delivery man.

What in the...? Her thoughts scattered. In one hand he held the handle to an animal carrier. In the other a large shipping bag.

"Ms. Stewart?"

She nodded, numb with confusion. She could see something wriggling through the openings in the carrier. The deliveryman stepped inside, set both items on the floor and thrust a small clipboard at her.

"I'll need your signature, ma'am."

Bri signed on the line, managed a smile and a murmured "Thank you" and closed the door behind him.

Carefully she picked up the carrier, for the first time noticing an envelope taped to one side. She'd get to the letter later, Bri thought, but first she peeked into the opening and exhaled a soft, "Ooh. Hello, there, little one."

The puppy inside gave a low whine, while the tail wagged in excitement. Though the dog didn't look much like him, Bri knew it was one of Boyo's litter, and it was adorable.

Setting the carrier back down on the floor, Bri tore the envelope from the side, ripped it open and began reading the letter from Tanner.

Brianna, this pup is not for you. I wrote this note before leaving for L.A. and gave it to Hawk, along with instructions. I'm sure you knew at once the pup is one of Boyo's. She was the runt of the litter. I asked Hawk to take Boyo to see his puppies as soon as he was well and to pick out one of the pups. Hawk called to tell me he had done so, and Boyo had immediately singled out the little female runt. She has had her shots, but she doesn't have a name. She is a gift for Dani—and her right to name. Inside the other package Dani will find food and supplies to get started. Also, there's a booklet with information about the breed.

Tell Dani she doesn't need to fear so long as the pup is with her. As you know, the pup will grow—not quite as tall as Boyo but tall enough. She will be loving, loyal and willing to give her own life for her mistress…as you know from experience.

Love, Tanner

Tears were running down Bri's cheeks by the time she finished his letter. Oh, how she loved this kind, compassionate, wonderful, sexy, beautiful and at times arrogant man.

Wiping her eyes with her fingers, Bri grabbed her purse, picked up the carrier and shipping bag and dashed out of the apartment.

Ten minutes later, she burst into her parents' home. Her mother was coming down the stairs, surprise obvious in her expression. "Bri, what's your hurry?"

"Dani," she answered. "Where's Dani?"

"Out by the pool, but— What do you have

there?" she called after Bri as she headed for the sliding door leading to the patio and pool area.

"Come, come," Bri called back, excitement singing on her voice. "Come see."

At Bri's hurried approach, Dani looked as puzzled as their mother. "Bri, what—" That was as far as she got.

"Look," Bri said, holding the carrier out to her. "This is for you."

"For me? But... Oh, my heavens! Bri, it's a puppy."

"I know." Bri laughed. "It's *your* puppy." As Dani began fiddling with the latch on the door of the carrier, Bri quickly added, "Wait. Before you take her out, I have this for you." She handed over the letter.

Dani began to read aloud. It wasn't long before she was blinking against a sting of tears. It didn't matter, because both Bri and their mother were also misty-eyed.

"Oh, Bri, what a thoughtful gift. Tanner sounds like a wonderful man."

"He is...." Bri's throat was so tight she could hardly get the words out. "Now you can take her out. And don't forget—you must find a name for her."

Dani carefully drew the dog from the carrier. "Oh, she's beautiful!" She cradled the wiggly ball of fur close to her, laughing when the puppy tried to shower every inch of her face with kisses.

Laughing with sheer delight for the first time since her shattering ordeal, Dani looked up at Bri and their mother. "I don't have to think about naming her," she said, laughing and crying at the same time. "Just look at her. What else could I name her but Beauty."

"Perfect." Bri laughed. "Now hand her over and let me get some of those kisses."

Bri stayed at her parents' for dinner. Over an impeccable meal, with Dani at her side, she explained what she planned to do.

There were some arguments that her plan was hasty and there was more than a little concern from her parents. Though she didn't say a word, Dani smiled and gave her sister a thumbs-up.

In the end, of course, Bri held firm. Early the next morning she stashed all her packed stuff in the trunk and backseat of her car and headed west.

Bri was going on a manhunt of her own.

It was late afternoon when Bri pulled her car into Durango after what seemed like forever on the road. Before signing in at the Strater Hotel, as she had done previously, she pulled into the first parking space she came across, dug her cell phone from her cavernous handbag and dialed Tanner's apartment number. To her surprise, he answered on the second ring.

"Wolfe."

Relief at knowing he was back safe washed through her. "Hello, Wolfe, how are you?"

"Brianna!" Could that be the sound of happiness she detected in his voice? "You got my message?"

Her brows wrinkled. "What message?"

"I called not ten minutes after I got home yesterday and I left a message on your answering machine."

Bri groaned. She had checked her home phone for messages every day except yesterday and today. "No, I didn't get it. I, er, I'm not at home, Tanner."

"Where are you, then?" His tone now held a definite edge. Where the heck did he suspect she might be, and with whom?

"I'm right here in Durango, just a short distance from your apartment."

He was silent for a moment. "Then get the hell here now. You hear me?"

She smiled. "Yes, Tanner, I hear you. I'll be there in a few minutes."

"You'd better be."

Her smile widened into a grin. He'd actually growled at her, like the animal whose name he bore.

Bri took only two things with her from the car. She was holding one of them in each hand when she rang his doorbell. It swung open at once, and she burst out laughing at the sight that met her eyes.

Tanner stood with one shoulder propped against the door frame, his long, shiny hair draping his shoulders. In one hand he held a bag of dark chocolate—purple-wrapped Hershey's Kisses. In the other he held the glittery gold cloth strips of the sandals she had worn the day he'd picked her up.

"Hi." He grinned at her astonished expression and stepped back, allowing her to enter.

"Where did you find them?" she asked. "I've been tearing my closet apart looking for them."

"They were stuffed under the front seat of the SUV." He laughed. "If you'll recall, you tossed them in the back when you put on your boots."

"Thank you for finding them. They're one of my favorite pairs."

"Mine, too." He eyed her hands. "And what have you got there?" He inclined his head, indicating the folded material she held in one hand and the large, round, old-fashioned hatbox in the other.

Bri was so busy drinking in the sight of him she had forgotten the items she held. "This, I believe, is yours." She handed over the folded material, which he couldn't help but recognize as his own hankie he had given her on their last night of the hunt.

"And this," she said, handing the box to him, "is a present from me to you."

He looked puzzled. "A present for me? Why would you buy me a ladies' hatbox from a bygone day?"

She gave him a look and an impatient sigh. "Open the box and look for yourself, Tanner."

Dumping the sandals, the bag of candy and his snow-white, neatly pressed hankie into her arms, he took the box and set it on the sofa. He untied the frayed laces holding the lid on and gave her a wary look.

"Nothing's going to jump out at me?"

"Oh, good grief, Tanner!" Bri shook her head. "You're a big, tough hunter. Open the silly box."

Laughing, he lifted the lid. His laughter gave way to an expression of wonder. Slowly, carefully, he lifted the buff-colored Stetson from the box. "Brianna… Why?"

"That one doesn't have a bullet hole in it." She gave him a teasing grin. "I bought myself one exactly like it."

"You're something," he said, plopping the hat on his head before pulling her into his arms and thanking her with a scorching kiss.

They broke apart for one reason—to breathe. When Tanner lowered his head to her once more, Bri raised a trembling hand to his chest to hold him back.

She drew a deep breath. "Tanner, wait. We've got to talk."

"We can talk later." He moved forward, backing her against the wall. "But first we've got more important things to do."

"No." She shook her head, bringing her other hand up to keep him a few inches from her. "No, Tanner. I didn't come here for sex." She gave a half laugh, qualifying her statement with, "At least not *only* for sex."

His eyes narrowed. "Okay, what do you want?"

"You."

"But you just said—"

"All of you, dammit!" She glared into those glittering eyes. "I want to be your partner…in every aspect of your life. In marriage, in work—and I do mean in the hunt—and, yes, sex."

Arching a brow, Tanner took on that austere statue-of-a-saint expression.

She arched a brow right back at him, although she couldn't match him for austerity. "And don't give me that look. It doesn't impress or intimidate me. Oh, Tanner," she murmured, lifting one hand to caress his face. "I love you. I want to be with you."

"It can't work," he said, shaking his head but covering his hand over hers to keep it where it was. "You'd be a nervous wreck sitting at home, waiting and worrying about me. And some jobs require me to be away for weeks. Hell, I was away over a month in L.A."

"You're not listening, Tanner." She scowled at him. "I said I want to be with you in every aspect." She slid her fingers slowly down his cheek, smiling as his tight expression softened. "That includes your hunts. You need someone to cover your back, and I intend to be that someone."

"You do, do you?" He moved closer, his body pressing into hers. "A ring on your finger and one through my nose, huh?"

"Oh, don't be silly," she said, smiling as she outlined his lips with her fingertip. "Nose rings are so yesterday." She gasped as he caught her finger between his teeth and sucked it into his mouth. With his body pressed tightly against her, she could feel his readiness for her and knew he could feel her shivery response. Time to bring out her last weapon.

"Tanner, I love you. And I'll continue to love you whether you're here or on a hunt. I would rather die with you on a hunt than live without you near me."

"You don't play fair," he murmured, dipping his head to taste her neck.

"Not when I'm playing for such high stakes." She arched her body into his, feeling the hard fullness of him against her. "Give me an answer now or I swear I'll be out of here in a shot."

"No, you won't." He raised his head a bit to smile at her.

"No," she admitted, snaking her arms around his neck to get closer still. "I won't."

He laughed. "You're still a little nuts, but I like you that way. Brianna, my love, will you marry me…and cover my back on our hunts?"

"Oh, Tanner, yes, yes, yes." She planted a swift, hard kiss on his smiling lips. When he reached for the buttons on her shirt, she caught his hand, held it still. "Wait, there's one more thing."

Tanner groaned. "Brianna, you're killing me here. I'm ready to go up in flames."

"Oh, my, we can't have that," she actually cooed.

"Then what is it?" He sounded like a man at the end of his rope.

"Could we please use a bed this time?"

Tanner roared with laughter. Sweeping her up into his arms, he strode toward the short hall to his bedroom.

"Oh, sweetheart, have I got a bed for you."

It was a king-size. Just perfect for two nutty lovers.

Tanner made love to Brianna with his hat on.

* * * * *

THE PLAYBOY'S PASSIONATE PURSUIT

by
Emilie Rose

Dear Reader,

It's not often a secondary character makes a lasting impression on me, but Toby Haynes would not go away. Even though he didn't get the girl in *Exposing the Executive's Secrets*, I couldn't get him out of my head. He seemed larger than life each time he swaggered onto the page, and I wanted to get to know him better. When an opportunity presented itself, I begged my editor to let me resurrect him for this Monaco series. Luckily for me she agreed.

The problem was that, despite growing up in North Carolina, the home of many NASCAR teams, I knew next to nothing about race-car driving. Toby, as previously established, was a NASCAR driver. My research into stock-car racing opened new doors, and I became a budding fan.

Hope you enjoy Toby's book and...I'll see you at the races. :)

Happy reading,

Emilie Rose

EMILIE ROSE

lives in North Carolina with her college
sweetheart husband and four sons. Writing is
Emilie's third (and hopefully her last) career.
She's managed a medical office and run a home
day care, neither of which offers half as much
satisfaction as plotting happy endings. Her
hobbies include quilting, gardening and cooking
– especially cheesecake. Her favourite TV
shows include *ER, CSI* and Discovery Channel's
medical programmes. Emilie's a country music
fan, because she can find an entire book in
almost any song.

Letters can be mailed to:
Emilie Rose
PO Box 20145
Raleigh, NC 27619, USA
E-mail: EmilieRoseC@aol.com

This book would never have happened without
Wanda Ottewell, my super-cool editor.
Thanks for loving Toby as much as I did and
for letting me bring him back to life.

Thanks go to Roxanne St Claire for trying to guide
me through the steep NASCAR learning curve.

One

Please don't let it be him.

Panic seized Amelia Lambert's heart, and then the organ lurched into a rapid, thundering rhythm like thoroughbreds breaking from the Kentucky Derby gate. Her gaze locked onto the back of the man standing at the registration counter, and a cold hard lump of dread formed in her stomach.

That sandy-blond hair, those wide shoulders, the muscular tush and long legs could only belong to one person. Someone she never wanted to see again.

Toby Haynes. Her dumbest mistake.

Why was he in Monaco *now?* She was supposed to have time to prepare for his arrival. Twenty-four days, to be precise.

She considered ducking behind one of the fat marble pillars in the glitzy Hôtel Reynard lobby until he left, but before she could translate thought into action he turned away from the desk and his gaze plowed right into hers. And then he smiled. That cocky, slightly crooked half smile had earned him the title of NASCAR's sexiest driver five years running.

She *hated* that smile.

Hated what it did to her. Hated how it made her skin tingle and flush. Hated how it made her toes curl. Hated how it tangled and heated her insides and anesthetized her gray matter.

Focusing on her as if she were the only other person around for miles, he sauntered toward her with a hotel key card in one hand and a black leather bag in the other. He stopped an arm's length away. An Atlantic Ocean too close, in her opinion.

"Hello, sweet Amelia," he drawled.

Her lungs failed at the intimacy of his leisurely I've-seen-you-naked inspection.

The man had enough magnetism to screw up compasses from here to Timbuktu. Throw in the fact that he possessed a risk-taking adrenaline-junkie personality that spelled doom for any relationship, and Toby Haynes was bad news all around. Never mind that he was every woman's dream lover in bed. A woman would have to be a masochist to get entangled with him.

Luckily she'd wised up.

Unfortunately not soon enough.

She tipped her head back to look into his silvery-blue eyes and tried to swallow the barge beached in her dry throat with only minimal success. "What are you doing here, Toby?"

"Vincent asked me to shadow you and your girlfriends until the wedding. Never cared much for following, but for you I'll make an exception."

Her stomach landed in her sandals, and chaos erupted in her brain as she scrambled to make sense of his words. Vincent was Vincent Reynard, heir to the Hôtel Reynard chain and one of Toby's race-car team's sponsors, as well as the groom-to-be to Amelia's best friend, Candace. Vincent happened to be footing the bill for Candace and her three bridesmaids to spend a month in Monaco planning the dreamiest wedding ever. The ceremony was scheduled to take place in four weeks.

"Why you?"

"I'm the best man. But then, you already know that. I recall you saying so. More than once." His Georgia roots oozed into his gravelly voice and over her skin like a humid southern breeze.

She could not believe she'd been dumb enough to feed his already Herculean ego with compliments.

But he had been that good.

And she had been that stupid. Being tipsy was no excuse.

And then she remembered Neal, her dearly departed fiancé, the man she loved with all her heart, and she felt like a traitor. Again. The same way she had that morning when she'd rolled over and spotted Toby's handsome face on her pillow.

Wait a minute. Panic knocked guilt aside. "*You're* Vincent's best man?"

"Yes, ma'am."

She would wring her friend's neck for withholding that crucial piece of information. "I'm Candace's maid of honor."

"Guess that means we'll be rubbing fenders. All those shared duties. We're gonna be tight."

This was bad. Very, very bad. Nauseating, in fact. She barely managed to contain her groan.

Toby slouched against the marble pillar beside her and

slid his key into his front pocket. The action drew Amelia's gaze over the taboo terrain of a generous masculine package encased in blue jeans so worn and faded she could tell which way the, um, *landscape* lay.

She suppressed a shiver as memories assailed her and gritted her teeth against the images burned on her retinas of how he looked naked, of what he felt like hot and bare and pressed against her, of how alive he'd made her feel on a day when she'd wanted to crawl into a dark cave and hide.

Her body smoldered and her hormones launched into a chorus line of kicks and spins. Those same stupid hormones had landed her in bed with him ten months ago, but that was a mistake she'd never repeat. Toby Haynes, like her father, was bent on burning a destructive trail along the fastest route to the grave.

Her journey climbed back up his flat stomach and broad chest and eventually reached his gorgeous tanned face, his let-me-at-you mouth and sexy bedroom eyes—eyes currently twinkling with satisfaction over her thorough inventory of his anatomy.

Darn. "Shouldn't you be driving in circles somewhere?"

His smile slipped but only for a millisecond. Had she not been staring at him like a deer caught in the headlights, she would have missed it. He blinked, raked a hand through his short, already disheveled hair and then hooked his thumb through his belt loop. His casual stance contradicted the tension carving shallow lines around his mouth.

"I have some free time. And it's ovals or tri-ovals or—"

"In the middle of the NASCAR season?"

"Yeah." He forced the word through a clenched-teeth smile.

Admittedly Amelia didn't follow car racing, but working as a nurse in a Charlotte, North Carolina, hospital near a speedway meant caring for several race-car drivers each year, and she'd learned a little about the sport whether she'd wanted to or not. Time off midseason was neither desirable nor good. It cost the driver points or money or… *something* that pushed most of the fools to check out of the hospital sooner than they should and often against doctor's orders. To earn an entire month off meant Toby had broken a major rule or been injured.

She took another quick appraisal of his muscle-packed body. He didn't look injured. He looked firm and fit and virile—*ahem*.

"What did you do?"

He shifted his jaw. "What makes you think I did anything?"

"Because you're a hardheaded, risk-taking daredevil. You drive like a maniac. And you don't miss races."

The corners of his mouth curled up—and so did her toes. "Been watching me, have you?"

Her face ignited into a ball of flame. She'd only watched part of one race. After the first wreck she'd had to turn off the TV. But Toby made the network news highlight clips every week and he'd done commercials both on TV and in print. She couldn't avoid seeing his handsome mug even though she tried.

She scowled and lifted her chin. "I have better things to do than watch grown men try to kill themselves."

"Like what?"

"None of your business. Go home, Toby. Candace, Madeline, Stacy and I can look out for each other. We don't need a babysitter. All you have to do is show up for the rehearsal and the wedding."

"No can do. My buddy asked and I owe him."

His buddy. Vincent.

She'd met Toby last year after a freak accident in his pit had burned Vincent over twenty percent of his body. Vincent had been airlifted to the hospital where Amelia and Candace worked in the burn unit. During Vincent's stay, he'd met and fallen in love with Candace. Toby had been a frequent and irritating visitor. Amelia had seen too much of him then and she'd already seen too much of him today.

"Vincent said the accident wasn't your fault."

The grooves beside Toby's mouth deepened. "I'm responsible for my team and anyone behind my wall."

If she had a dollar for every time she'd heard similar words, she could buy a private island in the Bahamas. She'd learned from her firefighter father and from her job dealing with the results of disaster that when the adrenaline kicked in, risk takers thought of nothing but the thrill of their daring deeds. They needed that rush the way a junkie needed a fix.

Toby lifted a hand to her cheek. She flinched out of reach but not quick enough to avoid a brief electrifying touch. "Like it or not, I'm going to be drafting you until after the wedding."

The fine hairs on her body rose in warning. She took a step back. "You said you didn't like to follow anyone."

His gaze rolled down her body and slowly back up. Her skin tightened and her nipples peaked. She folded her arms across her chest to hide the evidence.

"Depends on the view and the reason. Trust me, I won't be complaining."

How dare her pulse skip. She silently cursed her traitorous body. "Don't expect to take up where we left off."

"Tell me something, Amelia." He stretched out her name, long and low, the way he had when he'd groaned it during climax, and a heat wave engulfed her. "It was good between us. If I had any doubts, hearing you moan my name over and over deafened 'em. So why would you sneak out on a guy like that? And what's with the cold shoulder since?"

She squashed a trace of guilt and quickly glanced around to make sure none of the other hotel guests were listening. She'd refused Toby's gifts and hadn't returned his phone calls because she'd been afraid he'd sweet-talk her out of her common sense—and her clothes—again. The risk of falling for a guy just like dear ole Dad had been too high. She didn't intend to end up like her mother— stuck in a miserable marriage.

She wanted a man like Neal. Kind, gentle Neal, the fiancé she'd loved and lost to leukemia three years ago. She did not want a guy who'd haul his banged-up body home for her to put back together time and time again. Most marriages couldn't survive that kind of stress—a circumstance she witnessed on the job every day. With divorce rates at fifty percent, she had to use your brain to choose a partner or she'd end up in the wrong statistical column.

"Toby, what happened that night shouldn't have happened. You caught me at a weak moment. I'd had a rough week and too much to drink and I made a mistake. It won't happen again."

From the flare of his nostrils she suspected he didn't like being called a mistake. "You'd had two drinks."

"I'm not a drinker. I have a low tolerance level."

"You might call the first time a mistake, but that doesn't explain the next three. Sugar, you were hot for me—and not just that night. We'd been circling each other for months. You can't deny you wanted me. I caught you checking me out more times than I can count."

The accuracy of his words shot flames through her veins. "Then you can't count very high. And for your information,

I also crave éclairs 24-7. However I don't indulge often because too much isn't good for me. Neither are you."

"I was very good for you—every time. Granted, the first one was a little fast. But I didn't hear you complaining." The combination of his husky drawl and intense passion-darkened eyes nearly buckled her knees.

She stiffened her weak limbs and shaky defenses. She would not think about that night. Bad enough that the memory still invaded her dreams, she refused to let it take over her conscious hours. "Toby, I've heard about your conquests. Women are like races to you. You win one and then you pack up and fly to the next. You had me. It's time to move on."

"Can't do that, sugar. We're not finished."

The conviction in his words sent a shiver of desire rippling through her. He had her hot and bothered and weakening with only words. If she didn't scare him away, then she was going to be in serious trouble. Shock tactics might work. "Are you looking for a wife?"

He flinched. "No."

"Well, I'm looking for a husband and children, the white picket fence, the dog, the cat and the whole package. I won't deny you were an enjoyable interlude, but I am looking for Mr. Right and someone to share a porch swing with thirty years from now. You are nowhere close to qualified for the position, and I don't want to waste any more time on you. So back off."

She turned on her heel and beat a hasty retreat toward the elevator.

Waste time on him?

Toby fisted his hands and gnashed his teeth. Women didn't walk away from Toby Haynes. He loved 'em and left 'em on his terms and he always—*always*—left 'em wanting more.

Forget the bet. This had nothing to do with the wager he'd made to keep Vincent entertained during rough months of countless skin grafts and painful rehab and everything to do with Amelia Lambert—the first woman to mess up his foolproof system.

She'd left *him* wanting more. Nothing permanent like her fantasy house in the suburbs and happy ever after, mind you, because he didn't believe in permanence. He'd seen too many women walk away when times got tough and too many men blow when the pressure got too high. But he wanted more of her particular brand of five-alarm-fire sex. They'd combusted every which way including sideways that night, and having her dismiss the potent chemistry between them—dismiss *him*—chafed worse than sucking exhaust from the back of the pack.

He wanted her back. What's more, she wanted him, too. He'd seen the hunger in her green-and-gold eyes as she'd visually stripped him a few minutes ago, and his body had responded. Give him a few more laps around the mattress and then he'd be ready to drop the checkered flag on their relationship.

He took a minute to admire her slender figure and lean legs in a short white skirt and frilly, sheer peach-colored blouse over a fitted camisole instead of her usual shapeless hospital scrubs. Her hair, a wavy cinnamon curtain, swished between her shoulder blades with each step. His blood took a pit stop in his south end at the memory of the silky strands gliding across his belly and thighs—an experience he intended to repeat soon. *Very* soon.

He knocked himself out of neutral and straightened to tail her sweet, swaying behind. The sudden movement made the floor shift beneath his feet. Damn. He planted a steadying palm on the cool column. The vertigo vanished as quickly as it had appeared, but it reminded him why he was here.

Concussion. Couldn't drive. The doc claimed that by the time the wedding passed Toby should be back behind the wheel. Missing five races meant that, short of a miracle, he and his team would be eliminated from this year's chase for the championship. He didn't believe in miracles.

He'd been in the top ten for the past eight years and he didn't like losing. Every win proved his daddy wrong. Toby Haynes wasn't a worthless piece of crap. Too bad the old bastard hadn't lived long enough to eat his words.

Toby covered the ground between him and his target in long strides. "Hold up, sugar. We have to make plans. What in the devil is a Jack and Jill shower anyway?"

Amelia stopped abruptly and turned. "Why?"

"Because Vincent wants one and he put me in charge of it. And Candace sent me a link to a wedding Web site that says you and I are supposed to host some brunch thing to-gether, too. I have the e-mails. C'mon up to my room and we'll go over 'em."

He'd done his research and he knew exactly what his best-man duties were. Back when he'd thought he'd be rac-ing every weekend and blowing in only for the wedding, he'd intended to hire the best party planner in Monaco to set up a pair of bashes the bride and groom would never forget. Money was no object. But since he was stuck here he might as well use the situation to lure Amelia back into the sack.

Amelia folded her arms and gave him that prissy in-your-dreams look—the one that fired every cylinder in his engine. Nothing he liked more than a challenge, and the sweet little nurse had been a challenge from day one when she'd tried to bounce him from Vincent's hospital room after visiting hours ended. She hadn't stood a chance of ditching him then and she didn't now. What Toby wanted, Toby got. He hadn't made it from white trash to multi-millionaire by letting a few obstacles stop him.

He held out his hands and shrugged. "Hey, if you're not interested, I'm sure I can pull something together. They sell kegs in Monaco, right? And I bet the concierge can recommend a good stripper or two for the bachelor party."

Amelia's raspberry-red lips dropped open in horror. Bull's-eye. He'd missed riling her and bit the inside of his lip to stop a grin.

"You don't have beer kegs at bridal showers, Toby, and Candace would not appreciate strippers."

No kidding. But he loved Amelia's shocked whisper. Kinda reminded him of how she'd sounded when he'd dipped his head between her legs and licked her that first time. "No?"

She huffed out an exasperated breath. "Give me your list and go back to the States, back to your races and your bimbos and…whatever. I'll take care of everything."

If only he could go back.

"Nope. Gave my word. Never break it." If his good-ole-boy act made people underestimate him, that wasn't his problem. And if Amelia thought he'd give up his pursuit just because she played hard to get, then she'd seriously miscalculated how much he liked to win.

"Speaking of teamwork, I could use your help. Airline lost my luggage. Let me dump my bag upstairs and then you can take me shopping and do your worst." The airline had promised to have his bag to him within twenty-four hours, and he had a change of clothes in his carry-on. But he didn't have to share that information.

"I am not your personal shopper."

No, but she was one of those women who always helped out someone in need, a real sucker for a sob story. He'd learned that in the months of chasing her up and down hospital corridors.

"Admit it, you'd love to get me out of my pants. Again." He winked and she bristled predictably. "You've been here a day already. I know you women have scoped out the stores."

The glint in her eyes warned him he wouldn't score an easy victory. "I'm sure Gustavo, our concierge, can give you a map. If you want to discuss shower and brunch arrangements, then I'll make time to meet you in the café by the gardens later this afternoon. But right now I have plans."

Plans that didn't include him.

He ought to be frustrated by his lack of success. Instead the temporary setback only made him more determined to succeed.

The express elevator to the penthouse floor opened. She whirled around and stepped inside. Toby followed.

Her eyes widened. "Where are you going?"

"My suite."

She folded her arms and abruptly faced the doors. He was glad, because the swift ascent left him reeling. He braced a shoulder against the wall and widened his stance. The moment the brass panels opened again, Amelia bolted down the thickly carpeted hall. Toby straightened carefully, found his balance and followed more slowly, scanning the space to get his bearings.

Nine doors opened off the penthouse level. Two emergency exits. Six suites. One rooftop pool and hot tub for the private use of the penthouse-level guests. Amelia stabbed her key card into the door at the far end and a grin tugged Toby's lips. His room was next door. Convenient. *Thanks, Vince.*

He inserted the key into his electronic lock. "Knock on the wall when you're ready for me, sugar."

"Don't hold your breath." Amelia ducked into her room.

Toby's grin widened. Being sidelined for a month from the sport he lived and breathed no longer seemed like a fate worse than death. In fact, he could even say he was looking forward to it.

Two

Amelia slammed the suite door behind her—as hard as one could slam a door designed to operate silently.

She stalked into the luxurious sitting area and confronted her best friend. On second thought, maybe her *former* best friend. "Is there something you forgot to tell me?"

Candace tucked a lock of pale blond hair behind her ear and blinked her big blue eyes innocently. Too innocently. "Like what?"

"Like Toby Haynes is Vincent's best man and he's going to be a pain in my neck for the *entire* month, not just the weekend of the wedding."

"Oh, that." Candace made a show of straightening the pages of whatever wedding project she'd been working on.

"You knew. And you didn't warn me." Just as Candace had known about that miserable mistake Amelia had made ten months ago. Candace was the only one Amelia had told, and then only because she'd had to offer some explanation for suddenly switching to the Thursday-Sunday shifts— days when Toby would be at a racetrack somewhere.

"I didn't know until a couple of days ago. But it's been months since you two hooked up and split up, Amelia. You should be able to be civil to each other. Or if there's still something between you, maybe you can see where it leads."

Realization dawned and the betrayal winded her. Candace had a notorious reputation at the hospital for trying to pair up people. But because of their shared pain and shared past, Amelia had never expected her friend to practice that annoying habit on her. "You're matchmaking. With *me*. How could you?"

Candace's gaze softened. "Honey, Neal is dead. You're not."

Amelia flinched. "You don't need to remind me. I loved your brother. I still do."

"I loved him, too. And he loved you. You made the last year of his life better. Amelia, we don't have to forget him, but he's been gone three years and we have to move on. You spend most of your time alone in your apartment, reading romances or watching sappy old movies. You need to get out more."

"Not with Toby Haynes!"

"He's the only guy you've dated since Neal."

"We didn't date. We had sex."

"So you skipped a few preliminaries. Big deal. Besides, Vincent wants us to keep an eye on him."

"On Toby? Why?"

"Because of the wreck."

At a loss, Amelia shook her head. "What wreck?"

"The one last weekend that gave Toby a grade-three concussion. Vincent claims Toby's one of those alpha males who refuses to admit to any weakness, so he asked Toby to fly over here and keep an eye on us. But we're really watching him. Sneaky, huh?"

Vincent wasn't the only sneaky one. Amelia stabbed her fingers into her hair, yanked and silently screamed, *This cannot be happening*. "He looks fine."

"And since you worked in neurology before transferring to the burn unit, you know how deceiving head injuries can be. One of us—preferably you, me or Madeline—should be with him whenever he leaves the hotel, since we know what postconcussion syndrome looks like," Candace said. "And I have the name of a Monaco neurologist. Toby's supposed to check in regularly." She dug in her purse and offered a business card to Amelia.

Amelia took it with about as much enthusiasm as she would an open test tube of the Ebola virus. "I'm surprised you didn't ask me to share his suite."

"I was hoping you'd volunteer."

Amelia narrowed her eyes. "You'd better be joking."

Candace gave her an enigmatic smile.

"I could hate you for this."

"No, Amelia, you can't. We were almost family, and you can't hate family."

Ha. Shows what she knew. Amelia's parents detested each other. Their virulent screaming matches were legendary in the neighborhood. Her father might not be able to walk, but he sure could bellow and curse. And her mother didn't take his verbal abuse silently. More often than not, she provoked it.

"If he's so bad off, why did the doctors clear him for travel?"

"To keep him away from racing. There's some rule that says if a sick or injured driver can make one lap around the track and then hand the car off to a relief driver, he can still earn points. Or something like that. Vincent didn't want to risk Toby trying to make those laps when he's unstable."

Which only confirmed Amelia's opinion that adrenaline junkies didn't know what was good for them. If the man had to be forced to take time off when he was incapacitated—

"Consider taking shifts managing the best man as one of your maid-of-honor duties," Candace stated firmly.

If she didn't love Candace so much, she would tell her to take her maid-of-honor tribute and insert it like a suppository. "I *really* could hate you for this," she repeated.

"Nah, you're just miffed because you can't keep running. And because Toby makes you feel something."

Amelia didn't want to feel anything. Numbness was safer. It allowed her to make logical decisions instead of impetuous ones. If the right man ever came along to replace Neal, then he would gently coax her emotions back to life. He would not turn her into a quivering mass of screaming nerves on her coffee table, her floor, her bed and in her shower.

Toby had turned her into a stranger that night ten months ago. Someone passionate, impulsive, impractical and without restraint—a combination guaranteed to result in disaster.

Someone she never wanted to be again.

"Feeling lucky tonight?"

Amelia startled and gasped at the sound of Toby's low-pitched voice rumbling in her ear. His warm breath stirred the fine hairs on her neck.

How did he sneak up on her that way? He'd done so numerous times during the days when Vincent had been in the hospital. She wouldn't even know he was on the floor and then—bam!—he'd materialize behind her, whisper something outrageous in her ear and rattle her nerves like leaves in a hurricane.

She turned away from the craps table. Surprise stole her words and glued her feet to the carpet. Gone was the jean-clad invitation to sin she'd come to know and avoid. In his place stood a man sexier than any other in Le Sun Casino. Correction: sexier than any man in the entire Monte Carlo Casino complex. Maybe even in all of Monaco.

Toby had tamed his golden hair and shaved his stubborn block of jaw. He looked dashing, debonair, suave…all those words she'd read but never used.

Like the blond James Bond. Only better.

He certainly left her shaken *and* stirred. "I—I don't gamble, so luck doesn't come into it."

"No?"

"No, but that doesn't mean I don't enjoy trying to figure out how different games work." With a flip of her hand she indicated the black tux adorning his tall, broad-shouldered athletic frame to *GQ* perfection. "I thought you'd lost your luggage."

"I did, but our helpful concierge pointed me toward the shops when you refused."

She didn't feel guilty for that. Well, maybe just a twinge, given his concussion. She scanned the brightly lit circus decor of the room, looking beneath the colorful carousel dome in the center, past the numerous slot machines and other games of chance and over the finely dressed guests. She didn't spot her suitemates.

"Where's Candace?" The bride had agreed to take the first Toby-watching shift. Amelia had broken away from the group to wander around looking for celebrities before Toby joined them. She adored entertainment magazines, and

Monaco—the casino in particular—was packed with famous faces. Too bad it would be tacky to collect autographs.

"Candace said something about the three of them heading to the Café Divan for dinner and sent me after you. Hungry?"

"Not really. You go ahead."

His silvery-blue gaze coasted from her French-twisted hair to her bronze silk evening gown with its bust-enhancing lace bodice and chiffon godet skirt that gave the impression of curves—curves her matchstick figure didn't naturally have. He finally reached her ridiculously high heels and then took a leisurely return trip. She felt as glamorous as a Hollywood starlet in this gown—doubly so when Toby's appreciative gaze returned to hers.

"You look good, sugar. Good enough to eat."

Her skin scorched. Memories bombarded her. She snuffed them and mentally searched her barren brain for a polite way to send him back to Candace before she weakened. "Thank you."

But then she noted the groove between his eyebrows and his slight flinch when a woman beside him squealed over a win. "Do you have a headache?"

He shrugged. "S'probably jet lag."

Compassion she did not want to feel invaded her. Postconcussion syndrome often included headaches. "It's too soon for jet lag. That'll hit tomorrow or the next day. You should get out of these bright lights and away from the noise."

"Not leaving your side. Bride's orders."

Amelia stifled a frustrated growl over Candace's blatant matchmaking. She would chew out her meddling friend later for ditching her shift early, because there was no doubt what this was—a handoff.

Amelia nodded toward the exit. "Let's walk outside. The

fresh air might help your head. If it doesn't, I have acetaminophen in my room."

His lips quirked. "Inviting me to your room already?"

Smacking him wouldn't improve his headache, so she restrained the impulse. Barely. "You can wait in the hall."

"First let's find a quiet restaurant somewhere," he said. "I could eat."

Hope kicked in her chest. Ditching him couldn't be as easy as passing him back to Candace, could it? "Why don't you join the others? I heard the food's good."

"No point in staying in the casino. I don't gamble either."

Which was an odd thing to say given his occupation was a huge gamble *with his life*.

Within moments he'd handed a message and a big tip to a casino employee to inform Candace, Stacy and Madeline that he and Amelia were leaving. He guided her out of the building with a warm hand on her waist that she couldn't outrun no matter how fast she toddled on her heels.

The cool night air enveloped her. She struggled with her wrap. Toby lifted the filmy fabric. His fingertips brushed her nape and then he smoothed his palms across her shoulders and down her arms in a wide, warm nerve-tingling swath. She silently cursed her telling shiver and hustled down the sidewalk.

Twisting to dislodge the hand at her waist, she glanced back toward the postcard view of the building. "The casino is my favorite landmark in all of Monaco, especially when it's all lit up like this. It looks like a giant wedding cake."

A line of expensive cars circled the Place Du Casino, the kind of cars she'd only seen in movie magazines and on her long-term male teenage patients' hot-rod calendars. She shifted her gaze to the man walking so close beside her that their shoulders and hands bumped. Not surprisingly the Ferraris and Lamborghinis and other overpriced and overpowered toys held his attention.

His gaze caught hers. "Nice wheels."

"Testosterone, tires, trouble. Those three T's are the bane of the burn unit."

"Is that why you hate drivers?"

"I don't hate drivers," she answered quickly—too quickly, if his skeptical expression was an indication.

"Sugar, you were the frost queen to every driver who visited Vincent in the hospital."

"I was not."

One arched golden eyebrow argued silently.

"Okay, so I don't see the point in needlessly risking your life for sport. It's just…stupid."

His chuckle surprised her. She'd insulted him and his profession. Why would he laugh? "So that's why you're playing hard to get."

"I am not playing at anything."

He took her elbow and guided her past the fountains and sculptures of Casino Square and across the street. The warmth of his firm grip weakened her knees.

"Most women want me because I'm fast on the track and slow in the sack. But not you, Amelia. Since the driver thing doesn't flip your toggle switch, then it must be me that starts your engine. So what's the draw? My buff bod or my Southern charm?"

The teasing twinkle in his eyes made her pulse skip. A laugh gurgled from her throat before she could block it. "It's certainly not your humility."

"It's only ego if you can't deliver the goods. I can."

"Oh, *puh-lease*."

He pulled her to a stop on the sidewalk beneath an iron

lamppost. His gaze locked on hers and his big body loomed above her. "I did. And I will."

The intent look in his eyes stole her breath. He was going to kiss her if she didn't move fast, but her muscles seemed sluggish. Toby tempted her to ignore every last vestige of common sense and self-preservation.

Last time she'd fallen into bed with him looking for comfort, but instead of solace she'd found passion—passion far beyond anything she'd shared with Neal. And her body's betrayal had alarmed her. If she could feel so much for a man she didn't love and wasn't even sure she liked, how devastated would she be if she let herself come to care about him and then had to live through his self-destructive behavior?

She'd be her mother all over again.

She had to get rid of Toby Haynes. The sooner, the better.

He lifted his hand toward her face. Amelia ducked out of reach at the last possible second. Her brain thanked her. Her body did not. Her skin tingled and her breasts ached with the need to be touched. "Maybe we should go back to the hotel."

A salacious smile slanted his lips. "Now you're talking."

"And eat in the dining room." She gave him her best don't-mess-with-me glare, the one that snapped even the most quarrelsome patient back into line, but at the same time she noticed the lines around his mouth and eyes had deepened. He was dead on his feet, most likely with fatigue—another post-concussion symptom.

At times such as this she wished she'd chosen nursing for the paycheck. But, no, caring for others wasn't just her job, it was her vocation. Somewhere deep inside her an empathy switch engaged any time she saw someone in pain. That meant she couldn't walk away from this man and potential disaster no matter how loudly her internal warning sirens blared.

She took his arm and steered him toward the hotel. His bicep tensed beneath her touch, and she released him immediately. Glancing sideways at him, she asked, "Doesn't it ever get old?"

"What's that, sugar?"

"The come-ons. You're exhausted, Toby. If I accepted your invitation for a night of nooky, you'd be hard-pressed to follow through."

He looped an arm around her waist and pulled her close to the radiator-hot length of his body so fast she didn't even have time to gasp. "Try me."

Darn. There went that blip of her pulse again. She flattened her palm on his chest and tried to make light of the situation. "Not tonight. You have a headache."

Her flippant reply made the corners of his lips curl…and there went her toes, doing the same. Why, oh, why did a man so totally wrong for her have so much power over her libido?

And then he kissed her. She stiffened with shock at the initial contact with his mouth. Her stubborn muscles ignored her order to retreat and loosened. His lips were soft. Hot. Insistent. Persuasive. His tongue stroked her bottom lip, slipped inside and tangled with hers. Long fingers cradled her nape, trapping her—not that she'd managed to work up the strength to protest yet.

But she would.

In a second.

Or two.

His other hand painted a trail of goose bumps down her back and settled at her waist. His leather-and-lime scent invaded her lungs and his warmth invaded her body. Her reasoning powers left through the same open door.

Why him? Why did Toby Haynes—daredevil extraordinaire—have to be the one to sweep her off her feet? Why couldn't he be as gentle and considerate as the other men she dated, men who asked before each kiss and caress? *Because then you'd turn him down. Right?* Why did her body revel in his high-handedness?

She really had to stop him. But one kiss melted into two and then three. She clung to the lapels of his tux as her thoughts spiraled out of control. This wasn't wise. But he tasted good, felt good, smelled good. Every cell in her body hummed to life.

Toby shifted, leaning back against a nearby building and pulling her between his thighs. As if she weren't hot enough already, heat radiated off the stone wall, making her skin tight and dry. The lace of her bodice rasped her sensitive nipples with each shuddered breath. His hand slid lower, cupping her bottom, heating her flesh and pulling her closer. The hard ridge of his erection scorched her belly through the thin silk of her dress, shocking her into awareness of where she was, what she was doing and with whom.

Oh, God. Not again. Didn't you learn anything last time?

She planted her palms on his chest and wrenched her mouth free. His heart thumped fast and steady beneath her palm. Backing away, she wiped her damp mouth with the back of her hand as if that would wipe away the mistake she'd made.

"Find another playmate, Toby. I'm not interested."

His gaze raked her face, her body, lingering on her breasts, and then returned to her eyes. He didn't say a word, but his expression—and her racing heart—called her a liar. He slowly eased himself away from the wall.

She hugged her wrap around her and walked toward the hotel. Even if she were foolish enough to overlook his profession, she'd heard the other drivers who'd visited Vincent joke about Toby's short attention span with women and his legendary number of conquests.

Toby was all about temporary. She wanted forever. And she wanted forever without fear or conflict. Unfortunately her neglected hormones didn't understand the concept of choosing wisely.

She had to find a way to avoid being alone with him or else her month in this fairy-tale kingdom would feel like an eternity running from the castle dragon.

"I'm sorry," Madeline replied on Tuesday morning.

Disappointment wrapped around Amelia like a boa constrictor. The rapidly descending elevator left her stomach behind. "It's okay. I understand."

She hoped her suitemate didn't hear the dismay in her voice. "You have fun with your tour guide. And, Madeline, if a vacation romance with him is what you're after, then I hope it works out for you."

She turned her attention to Stacy, the third occupant of the elevator. Amelia had only met Stacy a few times before this trip and she didn't know her very well, but she had to enlist aid while Candace wasn't around to interfere and she couldn't be picky. "Stacy, any chance you'll have some free time to take a Toby-watching shift?"

Stacy tilted her head. "Explain to me what you meant when you said you 'accidentally' slept with him."

Amelia winced. Leave it to Candace's accountant to want a logical explanation instead of the sketchy facts Amelia had offered—namely that Toby was trying to pick up where he and Amelia had left off ten months ago and she wasn't interested.

"I'd had a rotten week. That Sunday I'd lost a long-term patient who left behind a grieving pregnant fiancée. Tuesday was the anniversary of the day Neal and I had planned to get married. And then Wednesday Candace and Vincent announced their engagement. Don't get me wrong, I was— *I am*—thrilled for them, but it was just too much all at once, I guess. That night Toby asked me to go to dinner after my shift, and against my better judgment I accepted and…well, you know the rest."

Stacy nodded and her turquoise eyes filled with sympathy. "All three incidents reminded you of what you'd lost, and you didn't want to be alone. Toby was there, and you're attracted to him so—"

"Believe me, I don't want to be attracted. He's totally wrong for me. He's reckless and overconfident and—"

"I don't think he's overconfident," Madeline interrupted. "Look at him. He's rich, gorgeous and successful. He certainly knows how to make a woman feel good. You could do worse. Candace is right, Amelia. You've been mourning too long. It's time to get back in the game. I wouldn't expect forever from Toby, but you should consider him for a vacation fling. You know, to oil your rusty hinges."

The idea both titillated and repelled her. "No, thank you. I'm not the fling type."

"Honey, anybody can be the fling type given sufficient motivation," Madeline said.

Stacy touched her arm. "I'll do what I can to run interference, but remember I'm not a medical professional. The only thing I know about concussions is what I've seen on the Discovery Channel, and that's not much."

"I'll tell you what to look for."

"Stacy, don't forget your delicious French chocolatier," Madeline added. "Franco might have something to say about how you spend your time."

Stacy blushed and ducked her head.

Amelia struggled to hide her grimace. From what she'd learned last night when the women had returned from the casino, both Stacy and Madeline had met men who might monopolize their non-wedding-planning hours. That meant Amelia would be on her own most of the time, because Candace certainly wasn't going to help her avoid Toby. In fact, the bride-to-be seemed determined to do the opposite.

The elevator doors opened. Dread knotted Amelia's stomach, but she squared her shoulders and walked with the others toward the small, private hotel dining room for the wedding-cake sampling. She could handle this. She wasn't emotionally fragile anymore. The anniversary of her nonwedding didn't hurt as much these days, and she'd avoid alcohol— both contributing factors to her stumble into Toby's arms.

She blamed her overzealous reaction to his kiss last night on the element of surprise combined with strolling down the moonlit sidewalks of Monaco—a magical place where princes really did marry commoners.

Even fairy tales have flaws, her practical side interjected. Monaco royalty hadn't exactly lived a charmed life.

Being swept off her feet was fine for fantasies and fairy tales, but choosing a mate for practical reasons instead of letting her hormones and pheromones rule gave her a better chance of having a successful marriage.

In the meantime, she'd simply devote herself one hundred percent to the wedding arrangements. A man's man like Toby Haynes would avoid the girlie stuff the way he would a full-body wax. Sure, he'd agreed to carry out his best-man duties, and he and Amelia would have to work together on the Jack and Jill shower and the wedding-party luncheon, but she'd bet her trusty Camry he wouldn't be caught dead sampling wedding cake, picking out flowers or choosing bridesmaids' dresses.

All she had to do was keep busy with maid-of-honor tasks and he'd stay out of her way.

And then Amelia stepped into the dining room and her plan imploded. Toby stood beside the linen-draped table, talking to Candace and a chef. He looked perfectly comfortable and devastatingly attractive in pressed khakis and a pale blue polo. His jaw gleamed from a recent shave and his hair was still damp from his shower.

His gaze met hers. He toasted her with a crystal glass, and one corner of his mouth lifted in a knowing smile.

She gulped. So much for Plan A.

Plan B, where are you?

Three

"**Y**ou can run, sugar, but you can't hide." Toby stuck his boot in the gap before Amelia could shut the door in his face Wednesday morning.

He pushed his way into her suite. She'd given him the slip after the cake thing yesterday and gone shopping with her suitemates. Today he'd stick to her tight little tush like a tattoo.

He gave her the once-over. Twice. She looked adorable in her prissy white ruffled nightie with pink cheeks and bedhead. He'd always found bedhead kinda sexy—especially if he was the one who'd caused it.

"Toby, it's early. Why are you here?"

The early-morning huskiness of her voice revved his engine.

"Found a couple of places for the parties. You need to see them before I sign contracts. The car will be here in thirty minutes. Need help dressing?" He didn't expect her to say yes, but if she did, the car would have to wait.

"I haven't even had coffee. Go away and come back in an hour." Shoving her hair away from her face with both hands, she wandered deeper into the sitting room. The sun streaming through the wide window made her long gown damn near transparent. He bit back a groan. Granted, Amelia didn't have the *Playboy*-bunny curves of most of the women he dated and bedded, but the curves she had were in all the right places and looked mighty fine at the moment.

Without looking away from the mouthwatering view, he unclipped his phone from his belt. "I'll ask the driver to have coffee waiting in the limo. C'mon, sugar, move your tail—unless prancing around in front of that window in your sexy see-through gown is an invitation for me to spend the day here with you."

She gasped, looked down and crossed her arms over her breasts and torso. "Go. Away."

"Not happening. Get dressed or undressed. Either works for me."

The flush on her cheeks deepened and her fingers fisted, but she didn't move.

"Need help making up your mind?" He stepped toward her.

She whirled on her heel, hustled through one of the four doors opening off the main room and shut the panel—hard.

He grinned. He could always count on Amelia doing the exact opposite of his usual women. Most would have dropped the gown—if they'd been wearing one when they'd opened the door in the first place—and invited him to spend the day naked.

She was hell on his ego but a good outlet for his frustrated competitive nature.

He made a quick call to order her breakfast and considered calling home to check on his teams, but he calculated the time difference and returned the phone to its clip. Nobody would be in the shop this late on a Tuesday night.

Thinking about the shop made him antsy. He started pacing.

He'd hired a relief driver to keep his car on the track and keep earning owner points. Daily e-mails from his crew chief kept him up to date on the kid's progress. But it wasn't the same as being there. With his teams. In the driver's seat. In the groove of the track. In the winner's circle.

But Vincent—damn his friend's sorry hide—had threatened to pull Hôtel Reynard's twenty million sponsor dollars not just from Toby but from Haynes Racing's other two teams if Toby didn't stay away from the track until the neurologist cleared him. Toby could find another sponsor, but he wasn't willing to lose Vincent's friendship. Especially when his buddy was right. Toby had no business risking himself or other drivers by getting behind the wheel when one little bump could upset his equilibrium and put him and anybody near him into the wall.

One of his laps around the sitting room carried him past the dining room table. A calendar caught his eye and halted his steps. Each square listed the wedding-planning activities for each bridesmaid by time and location over the next four weeks. Hair appointments, dress fittings, manicures, massages…

Toby pulled out his PDA and noted each of Amelia's assigned tasks. If she dodged him again, he'd find her. He'd barely stuffed the electronic organizer back into his pocket when her bedroom door opened.

He turned and his whistle died on his lips.

A white eyelet sundress with string straps crisscrossed

her chest, with a narrow ruffle leading from the V-neck down and around the hem, which hung just above her knees. A waist-high bow on her side cinched in the fabric and reminded him how delicate she'd been perched above him. Long, lean legs. Small, round breasts. Slender enough he'd thought he might snap her in two. And then she'd taken him inside and he hadn't been able to think at all.

If he pulled that bow, would her dress open for him? Would she be wearing plain white cotton panties like last time? And no way could she be wearing a bra under there. His pulse raced.

A matching eyelet headband kept her hair off her face, and low-heeled white sandals revealed shocking-pink toe-nails. Funny, before Monaco he'd only seen her two ways: Naked and in hospital scrubs. She'd even worn scrubs the night he'd taken her to dinner because he hadn't given her time to go home and change—her clothes or her mind.

He'd never pictured her in street clothes. But that was probably because he spent most of his time picturing her naked. She'd been so efficient on the job that her girlie-girl attire was a surprise. "Nice."

The white bangles on her wrist tinkled as she fidgeted with her purse. "Thank you. Where are we going?"

"Hôtel de Paris and a private villa."

"Why a private villa?"

"Thought the brunch should be relaxed instead of formal. We'll have it catered." He opened the suite door, motioned for her to precede him into the hall and then followed her out. "There are beds at either place in case somebody has too much champagne and needs to sleep it off."

"That's probably a good idea." She hustled to the elevator as if trying to outrun him.

He stepped in the cubicle beside her and braced a shoulder against the wall. As usual, the rapid descent caused the floor to buckle and pitch beneath him. Damn, he hated this. He didn't even want to consider what he'd do if the doc was wrong and the vertigo didn't go away.

It will go away. It has to.

"Are you okay?" she asked.

"Fine."

"Then why do you have a white-knuckle grip on the railing? Are you claustrophobic?"

"Sugar, I spend hours strapped in a race car. Drivers can't be claustrophobic."

She fixed him with her patented get-over-yourself stare.

"Balance problems," he admitted grudgingly several seconds later.

"From the wreck?"

"Yeah."

"Is it just sudden movements or all movement? Up and down? Or lateral, too?" She'd kicked into nurse mode. It turned him on.

Sad, Haynes. Sad.

"Sudden. Whichever way."

The elevator doors opened. She linked her arm through his elbow. "Lean on me if you need to."

He wasn't about to tell her the dizziness had passed— not when he had her close enough to smell the flowery scent of her hair and feel the warm softness of her breast against his arm. "Car should be out front."

Her sandals clicked-clacked across the marble floor. Another first. He was used to her in those god-awful ugly but silent nursing shoes. The tap-tap-tap of her heels danced along his already attentive nerves, jacking his awareness of her up another level.

The driver he'd hired opened the rear door to a black

Benz as they approached. Amelia's steps slowed. "You weren't kidding about the limo. I've never ridden in one. I guess you have?"

He shrugged. "Racing's a fast life. Not just on the track. Limos, jets, helicopters are all part of the deal."

"Rented, right?" Her voice sounded tight. Her hazel eyes couldn't get any wider. She stared at the car as if she expected it to bite.

"The limos are rented. The rest we own."

The shocked gaze bounced back to him. "You own jets and helicopters?"

"Haynes Racing Inc. owns two private jets and a chopper plus an assortment of haulers and motor homes. We keep pilots and drivers for each on salary."

"That seems a little…extravagant."

"Getting to and from racetracks and appearances is part of the job, and a lot of business is conducted during the ride. Most teams are similarly equipped. It's just transportation, Amelia. You get used to it."

"Teams? I thought you were just a driver."

Just a driver. His muscles knotted. She knew nothing about him. And she sure as hell didn't know about his old man's prediction that Toby would never amount to anything.

You're just a pretty face, Tobias. You'll never be nothing else. And when yer looks and charm dry up you'll be just a outta-work bum like me.

A drunk outta-work bum with a mean streak a mile wide and a razor-sharp tongue despite the slurring words.

Toby shook off the bitter memory. He'd scrapped and fought to make sure he wasn't "just a" anything. His talent, interests and finances were carefully diversified. These days you couldn't pick up a sports magazine without finding an article about him between the covers, and stories about HRI filled the pages of racing magazines and a few business journals. He loved every aspect of his business, from push broom to promotion.

Fans and fame had their perks, but he had to admit it was nice to be an unrecognized regular guy—for the most part—in Monaco. "I own HRI. We run three race teams and drivers."

Most women would be impressed with the wealth and power involved in being a team owner as well as a top driver. Apparently not this one. Amelia's lips pursed as if she'd sucked a lemon. She blinked and eyed the hotel as if considering going back inside.

He unhooked their arms and stroked a hand down her spine, stopping an inch short of her butt—not because he wanted to but because she was skittish. He nudged her forward. "Breakfast is waiting. Climb in."

She entered the limo slowly, her head turning every which way, as if she were afraid she'd miss some minute detail. He tended to take a comfortable ride for granted. There were always people to get him where he needed to go, and since he couldn't drive until his head cleared up, having a driver in Monaco was a necessity.

Amelia settled on the bench seat and caressed the dove-gray glove-soft leather slow and easy, as if committing each inch to memory. The way she'd stroked him that night. His muscles clenched. He released a pent-up breath on a silent whistle and followed her in, but instead of sitting beside her he settled across from her so he could watch her captivated expression.

"Sir?" The driver's voice forced Toby's attention away from Amelia's killer legs. Louis extended a tray with two coffee cups, a carafe and a plate of éclairs.

Toby took it from him. "Thanks, Louis."

"You're welcome, sir." Louis closed the door and circled the car to climb behind the wheel.

Toby sat the tray on the seat beside Amelia. The suck-a-lemon look replaced the enchantment on her face. "It won't work."

"What?"

"Trying to soften me up with my favorite foods."

Okay, so he wasn't above using whatever leverage he had to woo her back between the sheets.

"Just ordering something you said you liked." He filled the coffee mugs and then slid back to fasten his seat belt. "I'd rather be serving you breakfast in bed."

She rolled her eyes, buckled herself in and then reached for a china cup. "Give it up, Toby. I'm not going to sleep with you again."

"Ever hear it's not wise to challenge a driver? We're a competitive bunch."

The car eased away from the curb. She pinched off a corner of an éclair and popped it between her lips. The blissful expression on her face had him shifting for a more comfortable position, but the slow glide of her tongue sweeping her icing-covered lips convinced him there wasn't one. His pants were cutting off circulation to one of his favorite parts. He straightened his legs in the space between the seats.

Her gaze found his. "Why can't you accept that I'm not interested and give up?"

"Because you strip me naked with your eyes every time we're in the same room."

She choked on a bite of éclair, chewed rapidly and gulped coffee. *"I do not."*

Her scandalized whisper sparked another flashback to their night together. "Sugar, you can tease me all you want, but don't lie. Not to me. Not to yourself. You want me."

She opened her mouth to argue, closed it again and then frowned at him. Her fingers fussed with the ruffled hem of her dress, and each pleating fidget lifted her skirt an inch or two and flashed him a glimpse of smooth upper thighs. "I do not tease."

He couldn't help laughing. He nodded to her restless fingers. "You do it without even trying. And, sugar, you slay me. Every time."

Her gaze dropped to her lap. She flattened her hand and then looked at the bulge behind his zipper. Her eyes widened and her lips parted. She ducked her head and focused on finishing her pastry with the intensity of a brain surgeon at work.

How could a woman be so totally unaware of her appeal? And why did this scrawny little gal turn him on with zero effort when others couldn't do so with a bag full of tricks?

He'd find out. And once he did, like any magic trick, she wouldn't impress him once he knew the secret.

Toby Haynes was her worst nightmare.

An adrenaline junkie.

Times three.

It wasn't enough for him to drive at breakneck speeds. He enabled others to do so, too.

She couldn't get back to her suite fast enough and hustled down the carpeted hall with one goal in mind—putting a wall between her and her tormentor. She just couldn't figure him out. Why her? And what was up with this morning?

The staggering opulence of the villa and the Churchill Suite at Hôtel de Paris—the places Toby had chosen as possible settings for the luncheon and bridal shower—had set her romantic heart aflutter, but what rattled the most was how effortlessly Toby had fit into both places. He'd strolled into each venue wearing his faded jeans, battered boots and what felt like a silk shirt and looked right at home, whereas she'd been afraid to touch anything for fear of breaking something.

She stopped outside her door and scowled up at him. "You never had any intention of having a keg party, did you?"

His smile turned wicked and she knew she'd been had. Again. During those months visiting Vincent in the hospital, Toby had apparently relished getting a rise out of her. He'd provoked her at every opportunity.

"Is your good-ole-boy shtick just an act?"

"I grew up dirt-poor and barely made it through high school. Don't let a little spit shine fool you." He plucked her key card from her hand and opened her door. And then he put *her* key in *his* front pocket.

"Give me my key."

"Later. Let's hit the pool." He forced her into the suite by the simple act of moving forward. She could either hold her ground and end up plastered against him or get out of the way. A tiny reckless part of her wanted the former. Of course, she ignored that annoying, foolish voice and moved.

He closed the door, sealing them into the suite. All four bedroom doors stood open.

"Hello? Anybody here?" she called out. Silence greeted her and her heart sank. Her suitemates were out. So much for her plan to turn Toby over to one of the wedding party. She faced him. "I have things to do this afternoon."

"What could be more interesting than spending time with the best man?"

"I'd like to go sightseeing. Alone."

"I'll set something up. Tomorrow."

"I don't want to go swimming." Lovely. Now she sounded like a fractious child.

She hadn't visited the pool and rooftop garden yet, and while she'd like to, she'd prefer to save that experience for later, when Toby wasn't in the building. Or the principality. Wearing a swimsuit seemed half-dressed—and half-dressed was almost naked. And naked was not something she wanted to be around tempta—*ahem*—Toby.

"Not much point in having a private pool and hot tub if we never use 'em. And the sign says Clothing Optional." His eyebrows waggled.

Her jaw dropped open. She snapped it closed. He could *not* be serious. "Not interested."

He checked his watch—an expensive-looking ultrathin gold piece. "Lunch will be served on the patio poolside."

She folded her arms and stubbornly shook her head.

A muscle twitched in his jaw and his unblinking stare pinned her to the carpet. "I'm not supposed to swim alone."

Her molars clicked together on that blatantly manipulative statement even though he looked as though he'd rather eat worms than admit it. Duty sucked and Candace would pay dearly for this. Amelia wasn't sure how yet, but her friend would definitely pay.

"I will have lunch with you because I'm hungry and I'll sit in the garden while you swim *with your trunks on*. I have to deal with naked men at work all the time. I shouldn't have to suffer them on my vacation."

Wait. That didn't sound quite right.

And watching Toby's buff body wouldn't exactly be an arduous chore. Unfortunately. Keeping her common sense and hormones separated would be the real challenge. She needed to build a mental Wall of China between the two warring factions of her brain.

"Spoilsport." He winked. "But I'll make you a deal. I'll wear my suit if you'll wear yours."

She bit back a frustrated growl and barely resisted the urge to stomp her feet like the spoiled daddy's princess she'd been before her father's injury. "You are a master manipulator."

That smile—the toe-curling one she detested—slid across his lips again. "I'm a master of many things. As you well know. Making you sing, for one. How many orgasms did you have that night? A record-breaking number, didn't you say?"

Seeds of her mother's infamous temper cracked open inside her, and tendrils of fury sprouted, shooting for an outlet—her mouth. Her teen years had been filled with hurtful words shouted through the house, and it frightened her that she wanted—no, *needed*—to bellow and throw things at Toby. But she wouldn't. She had more control than that. But just in case, she turned on her heel, stomped into her bedroom and shut the door.

A knock sounded before she could lock herself in the bathroom. "If you're not by the pool in twenty minutes, I'm coming back and hauling you out. With or without your suit."

She threw her sandal at the door and then stared aghast and pressed her hands against her cheeks. She never had tantrums. Ever.

Toby Haynes brought out the worst in her, and that was why, no matter what he said or did, she could not afford to get involved with him again.

But how could she avoid certain disaster?

Focus on his injury.

Treat him like a patient.

You never have sex with your patients.

Amelia had ditched him again.

Ticked off, frustrated and determined to track her down, Toby exited her empty suite just as the elevator chimed.

Amelia stepped out of the cubicle and scowled. "Were you in my room?"

"Yep. Went to get you. Said I would." He took in the filmy black fabric covering her to midthigh, her bare legs, the sparkly sandals on her feet and the shopping bag in her hand. She'd changed into her swimsuit. Score one for the Haynes team. "Where have you been?"

"I had to buy sunscreen and get a new key since mine was stolen."

"Borrowed." He pushed open the door to the pool area and the sharp tang of chlorine filled his nose. "Water's waiting."

But Amelia didn't move. She tilted her head, sending her hair gliding across her shoulders. His gut clenched in memory of the caress of those silky strands.

Great. Now he had a hair fetish to go with his AWOL equilibrium and a ban from the track.

"You thought I'd stood you up, didn't you?"

He refused to reply.

"Not used to women saying no, Toby?"

No, he wasn't. In fact, he received more offers each season than an entire football team could handle—and he was usually the one who said no thanks.

"I want to swim. I may be sidelined from racing, but I still need to stay in shape." And according to the doctor, he needed a babysitter to do it. That irked the hell out of him, but if he wanted to make up lost ground when he returned to the track, he'd need to have his A-game ready. No slacking off in his training schedule. His balance issues meant most of his favorite sports were out of the question. Temporarily. He had to stick to swimming and working out in the hotel gym with a trainer.

Amelia's gaze, more green than gold at the moment, coasted over him, lingering on his bare legs. Every cell in his body sparked to life. She slipped past him though the door. He deliberately crowded her, savoring her gasp, her flowery scent and the brush of her body against his.

"You work out?" Her voice sounded a tad breathless. Good.

"Every day. Driving's more than just turning the wheel. A guy needs stamina—which I'm sure you recall is good other places besides the racetrack. What about you? You gonna be able to keep up with me, sugar? Here in the pool, I mean. We both know how well you handle me in other places."

She took off across the flagstones like a driver putting the hammer down in a qualifying race against the clock and called over her shoulder, "I can swim. How is your head? Any pain?"

"I'm fine. Looks like we have the pool to ourselves." Excellent.

She stopped ten yards away beside the deep end and faced him. "Does the bright light bother you? Are you having any other problems, like a decreased sense of smell?"

Her nurse voice clued him in, but still he asked, "Why?"

"Those, along with a compromised sense of taste, are common side effects of a concussion."

"I'm fine. But if you want to play doctor, I'm more than willing."

After giving him a disgusted eye roll, she turned a full circle to inspect the area. "This is beautiful. You'd never know we're on top of a building. It's more like an oasis, and with those tented double loungers I almost expect to see a sheikh stroll past."

Toby scanned what he hoped would be a setting for seduction to see what put that dreamy, awed note in her voice. Citrus trees and flowering plants overflowed from giant pots around the patio. The retractable roof had been opened to let in the sunlight. Despite being surrounded by four walls—walls you couldn't see because of the dense foliage—a gentle breeze rustled the leaves and stirred the air. Probably a well-concealed fan. It didn't do much to cool his overheated skin.

"Sheikh fantasies trip your trigger?"

Her nose lifted. "My fantasies are none of your business."

He loved it when she got snippy, because in the sack she was anything but uptight. He liked the contrast of the prim-and-proper nurse and the sensualist lover. "Wrong, sugar. Making your fantasies come true is my sole ambition."

He peeled off his shirt and tossed it on a lounger and then kicked off his leather flip-flops and rubbed his hands together in anticipation of caressing Amelia's pale, smooth skin. "Take off your top and let me help you with that sunscreen."

She stilled, and then a slow, smug little smile curved her lips as she deposited her bag in a chair, then reached into it and withdrew an aerosol can. "No, thanks. I bought the spray-on kind."

Sneaky. But he could get around that, especially since he knew she wanted to get her hands on him. Even now she checked out his pecs and abs and a flush darkened her cheekbones. His nipples and groin tightened.

"Then you can rub in mine. I love the feel of your hands on me." Hell, he craved it. He'd lost count of the times he'd woken up hard in the past months from dreaming about her touch. Not even other women had blunted his need.

But that was only because Amelia had ended the affair before he'd had his fill of her. It was like leaving pit road with less than a full tank of gas or only two new tires. You'd have to come back sooner or later.

"I'll loan you my spray." She unbuttoned her cover-up. Each released button jacked his tachometer up another notch. By the time she shrugged off the concealing shirt his heart was racing and close to redlining.

Have mercy. Her chocolate-brown halter tankini didn't show much skin, but that top offered up her breasts like an all-you-can-eat buffet. He couldn't wait to take a bite.

She stepped out of her sandals and bent to place them neatly beneath a lounge chair. His libido burned rubber in his gut at the sight of her butt in the brief bottoms. He clenched his fists on the need to cup her curves, ease the fabric down and slide into her slick heat from behind.

"I wish the food was here," she said as she straightened. "You could test it and tell me if your taste buds are altered."

He wanted to eat, all right, but food wasn't exactly what he had in mind.

"Don't you nursing types know you're not supposed to eat right before you swim?" His voice sounded hoarse. Eager to get his hands on her, he closed the distance between them. "Food's coming later. C'mon. Let's get wet together."

An irritated gurgle rumbled in her throat. She parked her hands on her hips, revealing a tempting sliver of pale skin between her top and bottom. "Do those ridiculous lines actually work for you?"

Yes, they did. Extremely well. Usually women giggled themselves silly over his good-ole-boy wit. But not Amelia.

Why was she playing hard to get? Despite what she'd said earlier, he didn't believe she only slept with guys offering the picket fence and the gold ring, because she'd slept with him before. Not that they'd done much actual sleeping that night. That could explain why he'd been comatose when she'd slipped out on him without a good-bye other than that cold note.

Did she like the chase? Had she dumped him so he'd have to pursue her again? Because there was no doubting she wanted him. She studied him the way a rookie does his first ride—with quick, shallow breaths, hungry eyes and twitchy fingers.

What game was she playing? Not one for which he had the rule book, that's for damn sure.

"You look good in that suit. Bet you look even better out of it."

She reached for him. Finally. Hallelujah.

But instead of twining herself around him she planted her palms on his chest and shoved. Toby wobbled and fought for balance. He caught Amelia's wrist and held on. If he was going in, she was coming with him.

The cool water closed over his head, muffling her shriek. For a second, the sudden movement disoriented him, but the silky tangle of her legs with his and his feet hitting the tile bottom centered him. He held her close and stared into her surprise-widened eyes through the clear water.

Tightening his arms around her, he pulled her close and kissed her. A hard press of his lips against hers. Nothing openmouthed or as hot as he wanted, because he didn't want to drown. At least not before he'd made Amelia Lambert pay for making him want her and walking away.

Four

You don't drown your patients, nitwit.

And you don't kiss them.

Amelia broke the surface, gasping for air and wondering where in the devil she'd left her common sense. Toby Haynes had once more goaded her into foolish behavior.

And that kiss… She wasn't going to think about it or how she'd almost coiled around him and kissed him back.

Toby surfaced a few yards away.

She tried to ignore her tingling lips and treaded water. "I'm sorry. I shouldn't have pushed you. Are you okay?"

"C'mere." He swam toward her with a predatory glint in his eyes.

Uh-oh. You're in trouble now.

She sculled backward toward the ladder with her gaze locked on the man pursuing her. "Toby, I don't think horseplay is a good idea for a man in your condition."

"You started it." He kept coming.

"You needed cooling off. I thought you wanted to exercise."

"I do. But right now I want payback. You pushed me. You owe me."

"Oh, *puh-lease*. I agreed to lunch, not to be mauled by you." Her hand bumped the ladder. She gripped the cool metal tubing, but before she could swing around and climb out, Toby grasped the rails on either side of her body, caging her between the steel of the ladder at her back and his equally hard body in front. His strong legs trapped hers beneath the water. Warm. Hairy.

"Mauled?" He practically growled the word. His eyes narrowed to silvery-blue slits. "I remember you liking my hands and mouth on you. 'Touch me everywhere,' you said. Correction—you begged."

Yes, she had. Shamelessly. Heat pulsed through her. Gulping, she kept her eyes trained on his face despite the temptation to grasp his broad, muscular shoulders, press herself against his chest and relive that night.

Provoking him wasn't her best move. And reminding him that sleeping with him had been a mistake didn't seem like the wisest course of action at the moment either. As much as he liked challenges, he'd probably insist on proving her wrong.

Get a hold of yourself, Lambert, and get out of this. He may be sexy, but he is also hazardous. To himself and to you.

But how? A challenge?

"I bet you can't beat me in five laps. Or should we make it one? Are you up to a race at all?"

His nostrils flared at the implied insult. "Yes."

"If I win, you lay off the tiresome cliché macho come-ons for five minutes."

"And if I win…" His eyes narrowed. "I get five minutes."

She frowned. "Five minutes of what?"

"Whatever I want."

Her heart rat-a-tat-tatted like a snare drum. She shook her head with enough force to send her wet hair flying. "No."

"I'm not talking about screwing you, sugar. Even at my worst I take longer than five minutes."

A fact she knew all too well. She shivered despite the warmth of the water and the bright sun shining directly overhead.

She didn't gamble, but this was a safe bet. Toby might have a size advantage, he might even be in good shape, but she'd been on the swim team in high school and during her first two years in college. Since then she'd maintained a gym membership and still swam a mile three times a week. His powerful legs would give him a better push off, but if sudden changes of direction were a problem, she'd beat him in the turns. Surely he'd be eating her wake long before five laps?

"You'll keep your hands and penis to yourself?" His hands had wreaked havoc on her control that night. As had the rest of him.

"If you insist."

"I do." She prayed she wouldn't regret this. "Okay. Deal."

He rolled onto his back, displaying his calendar-hunk chest, muscle-gridded belly and narrow hips in brief black trunks as he swam toward the shallow end. "Need a head start?"

"No." She wouldn't take that much advantage. "Do you?"

He chuckled. "Nah."

She breaststroked after him and realized that for the first time she was pursuing him instead of running in the opposite direction. The idea amused her.

Aroused her.

Worried her.

"Trying to psych me out, Amelia?"

She neutralized her expression. "Would it work?"

"Sugar, I play with the big boys. It's going to take more than an itty-bitty nurse to mess with my head."

She couldn't wait to humble him by beating him.

He reached the shallow end and stood. Water streamed from his body and glistened in his chest hair, reminding her of their shared middle-of-the-night shower ten months ago, of chasing droplets across his flesh with her tongue, of him doing the same to her. Goose bumps raced over her skin. Her breath quickened and her muscles tautened. She rolled her shoulders as she walked to the end of the pool, trying to shake off the time-robbing tension that could slow her pace.

Instead of lanes painted on the bottom of the pool to draw boundaries between her and Toby, the beautiful mosaic of tropical fish looked like a living coral reef beneath her. She knew from her guidebook that Monaco royalty had been heavily into oceanography since the 1800s. The legendary Jacques Cousteau had been director of the principality's Oceanographic Museum at one point. As soon as she could escape Toby, Amelia intended to tour the museum this afternoon. Without one irritating driver.

"Sure you're up to this?" she asked and placed a hand on the smooth rounded tile edge. "Five laps is a good distance."

"Chicken?" he countered, mimicking her crouch, and when she shook her head he said, "On three. One. Two. Three."

Amelia exploded off the wall. Toby bumped into her— not hard enough to hurt but enough to knock her off course. She sensed him stopping, standing, and heard him ask if she was all right, but she corrected her course and plowed onward without wasting precious seconds to reply. She wasn't an overly competitive person by nature, but this time she had to win. *Had to.*

He reached the first turn several lengths behind her, but by the second he was closing in. A quick turn and push and then—boom!—he bumped her again. Two things registered. First, she'd underestimated his swimming ability. And second, the turns knocked him sideways and into her path. She adjusted by widening the gap between them.

By the end of her third lap, allowing him five minutes of *whatever* started looking like a real possibility. A nightmare of possibility. She put everything she had into beating him. Her arms and legs protested her furious pace. Her lungs burned. But still he stayed abreast. She couldn't shake him—and she had to. Now. On this final stretch. But with the finish line in sight, he pulled ahead and she knew she was in trouble. She touched the side several seconds after him and slowly stood on rubbery legs.

What had she gotten herself into?

Toby leaned against the tiles, chest heaving, with a smug smile on his face and a promise in his blue eyes. The victor.

And she was the victim of her own foolish overconfidence. "The turns messed you up?"

"Yeah. You want to cry foul?"

"No." He would have beaten her whether he bumped her or not. "Okay, do your worst."

"I never do my worst."

The ego again. She sighed. "What's my forfeit, Toby?"

Before he could answer, the door opened on a pair of uniformed servers pushing a linen-draped table. Lunch had arrived.

"You'll have to wait and see." And with that he launched himself out of the pool in a rippling display of muscle, leaving her anticipat—*dreading* what was to come.

* * *

The fastest car didn't always win the race.

Toby's years in NASCAR had taught him that winning took patience, skill and strategy. Knowing when to hold your ground and when to make your move often meant the difference between first and forty-third place.

"Sure you want to stick with that no-hands rule?" he asked as he laid his cloth napkin on the table. His body idled like a perfectly set-up car waiting to be unleashed on a superspeedway.

Amelia's spoon clanked against her gelato bowl. "Yes."

"I'm good with my hands."

She inhaled deeply through her nose and exhaled again with exaggerated patience. "I know."

"And even better with my—"

"I *know,*" she interrupted. A flush flagged her cheeks, and her hazel gaze skidded away from their romantic alcove.

The servers had set up the table in the shade of one of the tents tucked beneath trees and then discreetly departed, exactly as Toby had requested. A breeze stirred the gauzy drapes and strands of Amelia's drying hair.

His taste buds had gone on strike, but not because of his concussion. He'd been too busy thinking about her slender figure beneath that bathing suit and debating how he'd get her naked without using his hands.

He deliberately rubbed his bare feet against hers again beneath the linen tablecloth just because he liked hearing her breath hitch and watching the color rise under her skin. Unless memory had failed him—and he hoped it had—Amelia was easily the most responsive lover he'd ever had. Instead of little hidden pockets of pleasure, her entire body had been one contiguous erogenous zone. No matter where he'd touched, she'd responded. He wanted her to again.

He dragged his big toe along her instep. She abruptly jerked her feet away and shoved back her chair, but the tightening of her nipples rewarded him.

He didn't doubt he could get her back in the sack with a little effort. Probably within the half hour if he used all his tricks. But he didn't want to have to chase her again tomorrow. This time he wanted to get her into his bed and keep her there until he was ready to let her go. That meant revising his plan, taking it slow and steady instead of pedal to the metal.

She'd be a delicious distraction from what he couldn't have, a race he could win and a hunger he could satisfy. God knows he needed a distraction from being away from the track and HRI.

"Toby, I have things to do today. What's my penalty?"

"I haven't decided yet. What are your plans for this afternoon?"

"Nothing you'd be interested in."

"Like?"

"Tourist stuff." She rose and shrugged on her cover-up. "Museums."

It stung a little that she didn't think he'd be interested in museums. Had she, like his father and countless others, written him off as a dumb jock? "I'll have the car waiting in thirty minutes."

"That's not necessary." She gathered her belongings. "And just for future reference, most women take more than thirty minutes to get dressed."

"Not you. You don't waste time caking your face with tubs of makeup that a guy's only gonna smear. After the museums we'll have dinner at the Italian restaurant Vincent's mother booked for the rehearsal dinner. She made reservations based on someone else's recommendation and she asked me to check it out and make sure it's suitable."

Resignation settled over Amelia's face, puckering her brows and tightening her mouth. He had her up against the wall and she knew it.

"Fine," she snapped through barely moving lips.

Strategy worked every time. Pretty soon Amelia would be his. But not today. Today he intended to enjoy the chase.

If anyone had told Amelia she'd enjoy the company of an egotistical, thrill-seeking, smooth-talking ladies' man like Toby Haynes, she would have suggested they have their head examined.

Her pulse skipped as he seated her at a corner table on the colonnade outside the dining room of the ritzy Italian restaurant. Her irregular heartbeat had nothing to do with the brush of Toby's lightly callused fingers against her nape as he lifted her hair over the back of the chair and everything to do with the breathtaking sunset over the Italian Riviera.

Who do you think you're fooling?

She sighed. Toby's seemingly incidental touches had tantalized, titillated and tortured her in the seven hours since they'd left the pool.

Seven hours. And not once had she wanted to smack him. She couldn't believe it. He'd apparently been on his best behavior, and if she was on edge, it was only because she kept waiting for him to collect her five-minute debt. She didn't doubt he would or that it would be physical. *Intensely* physical.

He might not have aggravated her with an unrelenting stream of flirtatious banter this afternoon, but he'd watched her. The way a predator watches prey it wants to consume. The way a man watches a woman he intends to bed.

The Oceanographic Museum and Aquarium had been

as fascinating as she'd expected. But a museum she hadn't intended to visit—one Toby had coerced her into—had been the highlight of her day. Prince Rainier's extensive collection of antique cars and carriages had entranced her, reminding her of royal processions, old movies and Hollywood glamour. There had been the traditional Mercedes-Benzes and Rolls-Royces she'd expected as well as more exotic cars she'd never heard of. Toby's knowledgeable commentary had only enhanced the experience.

He settled across the table from her. A crisp white shirt stretched over his broad shoulders, accentuating his tan. Fine tufts of golden-blond curls peeked from his cuffs and open collar. "Tomorrow we'll tour the Venturi factory."

She startled when the waiter opened her napkin for her and laid it in her lap before handing her a menu. You didn't get service like that back in Charlotte—at least not in the restaurants she frequented. "What makes you think I'll spend tomorrow with you? You're not my tour guide."

"Because Vincent sent me over here so the bridal party could babysit me, and Candace has dumped me in your lap."

Surprised by his perceptiveness, she shifted in her seat. "You figured that out, huh?"

"Doesn't take a rocket scientist. Vincent wants me away from the track—and he's not averse to calling in a few favors to get what he wants."

Did Toby also realize Candace was shamelessly matchmaking? The idea was too humiliating to contemplate. "What's Venturi?"

"Venturi is a sports car manufacturer here in Monaco."

"Can't stay away from gas-guzzling big engines?"

He leveled a patient look on her and she had to look away. Okay, so she'd been needling him. But she didn't want to like him and today…today she'd enjoyed his company a little too much for comfort. Dangerous territory.

"Venturi has built GT racers for twenty years, but the model I'm interested in is an electric sports car. I want to see how they packed performance into a battery-powered vehicle. I can't test drive it, but you can. I'll ride shotgun and you'll tell me how she feels."

"Do I even want to know how much this car costs?"

"Six hundred."

"Thousand? Dollars?" He nodded and she gulped. "That's a few too many zeros for me. I'll pass."

"You'll love it." The wine steward arrived and Toby asked, "Wine?"

"No, thank you." She didn't dare weaken her willpower with alcohol. He sent the steward away without ordering.

"You shouldn't let me stop you from having wine with your dinner, Toby. Candace said Mrs. Reynard chose this restaurant specifically because of its famous wine cellar."

"I don't drink."

She frowned. Teetotaling didn't fit her image of the fast-living adrenaline junkie she knew him to be. How had she missed that ten months ago? "Why?"

"My dad was a drunk. A mean one. Don't want to turn out like him." He stated it matter-of-factly and opened the menu.

A fissure formed in her preconceived notions of him. "I'm sorry. I didn't know."

"I don't advertise it."

"Did he…hit you?"

"Until I knocked him on his ass."

Sympathy squeezed her heart. You couldn't work in health care and not deal with physical abuse at some time, but it still disturbed her. No matter how fiercely her parents had fought, they'd never hit each other or her. Thrown things? Definitely. But not at anyone. Verbal arrows were their weapons of choice, but even those had been aimed at each other and not Amelia.

"And your mother?"

"Got tired of his abuse and left the day I turned fifteen."

She struggled with the urge to comfort him even though he hadn't asked for it. In fact, his brusque manner discouraged it. "Not a great birthday gift."

"Better than watching him smack her around." Toby signaled the waiter, who immediately rushed over, thereby killing that line of discussion. "Brave enough to let me order for you?"

"I…okay. But I won't eat anything weird or icky."

His smile said *Trust me*, and then he ordered in Italian, his voice deep and shockingly sexy. The waiter departed and Toby answered her surprised gaze with a shrug. "I have an Italian Formula 1 guy working on my engine team. He taught me enough to get by."

"I'm impressed." That wasn't a lie. Unfortunately.

"Good." His eyes narrowed. "Bet you had a mom, apple-pie and homemade-cookies childhood."

Amelia blinked at the quick change of subject. "You'd lose that bet. My parents married because my mother got pregnant with me. By the time I turned twelve, Mom had decided to make good on her repeated threats to leave my father. We were due to move out the week dad had his accident. Mom stayed to take care of him."

"What kind of accident?"

"My father was a firefighter. He went back into an inferno to save a fallen comrade. The other firefighter died, and my father ended up paralyzed from the waist down. Mom can't forgive him for putting his coworkers ahead of his family. And she makes sure he knows it every single day."

Stunned by her confession, Amelia ducked her head and studied her knotted fingers. Why had she told him that? She'd never discussed her dysfunctional family with anyone. Not even Candace, her best friend, knew the whole truth or Amelia's shameful secret.

For most of her teen years Amelia had secretly wished her mother would pack up and move out instead of staying behind to martyr herself caring for her injured husband. Life would have been much more peaceful if she'd left Amelia with her father.

But that was a boat of guilt she'd rather not row tonight.

Toby reached across the table. She abruptly leaned back in her chair to avoid contact. Accepting comfort from him had landed her in trouble the last time.

He narrowed his eyes. "You chose nursing because of your father."

"I liked helping him and making him comfortable." Looking after her father after school and on weekends had given her mother a much-needed break from being caretaker and her father a break from her mother's acid barbs and tantrums.

"Do you ever hear from your mother now that you're famous?" she asked Toby in an attempt to change the subject.

"She called. Once." The single hard-bitten word discouraged Amelia from asking for details, but it didn't stop her.

"What did she say?"

"She wanted money. What else?"

"I'm sorry."

The server placed their drinks and antipasto on the table and then left.

Toby nudged her foot beneath the table and winked. That invitation-to-sin smile slanted his mouth. "Hey, you're sitting across from NASCAR's sexiest driver. Lose the long face before you ruin my reputation. Unless you want to blow this joint and head back to my suite…."

The playboy had returned. That wasn't disappointment weighting her stomach, was it? Toby was a lot easier to resist when he was trying to get her naked than when he was being nice.

And then something clicked. She'd asked about his mother and opened a door—a door he clearly wasn't ready to let her pass through. "Do you act like a jerk to keep people at a distance?"

His head snapped back and his nostrils flared, confirming the accuracy of her statement. Something flashed in his eyes but passed so quickly she couldn't identify it. And then his expression turned salacious. "So we're gonna play head doctor? My couch or yours, sugar?"

She tried to rally her exasperation but failed. The damage had already been done. She'd had a peek past the charming facade Toby Haynes wore like armor and seen vulnerability. Seeing his pain made her want to help him.

For the first time in her life she cursed her compassionate nature. And she hoped it wouldn't get her into trouble.

Safety lay on the opposite side of that door.

Conflicting emotions tumbled in Amelia's head and agitated her stomach. She turned outside her suite with a quick but cool thanks-for-dinner-and-good-night hovering on her lips, but those words froze at Toby's closer-than-expected proximity. Her spine thumped into the jamb as she jumped back. He'd invaded her space while she'd been busy formulating a plan to escape unscathed.

Toby lifted a hand and leaned closer, but he only planted his palm on the wall beside her head. Scant inches separated their bodies, and his breath swept softly over her overheated face. But he didn't touch her. His gaze held hers, slid slowly to her lips and then returned to stare intently into her eyes for a dozen heart-pounding moments.

Would her five-minute punishment be a long kiss good-night?

She didn't want him to kiss her. His kisses muddled her thinking and made her act rashly. And yet she couldn't seem to persuade her leaden limbs to move her out of his way.

Her mouth dried. She swallowed.

His scent, a lethal combination of musky male and cologne, teased her nostrils. Warmth radiated from him, permeating the thin fabric of her dress.

Just do it. Make me pay already.

She wanted it over. The kiss. The embrace. This stupid fascination. The madness.

He reached past her with his other arm. She closed her eyes and steeled herself for the impact of his hand on her waist and his lips on hers, but instead of the heat and strength of him pulling her into his arms, her sluggish brain registered the hum and click of the electronic door lock. Her lids flickered open. Her key cut into her palm. That meant he must have used his—the one he'd stolen earlier.

He pushed the door open an inch and then shifted his leg to plant his shoe in the gap. The movement pressed the inside of his thigh against the outside of her hip. Hot. Hard. She vaguely registered the quiet cadence of the television coming from the sitting room. At least one of her suitemates was in.

He lifted her hand and wrapped her fingers around the knob. "Hold on."

And then he stroked a finger along her jaw and down her neck to trace the shoulder strap of her dress. Back to front. Scapula to clavicle. His slightly roughened skin raised goose bumps on her arms and shoulders, and her heart nearly battered a hole through her ribs.

"Be ready at nine tomorrow, sweet Amelia." Lowering his hand, Toby eased back and then he turned on his heel, strolled down the hall and disappeared into his own room. His door clicked shut behind him.

Her lungs emptied in a dizzying gush and her fingers contracted on cold metal. She sagged against the wall.

He hadn't kissed her.

She wasn't disappointed.

No. Uh-uh. She wasn't. Not even a little bit.

Just because she'd seen a less jerklike side of Toby today and she'd actually enjoyed his company for once didn't mean she liked him or wanted him to kiss her. Not tonight. Not ever again.

Liar.

She sucked in a sharp breath and plunged into the suite. Candace sat on the sofa surrounded by a rainbow of fabric samples.

"He knows," Amelia blurted. "Toby knows Vincent asked us to watch him. And he knows you've dumped him on me. His words. Not mine."

Candace's wily smile made Amelia's skin prickle. "I always thought Toby was smarter than he let on. That man can play good ole boy better than any Oscar-winning actor when it suits him. But he's smarter than that. If he weren't, Vincent wouldn't invest twenty-million bucks in his race teams every year."

"Twenty million?" Amelia squeaked. At Candace's nod, Amelia's purse slipped from her fingers and bounced on the coffee table. Toby lived in an affluent world she couldn't even begin to imagine. "One of you needs to take a turn with him tomorrow."

"We're all tied up. You're the only one free."

Amelia's temper stirred. "You have no intention of taking a turn, do you?"

"I'm busy. I have a wedding to plan."

"I'm your maid of honor. I'm supposed to be helping you."

"You are helping me by watching Toby. Vincent loves him like a brother. I can't let anything happen to him. And you're the one most qualified to ensure that it doesn't."

"Not fair. Madeline is a physician's assistant. She's had more training than me."

"Madeline has embarked on a holiday affair with her tour guide. Amelia, you know her ex did a hatchet job on her self-esteem. She needs this time to heal."

Unfortunately Amelia knew and agreed. Madeline's ex-fiancé, a doctor who'd worked at the hospital with them, had publicly humiliated her friend and destroyed Madeline's confidence when he walked out of their six-year engagement. Madeline deserved whatever happiness she could find.

The fight drained out of Amelia and an ice block of dread crystallized in her stomach. "I know she needs a boost right now. But, Candace, Toby's just like—"

She stopped. *Just like my father.*

This should be the happiest and most exciting time of Candace's life. If Amelia dumped her pitiful family history on her friend, she could ruin that. Could she live with being a wet blanket?

"I'm pregnant," Candace confessed before Amelia could make up her mind.

"What?"

"It's a secret. Please don't mention it to anyone. I'm avoiding Toby because I'm afraid he'll figure it out and tell Vincent before I can. I want to tell Vincent he's going to be a father in person, and that means not telling anyone until after I can do that. Can I count on you to keep my secret, Amelia?"

"But Vincent won't be here for weeks. He's tied up at the new hotel."

"Right. It's going to be hard keeping this quiet. I haven't been sick much, but I do sleep a lot. And—gag me—I am craving sardines. *Eeew*. It's like eating cat food, but I can't seem to get enough."

Amelia forced a smile. As happy as she was for her friend, she could feel a rising tide of panic. She'd been saddled with a man who could totally wreck her plan for a peaceful life, a man who'd already made her do impulsive and intoxicating things she regretted. A man who made her want to do those things again.

"Nobody will hear your news from me. Congratulations."

Candace stood and hugged her. "You're the best."

"That's what friends are for. But I will need some relief from Toby."

"I'll see what I can do."

But Amelia suspected whatever Candace arranged wouldn't be enough. She was on her own and in serious trouble.

Five

Toby Haynes had the machismo, charisma or whatever it was that sucked all the oxygen out of a room the moment he entered. The small confines of the car only intensified that effect.

"Are you crazy?" Amelia whispered as Toby folded himself into the passenger seat. "We can't just take a six-hundred-thousand-dollar vehicle and leave the country."

"It's insured. And the dealer knows where we're headed. He even recommended his brother's bistro for lunch. Work for you?"

She tightened her already white-knuckle grip on the steering wheel. "I can't think about food. My stomach is tied in knots. This car costs almost as much as I make in a decade."

"I've got you covered. Just enjoy the drive."

She wanted to. Impractical as it may be, she'd fallen in love with the adorable sports car on sight. The smell. The bold cobalt paint. The way the leather seats cradled her body like a spooning lover.

Don't go there.

The total absurdity of the price made sitting behind the wheel feel more like fantasy than reality. Forget Cinderella and her fancy pumpkin coach. *This* was a ride to be envied. Too bad Amelia had always been and always would be the sensible-sedan type when it came to actually purchasing a vehicle. And she never would have dared to test-drive a car she couldn't afford.

Toby leaned across her. His shoulder pressed hers and his springy hair brushed her chin. The clean tang of his shampoo combined with his nearness to make her head spin. He grabbed her seat belt and strapped her in and then turned his head. Scant inches separated their mouths.

Her breath caught and her skin tingled. "But—"

"Sugar, if you're as crazy about celebrities as Candace says you are, then you know you want to see Cannes."

"Well, yes, but…" She wanted to match her handprints to the ones in Allée des Stars, the French version of Grauman's Chinese Theater, where celebrities who'd attended the famous Cannes Film Festival had left handprints in concrete. But she'd planned to travel by train. Alone. Without the temptation of a man and a car she couldn't afford. And darn Candace for revealing her plans. "It's an electric car. What if the battery dies?"

"It's less than forty miles. We'll make it." He sat back and fastened his seat belt. "Quit making excuses and drive."

She bit her lip and wrinkled her nose. "You're not going to let me weasel out of this, are you?"

His eyes twinkled and his teeth flashed in a wolfish smile. "Not a chance. Let's go."

Part of her wanted to do as he suggested and live a little,

but her sensible side kept her foot on the brake. "They drive fast in Europe."

"A hundred and thirty kilometers per hour sounds fast, but it's only eighty-one miles per hour. You can't tell me you've never driven eighty on an interstate." His palm spread over her bare knee and squeezed, sending shock waves of sensation through her. "Amelia, I have every confidence you can handle this car as well as you handle me. C'mon, take me for a ride. You know you want to."

Take me for a ride. You know you want to. Heat imploded inside her. He'd said those same words ten months ago after rolling on his back and dragging her on top of him.

That night she'd ridden him until her thighs burned. And then, sated and drained, she'd melted over him like ice cream on hot apple pie.

She could not think about him and sex and still drive. She picked up his hand, returned it to his side of the console and put the car in gear. Her foot slipped on the clutch and the tires squealed. She flinched.

"Now you're talking. Let's see what this baby will do." He patted the dash.

She shot a worried glance at the salesman who'd given them the tour of the production facility and then the car keys. The man smiled and bowed as she left the parking lot, acting as if people drove away with six-hundred-thousand-dollar cars they hadn't paid for every day. Maybe the rich did. But she wasn't rich, and driving a vehicle that cost as much as a McMansion parked her heart in her throat and made her palms sweat on the leather-encased steering wheel.

Toby read the driving directions the salesman had provided, and all too soon Monaco faded from her rearview mirror and they merged onto A8. The car handled like a dream, and within minutes she got over her initial panic and relaxed. She felt a little like a butterfly breaking free of her cocoon. While she drank in the scenery of southern France, Toby focused on the dials and gauges and asked a steady stream of questions about how the car handled.

"Give her some juice," he prompted after they passed the exit to Nice. "Get a feel for her and then I want you to push her to the edge."

Amelia's heart stuttered. "The edge of what?"

"Control. I want to see what she's made of."

Something in his voice drew her attention. She glanced at him and saw a yearning in his eyes before he turned away. "You really miss this, don't you?"

He wiped a hand down his face. "Yeah. And it's killing me not to put her through her paces. But I wouldn't risk you, me or the other drivers on the road by getting behind the wheel before I'm cleared."

That didn't sound like an adrenaline junkie who never considered the costs of his actions or like a man who'd had to be forced out of the country to keep him off the racetrack.

Stealing quick peeks at him, she nibbled her lip and accelerated. Had she misjudged him? No. His career said it all. Drivers died at racetracks. And the NASCAR fans she knew watched for the excitement of the wrecks.

Car racing was a dangerous sport. Look at Vincent. He'd be scarred for life as a result of a racing mishap—and he'd been an innocent bystander. Toby had chosen a dangerous profession and he didn't even have the benefit of saving lives as her father had had to offset that risk.

They rode in silence past town names she could barely pronounce, and then she asked the question that had been nagging at her since she'd found out about his injury. "Have you considered what you'll do if you can't drive again?"

"No need to think about it. Doc says I'll be ready for qualifying in four weeks."

But the idea had occurred to him. She could see the concern furrowing his brow and tightening his mouth.

"Cars are like women," he said. "Some are loose. Some are tight."

And the playboy rides in again with a change of subject. This time she instantly recognized the defense mechanism for what it was, but she let him get away with it because maybe he wasn't ready to face the idea that his career could be over. In all likelihood, his concussion would resolve itself. But head injuries were tricky. There was a chance he wouldn't improve or that he wouldn't heal as quickly as he hoped.

Patients often had trouble coming to terms with learning that sometimes no amount of medical intervention or wishful thinking could return things to the way they used to be. Her father had fought for years before admitting he'd never walk again.

"Explain your sexist comment."

Toby chuckled. She wished he wouldn't. That low rumbling sound made it difficult to concentrate on anything but the man beside her.

"Racing lingo. Loose means her rear end wiggles. She slides out from under you on the curves. Tight means she won't go where you steer her. She's unresponsive. And like a woman, you need to read her every move and adjust your approach to get the most pleasure and performance out of her."

A disgusted noise climbed her throat. "Must you make every conversation about sex?"

"Sugar, I'm talking about the car. If you're thinking about sex, it's because you're fixated on that night. Same as me."

Gulp. Guilty. "Maybe you're giving yourself too much credit."

"Nah. You want me." Cocky. Confident. *Correct.*

She could lie and deny it, but what was the point when they both knew the truth? But this time she wouldn't let her wants make her forget the possible consequences.

She followed the signs to Boulevard de la Croisette and followed Toby's directions past palm trees and parks, luxury hotels, galleries and designer boutiques. According to her guidebook, this is where the stars shopped—and for a moment, riding in her borrowed carriage, she felt almost as if she fit in.

She found a parking space near the restaurant, pulled in and turned in her seat. "Wanting you is irrelevant. I told you—I'm looking for a husband and I refuse to marry someone with an occupation even more dangerous than my father's."

Toby's gaze held hers. "Nobody but you mentioned marriage. Amelia, you're hot, the hottest woman I've been with in a long time, but I'm not ever going to get married. A racing career's hell on a marriage. Drivers spend more time on the road than at home. Even if it weren't so tough, I don't exactly have a great example to follow. That doesn't mean we can't have a good time in Monaco. You can look for Mr. Picket Fence when you get home."

She should be offended. Seriously offended. He'd just admitted all he wanted from her was sex. Most guys at least tried to fake interest in more. Other than Toby, she'd always been one of those women who had to care deeply for a man before she slept with him, which meant—whether they faked it or not—there hadn't been many men in her bed.

But now that she suspected Toby used tired lines and

clichéd come-ons to keep his distance, she couldn't seem to muster outrage. Instead the temptation to do exactly as he suggested and dive into an affair tugged at her.

How totally unlike her pragmatic self.

She wouldn't consider his suggestion.

No. She wouldn't. Not even for a minute.

So why did the idea bedevil her like a bad case of poison ivy?

Amelia would have whiplash before she finished her dessert, Toby concluded.

Framed photographs of celebrities lined the restaurant walls. Movie and TV stars. Musicians. World leaders. Royalty.

An American sitcom star and his babe du jour occupied a table a few yards away, and in the back corner of the crowded beachfront restaurant an aging rock star was putting the moves on a woman young enough to be his granddaughter. Amelia's eyes were wide and awed as she tried to gawk without being obvious.

So why did these people rate the star treatment when she had no problem shooting him down? He could use a little of that hero worship if it meant getting her back into the sack.

On second thought, it was because she didn't brownnose and she hadn't slept with him because of who he was that he liked Amelia Lambert. Not that there weren't plenty of other reasons to be attracted. Such as her killer long legs, her sexpot mouth and her cute little butt.

Movement drew Toby's gaze away from the woman causing his blood to drain from his brain, and he spotted the restaurateur—the car salesman's brother—approaching with a camera.

Being a NASCAR driver meant being accessible to the fans no matter what you were doing or which continent you were on. The only place Toby had guaranteed privacy was inside his locked and gated estate. He pushed his empty plate aside and switched into promo gear.

"Monsieur Haynes, could I beg you for a picture and an autograph?"

"Happy to, Henri." And he meant it. Every fan, every autograph request rewarded him for years of hard work and sacrifice.

The man glanced at Amelia. "You and mademoiselle?"

"No, I'm not his girlfriend," Amelia answered too quickly for Toby's liking.

He dragged out his trademark grin. The camera flash temporarily blinded him. Even before the spots faded he accepted a black marker, signed the autograph-covered menu the manager put in front of him and then passed it back. He looked back at Amelia in time to see granddaddy rock star's hand descend on her shoulder. She stiffened and so did Toby. Her wide-eyed gaze bounced from Toby to the long-haired, big-lipped guy and back.

Toby's gut clenched and his lunch turned to battery acid in his belly.

"Great to see you, Toby," the musician said without bothering to introduce himself. "Nasty crash. You had me worried when you didn't drop the net and climb from the car. Glad to see you up and about. Used some of your footage in my last video."

"Right. I saw that. Good CD. We play it in the shop." But he'd take a sledgehammer to the disk if the guy didn't get his veiny, age-spotted paw off Amelia. She was his— for now—and he wasn't sharing.

"When will you be back on the track?"

"Chicagoland. I'm taking some personal time till then."

"I can see why you would." The guy's fingers squeezed Amelia's pale flesh and his lecherous gaze looked down her top.

Toby wanted to slug him.

What? Are you jealous?

Hell no. But he didn't like the guy looking at Amelia as if she were some groupie who could be had.

"I'll be watching the race. My money's on you." The guy returned to his jailbait chickadee.

"You know him?" Amelia whispered, her hand covering the area where the guy's had been. In adulation? Or was she wiping away the creep's touch?

"Never met him."

"But he seems to know you."

"That's the way it is in the public eye. People read about you and think they know you."

She bit her lip, lowered her hand and her gaze.

He remembered her fascination with entertainment rags and wanted his bitter words back. But he couldn't erase what he'd said, so he tossed a handful of bills on the table and stood. "If you want to see the handprints before we head back, we have to get moving."

The TV guy waved. Toby nodded but kept walking toward the exit. Several other patrons' heads turned as if they were trying to figure out who he was. Or maybe they were looking to see who *his* woman du jour was.

God knows he'd had his share of flashy, willing females on his arm, but he didn't like the idea of anyone shoving Amelia into that category and he didn't want the tabloids printing her picture or exposing her to that kind of talk. Most of the women he escorted wanted the exposure. He'd bet HRI Amelia wouldn't enjoy the attention.

She glanced toward the actor. "Do you know him?"

"No." As much as he wanted to get her away from public scrutiny and speculation, he realized star sightings were probably a big deal to her. Although he couldn't picture her yanking up her shirt and asking a guy to sign her boob. Toby had signed more cleavage than he could count. Fans asked for autographs on the damnedest things. "Did you want an introduction or autograph?"

"No. I don't want to intrude. Let's go." She didn't speak again until they'd walked a couple of blocks from the restaurant. There was a speculative quality to her gaze when she looked up at him. "I guess I never considered you one of them."

"Them?"

"A celebrity."

"Does that mean you want to jump my bones now that you do?"

The familiar gurgle of disgust burst from her lips, making him smile. He'd grown attached to that sound. He'd lain in bed too many nights thinking of ways to provoke it and then to turn it into that whimper she made when she climaxed.

"In your dreams."

"Every night, sugar." Sad fact—that wasn't a lie. His smile faded.

"Do you meet a lot of stars?"

"Enough. Drivers make appearances for their sponsors. NASCAR's big on fund-raisers and charity events."

Her eyebrows shot up. "Charity events? You?"

She didn't think much of him and that bothered him more than it should. Since his father, he hadn't worried about anyone's approval except his own. So why her? Why did this uptight nurse's opinion matter?

He didn't have the answer. The only thing he knew for sure was that his patience for getting her naked was shrinking fast while other parts of him weren't. Taking it slow and easy wasn't getting him anywhere in his quest to get her into his bed and out of his system. Maybe it was time to scrap that plan and turn up the heat.

"I support several charities besides the Haynes Foundation. I came from nothing. It's my duty to give back."

The sun beat down, reflecting off the sidewalks, glass storefronts and car windshields, driving shards of pain through his head.

"That's a really nice thing to do, Toby."

The approval in her soft voice made him feel ten feet tall and bulletproof. He wanted to kiss her so bad he couldn't see straight. Hell, he wanted to drag her into the nearest hotel and lose himself inside her long enough to forget the races he was missing and the fear that he might not be back in the car for Chicagoland. Or ever.

Amelia took his arm and steered him toward a shop. "The sunlight's bothering you. You need to buy some sunglasses before you get a headache."

Nurse mode. His engine revved. As much as he hated hospitals—and he'd seen the inside of several—it was disgusting how easily her efficient take-charge demeanor turned him on. But it was more than a sexual turn-on. Amelia looked out for him. In the casino, the elevator, the pool, here. How long had it been since a woman—including his mother—gave a damn about him except for what she could get out of him? But he didn't dare let himself come to like or expect it, because in the end she'd let him down the way women invariably did.

He should cut his losses and push her away.

But he couldn't. Not yet.

Not until he'd relieved this itch. And he intended to start scratching it.

Tonight.

"I want my five minutes."

Toby's words stopped Amelia in her tracks. Her hotel key card flipped out of her hand and tumbled, as if in slow motion, to the carpeted hall floor. Adrenaline raced through her veins, flushing her skin and quickening her breaths.

Buying time, she took advantage of Toby's slowed reflexes and knelt quickly to retrieve the card before he could. And then she straightened ever so slowly before meeting his gaze. "Now?"

"Now."

She tried to gauge his mood by his tone and failed, tried to guess what her penalty would be from his expression with no better luck. His set jaw and level gaze gave nothing away. Nor had he said anything on the drive back to Monaco to hint at his intentions. In fact, he'd been unusually silent.

She wanted to fabricate an excuse for why this wasn't a good time, but the creative side of her brain was too busy running amok considering what he could do with five minutes to come up with logical reasons.

Making that wager had been stupid. Stupid. Stupid. *Stooopid*. She didn't gamble, didn't bet. Heck, she'd never even joined the nurses' pool to buy lottery tickets. But she'd foolishly made an exception by wagering with Toby because she'd believed winning a sure thing.

And now she would pay for her recklessness.

"I, um…guess you could come in. I don't know if my roommates are in or out or—"

"My room."

Her mouth opened, but she couldn't speak and could barely drag a breath into her constricted chest. He strolled down the hall, extracted his key from the pocket of his khaki pants, unlocked his door and pushed it open. A tilt of his head indicated she precede him.

This was a mistake. But a promise was a promise. Wobbly legs carried her forward. Doubt sucked each step like deep mud.

Entering cautiously, she scanned his sitting room, noting the earthy Tuscan colors that were so different from the lighter, more feminine decor of the suite she shared with Candace and the bridesmaids. She halted beside the cognac-colored L-shaped leather sofa separating the sitting and dining areas. A wide balcony and a door leading to the bedroom were the only exits—neither a viable means of escape.

He stopped behind her, close but not touching. Her mouth dried. She dampened her lips and focused on the blue sky beyond the glass balcony doors. "What's my penance?"

"Eager, sugar?" The words were low, barely audible, like the rumble of thunder in the distance.

The fine hairs on her body rose as if an electrical storm crackled nearby. "Eager to get back to my room, yes."

"Drink?"

"No, thank you." She clutched her purse tighter. The lace edging the scooped neckline of her teal top rasped against her skin like a calloused fingertip with every shallow breath, and the hem of her denim skirt teased the back of her thighs like a lover's caress.

She'd been wearing this outfit for eight hours. Why had it suddenly become a source of tantalizing friction?

Because Toby was right. She'd fixated on that night, her mind rutted in a treacherous path that could only lead to trouble. Being alone with him made her think of sex. Of intense pleasure. Of impulses best ignored.

He reached around her, took her purse and tossed it on the coffee table. Her fingers fisted and her muscles tensed. She was a mature twenty-seven-year-old woman who dealt with life and death on a daily basis. She could handle five minutes of whatever Toby Haynes dished out.

She cleared her tight throat. "Do you have a timer?"

The air stirred as he shifted behind her and then she heard a click and a metallic chink. Toby's muscled forearm, tanned and sparsely dusted with dark golden curls, entered her peripheral vision. He offered his watch. His other arm encircled her and he pointed at a tiny button.

"Push that button when you're ready to start."

She took his watch in her hand. The gold carried the warmth of his body and burned her palm like a hot ember. "Y-you promised no hands and no p—"

"I remember." He lowered his arms and moved closer. Heat blanketed her back even though he didn't make contact. "Whenever you're ready."

She'd never be ready.

"Couldn't I just do your laundry or something?"

"Hotel does that."

Her thumb trembled above the button. *Five minutes. Get it over with.* His leather-and-lime scent surrounded her, and his breath stirred her hair. *Do it.* Her thumb contracted, starting the second hand. She concentrated on that tick-tick-tick and willed her heart to slow to the same steady beat. No such luck. It hammered three times as fast.

Toby's breath teased the sensitive skin beneath her right ear and his chest molded her back. The barrier of clothing did nothing to lessen the transference of heat. Sparks scattered through her bloodstream.

"You smell good."

"Um, thanks," she croaked. "Toby, this is not a good idea."

"Five minutes. Of whatever I want. You agreed." He nuzzled her temple, pressing his face to hers. His late-afternoon beard scraped deliciously against her cheek, contrasting with the smoother skin over his cheekbone. Soft lips teased the shell of her ear. The nip of his teeth on her earlobe startled a gasp from her.

Damn that promise. But if she held her ground and quit running, then maybe he'd quit chasing and give up the seduction attempts.

She kept her eyes open and tried to remain rigid and unresponsive as he trailed feathersoft kisses down her neck and across her shoulder. But she couldn't stop the tendrils of desire winding along her synapses. He painted a design on her skin with his tongue and then blew on her damp flesh, sending a shudder undulating through her.

Her lids grew heavy. Forcing them back open, she bent her head to check the watch. Only sixty seconds had passed.

He burrowed his way beneath her hair to nibble her nape. Goose bumps raised her skin. Her breasts tightened. Ached. She wanted to lean against him, to surrender and turn in his arms. Instead she clamped her bottom lip between her teeth, stiffened her spine and lifted her chin to study the smooth ceiling.

His tongue laved the pulse point on the opposite side of her neck. He sipped from her jaw, the hollow of her cheek. She wanted to turn her head, wanted to join her lips to his, because heaven knows the man was a champion kisser. He stepped away, saving her from making an enormous mistake. And then he circled in front of her. His hunger-filled gaze devoured hers.

With his hands fisted beside him, he closed the gap between them, sandwiching the hand she'd clenched around his watch between her navel and his erection. She shifted her hand away from the burning contact, unintentionally stroking his length. He sucked in a sharp breath and then leaned forward and kissed her brow, her nose, the corner of her mouth.

Her lids fluttered shut. He was really, *really* good at this. She longed to touch him, to twine her arms around him, pull him close and surrender her mouth.

You're weakening. Restrain your impulses.

She turned her head and forced her sluggish brain to look at his watch and calculate time. It wasn't easy. Two minutes left. She needed something to concentrate on besides the magic of his touch. She started counting down the seconds. One hundred twenty. One hundred nineteen. One hundr—

Soft hair brushed the underside of her chin and then his tongue traced the lace edge of her top from one collarbone to the other, dipping low to lave the cleavage created by the push-up bra Candace had insisted Amelia buy. A moan slipped past her lips.

Um…one hundred, um…seventeen. One hundred sixteen. One—

He bent lower and nuzzled her nipple through the fabric of her top. His teeth scraped the sensitized tip and his breath heated her flesh. She felt the caress deep in her womb and her thoughts scattered. The strain of resisting the urge to hurl herself into Toby's arms and his bed made her tremble.

She lost count. Where was she again? One-fifteen? One-ten?

And then he straightened. Time's up already? A sigh of relief—and maybe just a twinge of disappointment—gusted from her lungs, only to be dammed by his mouth. He kissed her hard enough to force her head back, granting him deeper access, and then he angled his head and swept his tongue between her lips to tangle with hers. Slick. Hot. Ravenous.

Her heart stumbled into a sprint. His chest scorched her breasts. The cool metal of his belt buckle stamped her belly above the hot column of his erection. His thigh pressed between hers, creating a delicious friction against her center. She shifted her hips and pleasure bolted through her. Heat poured from him into her every pore, flooding each cell with hunger.

She wanted him. Wanted his touch, his possession, more of the driving need pulsing against her abdomen. No other man had ever aroused her to such an intense craving. No other man had ever wanted her with such obvious restrained hunger.

An annoying bleep penetrated her desire-fuddled brain. She ignored it, but Toby slowly lifted his head. She blinked, trying to gather her wayward thoughts, and tracked the sound to the watch in her hand—the hand currently tucked in the small of Toby's back.

He wasn't holding her and hadn't needed to. She'd wound her arms around his middle and plastered herself against him.

She didn't even remember moving. She snapped her arms back to her sides. Toby pried the watch from her numb fingers and silenced the annoying alarm.

Horrified by her lack of control, she staggered backward gasping for breath. One step. Two steps. Three. The coffee table bumped her calves, halting her.

"I—I have to g-go."

Toby's chest rose and fell as rapidly as hers. His dilated pupils almost obliterated his silvery-blue irises, and moisture from their kisses dampened his lips. "Stay."

She wanted to. Dear heavens, she wanted to. But she

couldn't risk letting her hormones make her decisions. Shaking her head, she skirted the table, scooped up her purse and backed toward the door. "I can't do this."

"Amelia—" He lifted his hand and moved forward.

She clutched the doorknob so tightly her knuckles ached. "You're too much like my father, Toby. And I, apparently, am too much like my mother. Trust me, that is a horrible combination, and I won't end up like them."

Six

Amelia had barely slept. How could she when she'd realized she was no better than her mother at controlling her impulses?

If Toby's watch alarm hadn't gone off, she would very likely have ended up in his bed, and that would have carried her one-hundred-eighty-degrees away from her goal of finding a gentle lover who would cherish her forever, one who wouldn't undercut her self-esteem with low blows and cutting insults or thoughtlessly risk his life.

And this time she couldn't blame her lack of restraint on alcohol or a disastrous week. This time the weakness lay solely within her.

She sat at the table in her suite Friday morning sipping café au lait and staring blindly at the Mediterranean while waiting for her roommates to join her. She loved their morning gatherings. As an only child, she'd experienced nothing like the camaraderie she'd found with Candace, Madeline and Stacy. Would she have felt a little less like the rope in a tug-of-war match if she'd had siblings to share the load?

Doesn't matter. The past is over. Focus on the future.

Candace wandered in looking pale and queasy. "G'morning, Amelia. You know, mothering us is not a maid-of-honor duty, but bless you for calling room service."

"Good morning." Amelia poured her friend a cup of steaming hot chocolate and pushed it across the table along with a plate of toast. Candace sipped with her eyes closed and then cautiously nibbled her bread.

Once Candace had regained some color, Amelia asked, "What's on the agenda today? I didn't see anything on the calendar except my massage this afternoon."

"We have to make a final decision about bridesmaid dresses this morning. Afterward we'll go to the Oceanographic Museum and then have lunch. Afternoon's your own. We'll meet up again at midnight for an excursion to Jimmy'z, the dance club in the Monte Carlo Sporting Club. The place is famous for celebrity sightings. You ought to love that."

"Sounds fun." Even if she wasn't exactly the clubbing type.

"You've seen the museum. You can skip it if you want."

"Will Toby be joining us?"

"He's spending his morning with Vincent's personal trainer. I don't know about tonight, but I'd guess with his equilibrium issues, dancing will not be high on his agenda."

An entire day without temptation. Tension drained from Amelia's limbs. "Then I'll join you. The museum is worth a second visit."

Stacy wandered in and headed for the coffeepot. "Hi."

The women chorused a greeting. Seconds later the outer

suite door opened and a sweat-dampened Madeline entered wearing her running gear. She lifted her hand in a silent wave and crossed to the minifridge for a bottle of water.

"Working up a sweat with your sexy tour guide?" Candace asked.

"No. I was running off some of the rich food we've been scarfing down."

"That's too bad. I was hoping—"

Madeline groaned. "Please don't start matchmaking. Not everyone is looking for hearts and flowers and a husband."

Candace shook her head. "How can you not believe in love in a place like this?"

Madeline sipped her water. "I never said Monaco's not a very cool place. I can see why Vincent likes living here when he's not away on a job. But, despite the castles and princes, I'm not going to get caught up in the fairy tale."

"You could fall for your sexy tour guide," Amelia teased.

"Not a chance."

Amelia's heart ached for her friend. "Madeline, I hate to see you give up on love just because of one bad experience."

Madeline pointed the bottle in Amelia's direction. "Before you condemn me for not believing in forever, look in the mirror. You don't do long-term relationships either. In fact, you are the queen of short-term."

Taken aback, Amelia blinked. "What are you talking about? I was engaged."

Madeline flashed an apologetic smile toward Candace and then settled across the table from Amelia. "You know I love you like a sister, right?"

Uh-oh. Anything following that preface wouldn't be good. But she'd known and trusted Madeline almost as long as she had Candace. Bracing herself, Amelia set down her coffee cup. "Yes."

"I see a pattern in your relationships that I'm not sure you recognize."

"A pattern?" she parroted.

"You knew Neal's poor prognosis before Candace introduced you and yet you fell for him."

"Well, yes, but—"

Madeline held up a hand. "And you knew the Navy recruiter you dated before Neal was due to be reassigned in six months. We know you're not going to move away from Charlotte and your family as long as your father's alive, so a future as a military spouse was a no-go."

"*Okay,* so that's two, but—"

"Before the lieutenant you dated a visiting university professor who was only in town for summer session. And don't get me started on the guys you dated in college. You only went out with the ones scheduled to graduate and move out of state soon."

Amelia fought the urge to squirm in her chair. Was it true? Had she unintentionally sabotaged her relationships? Of course not. She wanted happily ever after and she'd been actively searching for Mr. Right.

"I believe in love and marriage," she protested.

"And yet you repeatedly chose dead-end relationships."

"She's right," Candace added, shocking Amelia further. "I didn't see it until Madeline pointed it out, but you've always chosen guys who aren't going to be around long-term."

Panic seized Amelia's throat. "No. She's not right. I believe in fate, destiny, kismet and all that stuff. There's a soul mate out there for everyone, and I'm actively searching for mine. I've just been…unfortunate."

"I think you're afraid to commit," Madeline speculated.

"I'm not afraid. I'm careful. Love comes from the head first and then the heart follows. You have to find a person who's like you in temperament and goals, one who wants the same things out of life, and then you carefully move forward. Like Candace and Vincent have. Like Neal and I did."

"What about opposites attracting or sexual chemistry?" Stacy asked.

Amelia's parents had been opposites. The working-class jock and the pampered honor student who'd tutored him in high school. Her mother's dream of attending a private college and then medical school had died when she'd accidentally become pregnant. Amelia's father had gone on to have the firefighter career he'd always wanted. The inequity had caused friction in the marriage.

"Once the novelty wears off, the things that initially attracted you will begin to annoy you, and love will turn to hate when the sacrifices become too great. Sexual attraction blinds you to those irreconcilable differences."

"Are you saying you'd marry someone without sexual chemistry?" Candace asked in a carefully modulated voice.

Amelia tried not to cringe. She wouldn't discuss her and Neal's disappointing sex life with his sister. Besides, it hadn't been Neal's fault. He'd been dying, and you couldn't expect a dying man to be good in bed. She selected her words carefully. "I'm saying sex is not the most important thing."

"It's in the top three, right behind love and trust," Candace insisted. "If the sex is bad, the rest falls apart."

"Franco and I have, um…chemistry," Stacy said with a blush, and Amelia wanted to kiss her for drawing the fire to herself and away from Amelia. "But we've agreed our… er…relationship will only last as long as I'm in Monaco. I've never had a relationship based solely on sex before. It seems…" She shrugged.

"Safe?" Madeline suggested. "You'll have a great time

and he won't break your heart because you know it's going to end here. It's a win-win situation."

Stacy chewed her lip. "I guess so."

Madeline's emerald gaze skipped between Stacy and Amelia. "You two may be going about it in different ways, but you're both protecting your heart with short-term affairs. Same as me."

She covered Amelia's hand. "You say you believe in romance, but I see you making sure no guy sweeps you off your firmly planted feet. There's nothing wrong with that as long as you recognize what you're doing."

Could Madeline possibly be right?

Her friend rose and pitched her empty water bottle into the trash. "Amelia, we all know Toby's a player, but you two strike enough sparks off each other to light California. The way I see it, you have a choice. You can either live in the moment and enjoy the electricity while it lasts or play it safe and hold out for a fairy tale that might never happen. The question is, which one will you regret the most?"

Amelia didn't have an answer and she suspected she resembled a goldfish with her mouth opening and closing but nothing coming out. She wanted to argue, to prove Madeline wrong. But a rebuttal wouldn't form. Doubts, however, bloomed like wildflowers after a desert rain.

"How do you know we strike sparks off one another?"

"Because I stepped off the elevator Wednesday night when you and Toby were standing outside our door. You were so engrossed in each other I don't think either of you heard the elevator ding or saw me in the hall. Rather than get zapped by the current between you, I got back on and went downstairs to the bar, where I hooked up with Stacy."

Madeline held her palms up by her shoulders like balancing scales. "Live or dream? Fun or fantasy? What's it going to be, Amelia?"

Naked and alone, Amelia lay facedown on the table and squirmed under the sheet covering no more than an eight-inch-wide swath across her bottom.

She'd never had a massage, and the idea of someone other than her doctor getting up close and personal made her uncomfortable. But this "treat" was a gift from Candace, and her friend had promised when she'd scheduled appointments for each bridesmaid at Hôtel Reynard's top-rated spa that a massage would be a relaxing and rejuvenating experience.

A little stress reduction couldn't be a bad thing, Amelia admitted. Having to fight the illogical push-pull of her attraction to Toby all week had been challenge enough. Combining his tempting presence with Madeline's eye-opening evaluation this morning threatened to make the knot of tension between Amelia's shoulder blades a permanent fixture.

Yesterday's kiss hadn't helped. If Toby's watch alarm hadn't gone off—

Don't go there.

She'd excused herself from the bridal party after lunch and headed directly for the spa rather than risk bumping into Toby in the upstairs hall. She couldn't face him with her mind in turmoil. But when the receptionist had escorted her into this candlelit room, told her to strip, lie down and cover only her buttocks with the sheet, she'd almost decided she'd rather deal with Toby than expose herself to a total stranger.

Better the devil you knew…

Three things had kept her from chickening out. One, it would have been inconsiderate to cancel at the last moment and to refuse Candace's gift. Two, Candace would be charged for the expensive massage at this late date whether Amelia had it or not. And three, Madeline's accusation that Amelia was playing it safe was a little too accurate for comfort.

Exhaling a series of long, slow breaths, Amelia willed her limbs to loosen. *Relax. The masseuse is a professional. He or she doesn't care what you look like naked.*

She'd almost convinced herself when the door opened and a draft of warm sage-scented air swirled over her skin. Her muscles clenched all over again. She pressed her face firmly into the horseshoe-shaped pillow. If she concentrated on visually tracing the veins in the marble floor beneath the table and didn't look at the masseuse, then maybe this wouldn't be as embarrassing. "G-good afternoon."

"Back atcha, sugar."

Toby! She jerked her head up just in time to see him drop the towel encircling his hips. Her lungs seized and her heart stuttered. It's a wonder he couldn't hear it knocking against the table. His gaze caressed her face, her naked back and her legs before traveling back up to linger on her upper torso.

She flattened her breasts against the table. "What are you doing here?"

His penis thickened, lengthened and rose from his dark golden curls, drawing her attention the way a new intern attracts nurses. Her internal muscles contracted.

"Massage. Same as you. Keep looking at me like that and I'm going to have trouble lying facedown."

"Then leave." Shielding her breasts with her arm, she forced her gaze back to his face. "This is a private massage."

"A private *couple's* massage," he corrected. "You and me, side by side, being rubbed in all the right ways. I changed the reservation."

She could kick him…and herself. She'd thought it odd that the room contained two tables, but she hadn't asked for an explanation. If she had, she could have avoided this. "Do not turn this into something sexual, Toby Haynes."

"I dare you to lie there while the masseuse does her thing and know that I'm naked right beside you getting the same treatment and not get turned on. By the time we're done you'll be wishing it was my hands on your body and that we could lock the door and finish each other on the table."

She did not need that image in her head—the one of Toby pulling her to the padded edge and plunging deep inside her the way he had on her coffee table. And if her cheeks were half as red as they were hot, then he'd know how strongly his words had affected her.

She glanced at the door. No lock. Good. That meant she wouldn't be tempted. Not that she was. Not even a tiny bit.

He sat on the table beside hers, knees splayed, palms planted beside his thighs, which left his privates at eye level. He made no attempt to lie down or cover himself with the sheet. The man had absolutely no modesty.

With a body like that, who would?

And she was trapped. She couldn't get up and leave without giving him an eyeful. She averted her gaze from his long, thick shaft. "Go. Away. This is supposed to be relaxing."

Mischief twinkled in his eyes. "Do I make you tense?"

As a bowstring. "If Candace sent you, I will strangle her."

"Lucky for her, joining you was my idea. I'd hate to have to explain to Vincent that the maid of honor knocked off his bride because Candace was matchmaking."

He knew. She wanted to crawl under the Egyptian-cotton-draped table. Could she possibly be more humiliated? Nope. "Joining me was a bad idea. And cover up, for pity's sake."

His grin widened. "If you insist. No need to get prissy. It's not as if you haven't seen and tasted everything I have."

Her cheeks erupted with a fresh wave of lavalike heat, and her mandible locked. "That. Night. Was. A. Mistake."

"So you keep saying. But repeating the words doesn't make 'em true. And your eyes…well, let's just say lying's not one of your talents." He picked up the sheet and lay down—carefully. She tried not to ogle his perfect honeydew-melon rear before he covered up. Tried and failed.

He rolled onto his side, propped his head on his hand and sought her eyes. "Ever had a massage?"

She couldn't help following the line of hair bisecting his abdomen and disappearing beneath the sheet. "No. Have you?"

"Yep. Occupational hazard. Loosen up or the massage won't feel good."

She shoved her face into the pillow and muttered, "I could do that a lot better if you'd leave."

"We could always cancel and take this upstairs to my suite. I give one hell of a good massage."

"No doubt you've had lots of practice," she grumbled in disgust. "Forgetaboutit."

"You don't know what you're missing. No wait—you do. Am I too much for you, A-mel-i-a?" There he went again, stretching out her name like an orgasmic groan. "Because I could have sworn you were with me every second of that night. Sure felt like it when your body was contracting around mine and squeezing me so tight I thought my…*brain* would explode. And I could've sworn I heard you say—"

"Roll over and shut up or I'm leaving." She lifted her head enough to glare at him. If blood could simmer, hers would. From anger but also from arousal. Which only made her angrier.

"Nah, I don't recall you saying that. It was something more along the lines of—"

The door opened before she could make good on her threat to leave. A man and a woman entered and introduced themselves as Lars and Nina. Amelia tensed and chewed her bottom lip. She hoped the big blond guy was Toby's. But Lars crossed to the shelf at the head of Amelia's table, and her hopes crashed and burned.

The abstract idea of having a strange male massage her hadn't bothered her too much, but actually having his crotch inches from her eyebrows and his hands preparing to touch parts of her the sun never saw made her *extremely* uncomfortable. She wanted to bolt.

"No," Toby barked, making Amelia jump. His jaw muscles looked like marbles beneath his tanned skin. He pointed to Lars. "You're over here. Nina's over there."

Lars shook his head. "Mademoiselle Meyers specifically requested me for Mademoiselle Lambert."

"I'm overriding that request," Toby insisted. "Switch or Mademoiselle Lambert and I are outta here."

She really ought to object to his high-handedness. But her lips remained sealed.

The spa employees exchanged a look, then changed positions. Relief sagged through Amelia. And then a peculiar idea slipped under her skin like a hypodermic needle. Toby didn't want the guy touching her. His possessiveness sent a thrill through her. And wasn't that insane since she didn't want him to be possessive? But the tingles in her extremities couldn't be denied.

Maybe he'd seen the panic on her face and had done the gentlemanly thing. Warm fuzzies joined the tingles.

Or was he one of those guys who fantasized about two women and a ménage à trois? Her lip curled in disgust. The tingles and warm fuzzies evaporated.

She dropped her face into the pillow with a silent groan. She'd better cling to the last idea if she wanted to keep her distance from Toby Haynes.

Do you want to keep your distance?

She chewed her bottom lip. Before this morning the answer would have been an easy and unequivocal yes. But Madeline's comments haunted her.

Had she sabotaged her search for Mr. Right by only dating Mr. Right Nows?

Looked that way. And how could she not have noticed that?

Did the short-term nature of her relationships mean she hadn't cared about the men she'd been involved with? No. But she had to admit she'd never pictured herself sharing side-by-side rockers at the retirement home with any of them.

Not even Neal.

That disturbing revelation rattled her so much she barely registered the warm oil on her shoulders or the firm hands working it into her skin.

"Go easy on her. It's her first massage," Toby said.

Amelia turned her head sideways and found Toby watching her. His back glistened with oil. Lars's big hands dug deep into muscle, but Toby didn't flinch.

For ten months she'd been running from Toby Haynes and the passion she'd experienced in his arms, and yet avoidance of a problem had never been her style. She faced difficult issues head-on. The way she had her father's paralysis, her mother's subsequent caregiver-stress issues and Neal's debilitating disease.

If she didn't get a handle on her aberrant feelings, her desire for Toby could devastate her future plans. He was everything she *didn't* want in a man. Except physically. And yet he'd monopolized her thoughts for an entire year. There was something terribly wrong in that.

Toby lifted his hand, reaching across the space between their tables.

Amelia hesitated. Perhaps Madeline was right and dealing with her illogical attraction here in Monaco, the land of fantasy and fairy tales, was the answer. Toby didn't want a future with her any more than she wanted one with him, and if she let her passion for him burn hot, it would quickly burn out because it wasn't based on anything more substantial than lust.

A nice, controlled burn. That's what she needed. And when she returned to the real world—work, home and family—her problem would be solved and she'd be one step closer to finding a gentle, caring partner with staying power.

She reached across the intervening space and linked fingers with her temporary obsession.

And prayed she could contain the blaze.

If he got any harder, Toby figured his erection would jack his hips off the massage table like a race car waiting for a two-tire change.

No doubt Lars, of the meat grinder hands, knew it. Why else would the guy have tried to mulch Toby's muscles into hamburger for the past thirty minutes? The jerk was probably pissed he'd missed out on feeling up Amelia.

The second the door closed behind the departing masseuses Toby tossed off the sheet, swung his legs over the side of the table and sat up. Rolling his shoulders, he checked for permanent damage.

He studied the back of Amelia's head, the way her silky cinnamon hair parted and trailed over the table. After holding his gaze and his hand throughout the massage, the minute the massage ended she'd planted her face in the pillow.

"You okay, sugar?"

Amelia's back rose as if she were taking a deep breath and then she pushed up on her elbows, giving him a tantalizing glimpse of one pale breast. His dick twitched in appreciation.

"I'm fine." White teeth dented her bottom lip. And then she sat up—sans sheet—making no attempt to conceal a single delicious inch of creamy skin from his view. His heart and groin pulsed in tandem. She noted his roll-cage-hard condition, averted her face and licked her lips—which only increased his discomfort.

Her nipples puckered, begging for attention. He wanted to taste them and then trace every sheet-wrinkle impression across her thighs, belly and breasts. With his tongue. The curls between her legs had been tamed into a tight, tiny triangle since their last encounter. Sexy. Oh, yeah, definitely sexy.

Her hands fisted in her lap. "Can we go upstairs now?"

"Your suite or mine?"

Her gaze didn't get anywhere close to meeting his. "Yours."

He nearly fell off the table. He'd expected her to red-flag him and blister him for delivering yet another line. But he wasn't dumb enough to question his luck. All right, he was dumb enough. But he could wait till later for his answers.

Not wanting to give her a chance to change her mind, he stood.

She slid off her table more slowly, snatched up a towel

and covered herself. Her movements were jerky instead of the smooth, efficient and graceful ones he'd come to associate with the slender nurse.

"Amelia."

She paused and, clutching the ends of the Turkish towel to her breastbone, stared at his chin. Tension tightened her features and a white line cinched her lips. She looked pale and anxious instead of flushed and aroused.

He threaded his fingers through her soft hair and tugged until she met his gaze. Her lashes quickly descended, shielding her eyes, but not before he made a surprising discovery.

She's shy. And nervous.

Something inside him softened, and for the life of him he couldn't think of anything to say to ease the situation. No lines came to mind. No come-ons. No flirtatious, teasing banter. He drew a complete blank. A first for him. As Amelia had accurately guessed, words were his tools. He used them to draw people in or push them away. Now he had none.

So he did the only thing he could think of. He kissed her. Her eyelids. Her cheeks. Her nose. Restraining his hunger, he sipped from her lips until her mouth softened beneath his and the stiffness eased from her muscles—and invaded his.

She leaned into him and then her hand curved over his naked hip, jolting him like a jump-started battery. He lifted his head and sucked air. He wanted to act out every fantasy that had starred her and had disturbed his nights, but he didn't want to be interrupted and he couldn't guarantee that here. So even though letting her go was the absolute last thing he wanted to do, he stepped away.

He yanked a thick hotel robe off the rack by the door and draped it over her shoulders. While she slid her arms into the sleeves, he stuffed his into a second robe and loosely tied the belt. After lacing his fingers through hers, he towed her out of the massage room and into the dressing area. His heart beat faster with every step, as if he were climbing a rock face instead of walking a flat floor.

Eight louvered doors surrounded a splashing water fountain designed to instill tranquility. In his case it failed. Big-time. "Grab your gear and let's go."

"Shouldn't we shower off the oil first?" she asked as she paused by the door of the room beside his. He ducked in, scooped up his clothes and rejoined her.

"We'll do it upstairs. Together." Because if he didn't get her out of here, he was going to lose what little patience he had left. Who was he kidding? He'd already lost it.

"On second thought…" He advanced, backing her into the six-by-six cubicle, and kicked the door shut. He flung his bundle of clothes in the corner, yanked her into his arms and covered her mouth with his. Craving the sweet taste of her, the slickness of her tongue, he delved deep without preliminaries.

He opened her robe, found her satin-soft skin and tightly beaded nipples with his palms. It wasn't enough. He needed more. Her skin. Against his. He ripped open his robe and pulled her close. Hot. Oh, man, she was hot. She whimpered into his mouth at the press of flesh, and he'd bet his trophy case steam poured from his ears.

When his lungs threatened to explode he lifted his lips a fraction of an inch. "Can you be quiet this time?"

She blinked and then her eyes widened. A flush painted her face and neck. She glanced at the closed door and ran her tongue over her damp, swollen lips.

"You mean you'd—we'd—*here?*" The last word was little more than a squeak.

Desire choked him. He jerked an affirmative nod.

Her gaze bounced to the door again and then back to him. "B-before we, um, do this I need to make something cl-clear."

"Shoot." Hell, he'd agree to practically anything to get inside her right now.

How did she make him this crazy when no other woman had? He cupped her waist and walked her backward toward the padded bench.

She splayed a hand on his chest, lighting five fires with her fingertips. "I—I'm not looking for a long-term relationship with you, Toby. This affair ends the minute we leave Monaco. You can't call me or try to see me after we get home."

His steps faltered. She was giving *his* speech. And being on the receiving end was about as much fun as a rectal exam. *He* was the one who set the limits on his affairs.

What does it matter who says the words as long as you both abide by the rules?

"Deal."

Amelia inhaled deeply, squared her shoulders and then met his gaze. "Okay, then. I'm ready."

So was he. Ready to blow, that is. He wanted her that bad.

That wasn't good. *Get a grip, man.*

He skimmed his palms down her back and over her smooth buttocks. He cradled her thigh and lifted until she rested one foot on the bench. Stepping into the V of her legs, he stroked his erection against her damp curls. Her welcoming slickness had him whistling air through his clenched teeth.

"This is gonna be fast. Hard and fast. Are you still on the pill?"

She planted both hands against his ribs. "Yes, but don't you have a condom?"

"Not with me."

Her face and body tensed, her withdrawal obvious even to his lust-fogged brain. "I won't take chances. Especially not with a man like you."

A man like you. The words hit him like a sucker punch. What in the hell did that mean? She didn't think he was good enough? She thought he dipped his stick indiscriminately?

"I'm careful and I'm clean."

"The pill isn't one hundred percent effective. I'm not willing to risk a pregnancy."

Pregnancy? Neither was he. He never intended to get married or have kids. He refused to risk letting anyone down the way his folks had him. God knows he didn't know how to be a father.

"Then we're good to go, because neither am I. But we'll have to take this show on the road. I have what we need upstairs."

Seven

She was going to have sex with a man she didn't love. Amelia wasn't even sure she *liked* Toby Haynes.

Oh, sure, her body craved his. But her body wasn't in charge here. She wouldn't let it be. And once this series of encounters ended she'd go back to being her sensible, practical self.

Yes, he made her feel good. But she'd keep her head this time.

Averting her eyes from the dressing room mirrors, she tried to ignore the naked man bumping elbows and hips with her as she buttoned her top in the cramped space. She reached for her panties, but Toby snatched the pale pink cotton out of her hand and stuffed it in his front pocket.

Amelia stared at the tiny bump next to the much larger bulge of his erection. She blinked and then met his gaze. "Give those back."

"You don't need 'em."

"You expect me to waltz through the hotel without my underwear?"

His wicked grin made her insides fizz like a shaken soda pop. "Yeah."

"You're wearing yours."

"That's so you can peel them off. Later. Real slow." He captured her hand and stroked her palm over the thick, hard denim-covered ridge. Her heart skipped wildly. "See how much I'm looking forward to that?"

She tugged her hand away, but the residual heat spread from her palm to her cheeks and then pooled where her panties should be. She pulled her skirt over her bare bottom. The button and zip challenged her uncooperative fingers, but finally she managed to get the job done.

She couldn't help second-guessing her decision. About this affair. About leaving this dressing room semidressed. About…well, *everything*.

Toby Haynes was too much like her father. But this wasn't about forever. This was about fitting the last piece of the puzzle in place. As soon as she found Mr. Right her life would be perfect.

But first she had to deal with Toby.

The last time they'd slept together she'd been weak and needy and allowed herself to be swept away on a storm surge of emotion and impulse. Impulses were mistakes. But this wasn't an impulse. This was a calculated plan designed to eradicate all traces of her attraction to this egotistical, thrill-seeking, smooth-talking ladies' man from her system the way an antibiotic does an infection. She was stronger now. Strong enough to hold her own and cure this temporary obsession.

Toby's big hand captured hers. With a feeling of inevitability she followed him out of the dressing room. This encounter had been brewing since she'd first set eyes on him in the hotel foyer.

No, she admitted grudgingly. Since the first night she'd gone toe-to-toe with him in Vincent's hospital room.

She'd informed him visiting hours were over and he'd have to leave. He'd said, "Not unless you carry me out. My buddy needs me and I'm staying."

Vincent had been heavily sedated at the time and probably hadn't even known Toby was there. She should have called security and had Toby removed. But Vincent's family hadn't arrived yet, and she'd have hated for her patient to awake alone and in pain. Add in the concern lining Toby's face, and she'd bent the rules. She'd let him stay.

She hated to admit it, but his loyalty to Vincent in the months following the accident had impressed her. When he wasn't on the road for a race, Toby had been by Vincent's side, keeping his friend entertained and motivated through each stage of recovery and every setback.

Toby led her out of the spa and across the vast lobby. Amelia felt incredibly naked, as if everyone around them knew of her underdressed state. Her skin burned. Her palms dampened, and it shamed her to admit they weren't the only part of her growing moist.

They stopped in front of the penthouse elevator. Toby's eyes found hers. The hunger straining his expression dried her mouth and weakened her muscles. He drew circles in her palm with his thumbnail, scraping up arousal from deep inside her and distracting her from her pantiless predicament—but not so much that she didn't wonder if the concierge who acted as a gatekeeper to the upper floor couldn't guess she and Toby were headed upstairs for sex.

The brass doors opened. Toby towed her inside, propped

himself in a corner and pulled her into the crook of his arm. Would he kiss her again on the ride up? Would he do more than kiss her? Did she want him to? Her pulse pounded a resounding *yes* in her ears and much lower.

Just before the doors closed, a third occupant entered the cubicle.

That meant no kisses. She wasn't disappointed. Not at all. Uh-uh.

Liar.

The Mafia-dark burly guy wore a suit and an earpiece microphone thingy. Was that a gun under his coat? Hotel security? A bodyguard for someone famous? His probing gaze inspected both her and Toby from head to toe. Supremely conscious of her nakedness Amelia squeezed her thighs together and fought the blush she was sure must be creeping up her neck. And then the man backed into the opposite corner and faced the doors.

Had Toby noticed the weapon? Amelia sought his gaze and the bottom dropped out of her stomach. If a man could undress you with his eyes, then she'd be stripped bare and they'd be making love in the elevator. Had that been his intention when he'd stolen her panties? She wasn't wearing a bra—almost never did. What was the point when she didn't need support? That meant only two pieces of fabric separated her from his touch.

Her skin tingled and her internal muscles clenched. For a split second she wished they were alone, but then reason reasserted itself. There were probably security cameras in the elevator, and the last thing she needed on this trip was to be arrested for indecent exposure and who knows what else. Not to mention the lack of a condom.

Tell that to her moistening parts and desert-dry mouth.

What felt like an eternity later, the elevator opened on

the penthouse level. The suit exited first and headed down the opposite end of the hall. Toby straightened—carefully, Amelia noted. She followed him out. She had to take two steps for each of his long strides, and each quick tread sent a teasing draft up her skirt. He inserted the key card into the lock and then shoved open the door of his suite.

Last chance to change your mind.

No. This plan would work. It had to.

Scraping her courage together, Amelia put one foot in front of the other. She'd barely crossed the threshold when Toby palmed the door shut and leaned against it. He snagged her waist with one hand and hauled her between his splayed legs, fusing her hips to his. The fingers of his other hand speared through her hair, bringing her mouth to his in a hard, brief and blistering-hot kiss, a tangle of tongues, a gnashing of lips and teeth.

Her head was spinning before he swept her off her feet and stalked toward his bedroom. She snaked her arms around his neck and struggled to regulate her breathing, but it was a lost cause. He dipped. Believing him about to drop her, she squealed and tightened her arms, but instead he grasped the spread with the hand beneath her knees, ripped it back and then laid her in the middle of the cool Egyptian cotton sheets and followed her down.

His thighs separated hers, hiking up her skirt to an indecent level, and then his denim-covered erection pressed her bare center. The rough fabric abraded her tender flesh in a delicious way, and when he flexed his hips, a bolt of pleasure shot through her, stealing her breath. He braced himself on straight arms above her and then, biceps bulging, slowly lowered his torso until he blanketed her with heat, stopping with his mouth a scant inch from hers.

"Save the screams for when I'm inside you."

His ego truly was astounding. "You think you can make me scream?"

"Guaran-damn-tee it."

And she was just as determined to make sure he didn't. This wasn't last time. Her will wasn't weakened by alcohol or grief.

His mouth feathered over hers in the briefest of teasing kisses. She tried to arch up for more, but his chest held her down. He touched down for another butterfly sip and then rolled to her side, leaving one leg thrown across hers. A big palm spread across her navel and swept upward to the buttons of her lace blouse.

"I like your girlie clothes. I like getting you out of 'em even better."

He started at the bottom, releasing one button, folding back the plackets and then exploring the exposed triangle of skin with his lips, with his tongue. He painted a damp trail along the waistband of her skirt and then blew. The shocking contrast of hot tongue and cold air elicited a wave of goose bumps. The second button gave way. Her rib cage received the same sip-lave-blow treatment with equally mind-melting results. The third button opened. He nibbled a tantalizing path along the underside of her breasts, and her nipples tightened, tenting her thin blouse.

The fourth and final button slipped free, but he didn't hurry to claim his prize—if her small breasts could be considered a prize. His chin, covered in afternoon stubble, scraped a shiver-inducing line along her sternum. She arched her back, lifting herself toward his mouth.

"Something you want, sugar?"

He knew what she wanted. Why make her ask? "Touch me."

"Where? Here?" He nipped her jaw, her earlobe. "Or here?"

He had to feel the pulse in her neck pounding beneath his lips. She fisted her fingers in his short hair and urged him in the right direction. "My breasts."

A quick rasp-rasp across her chest as he shook his head made her want to growl in frustration, until she realized he wasn't saying no. He was nudging fabric out of his way with his chin. His stubble lightly scraped her nipple once, twice. He circled her areola with a sandpaper caress.

She groaned and squirmed as heat and tension spread through her. "Yes. There. Please."

He rewarded her request with the hot, wet suction of his mouth, making her hips bow off the bed as desire yanked deep inside her. He settled her with a big, warm palm on her thigh. And then that hand climbed higher, approaching her exposed sex at a snail's pace. *Faster, faster,* she wanted to cry, but his teeth snagged her nipple, holding it captive for the flick of his tongue, and the words vanished.

He switched to the opposite side, giving equal attention to her neglected flesh, sucking, laving, scraping. And then his hand reached her curls. He gave a gentle tug and she gasped. How could pulling hair be sexy? And yet she was about to come unglued. He traced her damp seam, down, up and then back again and again, approaching but always stopping just short of the spot that could send her over the edge. She dug her fingers into his muscle-corded shoulders and rocked to meet his fingers. She couldn't help herself.

He lifted his head. "In a hurry?"

She licked her lips and tasted him. "Aren't you?"

"Oh, yeah." His killer grin twisted her insides and her toes contracted.

He bent his head and covered her mouth. His tongue found hers at the same instant his fingers struck gold. Orgasm crashed through her in wave after wave. The thigh he'd thrown over hers held her captive for the onslaught, and his kisses muffled her cries.

She dissolved into the mattress, sated and yet still wanting. Wanting him. Too much. So much it scared her. So much it reminded her that she was losing control.

A little foreplay was a good thing, necessary even, to make sex comfortable. But too much was…dangerous. Uneasiness crept over her like a spider web. She struggled to gather her shattered composure.

He flicked open the button of her skirt, lowered the zip and then tugged the garment down her legs and pitched it onto the floor. His heavy-lidded gaze caressed her, making her feel sexy instead of skinny. No other man had ever looked at her that way—as though she was the woman he wanted instead of the one he could get.

He cupped her breasts, thumbed the pebbled tips and then shifted his body back between her legs. His broad shoulders held her open and exposed, and then he lowered his head and did with his tongue what his fingers had done seconds before. He drove her out of her mind, carried her high and then pushed her off the edge.

And she couldn't stop him.

Even before the aftershocks faded, he rose onto his knees, pulled his shirt over his head and reached for the waistband of his jeans.

Time to regroup. She arched up and covered his hands. "My job."

The fabric stretched tight over his distended flesh. Determined to torment him the way he had her and to shift the balance of power back where it should be, she trailed her short nails across his chest, circled his tiny nipples and then raked up and down his fly.

Toby's jaw muscles knotted. His back bowed and his fists clenched. "Be quick about it," he ordered in a strained voice.

He'd made her weak, and she had every intention of returning the favor. "What's the matter, Haynes? You can dish it out, but you're not man enough to take it."

He scowled. "I can take it and I can take you—which you'll find out as soon as you get these damn jeans off."

She lowered the zipper one tooth at a time and then slipped her fingers into the opening to cup and stroke cotton stretched over rigid heat. The cords of his neck tightened visibly. She eased his pants over his hips and then wedged a fingertip beneath the elastic band of his briefs and circled his waist to tease the crevice of his buttocks.

His thigh muscles knotted, trembled. He muttered a blasphemy.

Easing the elastic out of the way, she uncovered the engorged head of his penis and glanced up to find Toby watching her. He gulped and a surge of power filled her. Ever so slowly, without looking away from the need in his eyes, she parted her lips, dampened them with her tongue. His breath hitched. She lowered her head and licked him. Air whistled through his clenched teeth. But he didn't blink.

She shoved his briefs to his thighs, curled her fingers around his thick shaft and licked his satiny length, bottom to top. His hands cupped her head, fingers tangling in her hair. Again and again she bathed him and then took him into her mouth.

"*Yesss,*" he hissed.

She'd never met a man who didn't like this. The difference was this time she liked it, too. Liked his taste. His scent. His heat. She liked making Toby shake, making him swear—which he did more creatively with each swirl of her tongue. She relished pushing him to the edge more than she ever had before.

"Stop." He uttered the word so low and deep she barely understood him. His fingers tightened on her scalp, pulled. "Stop," he repeated louder, clearer, when she ignored him.

"Dammit, stop." He caught her shoulders and forced her to release him and then tumbled her backward onto the bed and slammed his mouth over hers. The kiss bordered on savage. He took her mouth, took her breath. But he didn't take her. His erection scorched the inside of her thigh. She was open and wet and protected from pregnancy. He could have plunged deep even without the condom she'd insisted upon. But he didn't.

Finally he released her mouth and vaulted from the bed. "Witch."

The approval in his tone and in his hot blue eyes belied the insult and sent a thrill through her. Had any man ever wanted her with such naked hunger before Toby? No. And the intensity of his need both excited and worried her. Worried because she felt it, too.

He shucked his clothing in record time, yanked open the bedside table drawer and retrieved a condom. After sheathing himself, he climbed back onto the bed, hooked her knees over his bent arms, yanked her hips forward and impaled her.

Her lungs emptied on a rush as he filled her. Barely giving her time to adjust to his size, he withdrew and then drove deep again and again, taking her on a wild, fast ride. The pleasure was too intense. Too unrestrained. She struggled to rein it in.

She caressed the supple skin of his chest, his thighs, his buttocks—any erogenous zone she could reach.

"Stop," he groaned again.

But she didn't. Arousal tightened inside her, so she re-doubled her efforts, mapping his body, seeking out his plea-sure points until he cursed and released her legs only to grab her wrists and pin them on the pillow beside her head.

He leaned down, his gaze drilling hers.

"Don't. Rush. Me." He punctuated each word with a hard thrust and then stilled deep inside her. He swiveled his hips, creating a delicious friction against her sensi-tive flesh. She felt her control slipping and rallied to regain the upper hand by arching her back and taking him even deeper.

He dipped, captured a nipple between his teeth and tugged just hard enough to make her gasp. The love bite reached deep into her womb. Again and again he tormented her breasts and swiveled his hips, until she lost the battle for control and a tsunami of an orgasm slammed through her. He pounded into her as successive waves of ecstasy robbed her of strength and reason. His groan barely pene-trated her overwhelmed state. And then all was still except for their gasping, shallow breaths.

Sanity slowly returned and she realized she'd done it again. She'd lost it. Completely. She'd always focused on bringing her partners pleasure and had never really worried about her own. Making them lose control first meant she didn't have to worry about losing hers. Toby refused to let her sacrifice her satisfaction for his.

Sacrifice.

An invisible icy finger dragged down her spine and ev-erything within her froze except for the panicked thump-bump of her heart.

Sacrificing and martyring were two sides of the same coin.

A martyr.

When had she started emulating her mother?

* * *

"Want to tell me what that was about?" Toby's husky drawl yanked her out of her shocked stupor.

"What?"

"Trying to get me off before you finished."

Her barely cooled body filled with uncomfortable prickly heat. She must have drawn the wrong conclusion. And as soon as she could get to her room she could analyze this…encounter and figure out what was really going on.

She focused on his square chin. "That's crazy. I had orgasms." She wiggled, but it was like trying to slide out from under a boulder. "Let me up. I have to dress for dinner with my suitemates."

Toby didn't budge. His hands and hips kept her pinned to the bed. "You had two alone. You needed one with me. Inside you."

"A technicality. Now move." Still avoiding his gaze, she bowed her back.

"You were trying to get me to lose it while you lay there cool as a cucumber, pushing my buttons. Same as last time."

And just like last time, he'd refused to give up until she'd lost it. Her cool. Her control. Her mind. And this time she couldn't blame her lack of inhibitions on booze or grief.

She needed to get out of here. Needed to think. She struggled again to no avail. He held her down as easily as he would a butterfly. His grip didn't hurt, but it was inescapable.

"You're mistaken. Now please get up."

"Sugar, I'm not getting off you until you level with me. And if you don't quit squirming, we'll be here till breakfast. Maybe longer." He rocked his hips. His thickening erection knocked the breath from her lungs—in surprise and in a shocking burst of arousal.

"I need to use the bathroom," she lied.

"Then talk fast. As soon as you tell me why you don't like coming I'll let you go."

She wanted to be somewhere else. Anyplace else. "I never said that."

"The women I know like getting off. With me. Without me. Whenever and wherever they get a chance. Why do you fight it?"

"I don't."

He leaned down, aligning his nose with hers and forcing her to look into his eyes. His hips pistoned again, and her breath hiccuped as a bolt of unwanted hunger shot straight to her core. "It'll take me less than two minutes to prove you're lying."

The man was cocky, confident…and very likely correct.

She could continue fighting and suffer the consequences or get this over with.

"I don't like losing control," she admitted reluctantly.

"Isn't that the whole point of sex?"

She'd known he wouldn't understand. Nobody would. That's why she'd never tried to explain her conflicting emotions about her dysfunctional family.

She bit her lip and struggled to formulate an acceptable—if not quite accurate—explanation. Toby threaded his fingers through hers still pinned to the pillow, withdrew from her body almost completely and then slid back in. He set a slow pumping pace that kept her brain from forming coherent sentences.

"I can't think when you do…that."

"Don't think. Just talk."

"I thought men didn't like to talk after sex."

"In case…you didn't notice…we're not finished. And I'm not most men. Talking fine-tunes…performance. I talk to my crew…when I drive…and my partner in bed. That way…everybody's…on the same page…and we all get… what we want." His shortened breaths made the words come out in choppy bursts.

Her extremities tingled and her toes dug into the luxurious sheets. Another release hovered disgracefully close, and she trembled with the effort to shut it down. *How does he do that?* She had to get rid of him before she became addicted to the way he made her feel, and the only way to do that was to give him what he wanted—the ugly truth.

"My parents hate each other. My mother has a temper. When she lets go, the whole neighborhood hears."

"She hit you?"

Given his upbringing, she wasn't surprised he'd ask that. "No. Never."

"Stating the obvious—you're not your mother." The tendons of his neck corded. His arms trembled.

"But I'm m-more like her than I want to be. Especially in bed with you."

He swiveled his pelvis and her insides wound tighter. A muffled moan slipped between her lips. She couldn't believe they were having sex and talking about her parents simultaneously. The ick factor should be grossing her out, but the powerful surges of Toby deep inside her kept her too distracted with wave upon wave of arousal to maintain rational thought processes.

And *that* was exactly the problem.

"Genes are there. But you have control. Over decisions. Over choices. Don't have to repeat…her mistakes. You choose…to race clean…or dirty."

A drop of sweat rolled from his forehead down his lean cheek. It dripped from his jaw and landed on her breast. He dipped and lapped it up—only he didn't stop with that single sip. His tongue circled her nipple, teasing but not hitting the sensitive center. The opposite breast received the same neglectful attention. Her nails dug into the backs of his hands. She wanted to scream in frustration. But she wouldn't.

"I don't like her when she loses control," she confessed in a rush and immediately wanted the shameful words back. What kind of person didn't like her mother?

Toby's body stilled, but instead of looking repulsed by her admission, his expression softened. The understanding in his eyes tugged at something deep inside her.

"You don't have to like somebody to love 'em, Amelia."

He knew. He knew what it was like to have a parent you both loved and hated. In that instant she felt a connection with Toby that she'd never experienced with anyone else. Not even Neal. The realization sent a frisson of alarm skittering through her.

How could someone who embodied her worst nightmares understand the emotions tormenting her? It wasn't fair. Her eyes stung at the injustice of being so in tune with a man she didn't love and could never trust her heart to because of his daredevil personality.

"And bed is the one place it's okay to let go. Let go for me, sugar." Then Toby's mouth slanted over hers, and the ride turned as fast and furious as the past five minutes had been slow and steady. Her reeling senses welcomed the desire distracting her from her tumultuous thoughts, and when he released her hands to cup his under her buttocks and drive deeper, she wound her arms around him instead of pushing him away.

Another orgasm burst upon her like a flash fire. Slowly the embers cooled and the haze cleared from her brain, and then she discovered a heartbeat too late that she'd miscalculated.

Her plan for a careful, controlled burnout of the passion between them was in danger of going up in smoke.

She was falling for Toby Haynes.

And she had to stop it. Right now.

Eight

She'd hung him out to dry. Again.

Toby had never met a woman he couldn't figure out. But Amelia Lambert stumped him. As crazy as she apparently was about celebrities, she wasn't impressed with him. That irked him, for some damn fool reason. Did she have any idea how rare it was for a guy to accomplish what he had and at his age? How hard he'd worked to make HRI a force to be reckoned with in racing?

She wasn't interested in having her picture taken with a NASCAR driver, in bragging rights of having screwed one or in boosting her career via his. And he'd had dozens of women try to squeeze a wedding ring out of him. Amelia wasn't one of them.

So what did she want from him? And why did she act as though being with him was a chore? Sure, he knew she'd been assigned to babysit him. But, c'mon, she wanted him—a fact made clear by every heart-revving glance she sent his way and that round of set-the-sheets-on-fire sex.

For a second this afternoon something intense had flared between them. *Too* intense. He didn't *do* intense. Except in racing. The vulnerable look in her eyes had driven him from her arms and her warm, flushed body immediately after sex. He'd retreated to the bathroom to fill the big whirlpool tub for round three. And his cell phone had rung.

By the time he'd finished talking to his team manager, Toby had needed to distract himself with mind-numbing sex, but his sheets had been cold and Amelia long gone.

He scanned Jimmy'z. The club was packed. Before the crash, he'd have enjoyed losing himself in the music and dancing. But tonight the noise reverberated off the walls loud enough to make his eardrums vibrate the way a pounding rubber mallet does a dented fender. And he couldn't dance without falling on his ass.

It had been two weeks since the crash and his balance wasn't any better. Would it ever be?

He shut down that line of thinking. He hadn't achieved this level of success with a negative attitude.

It took him fifteen minutes to locate Amelia on the crowded floor beneath the flashing multicolored lights. Watching her move to the insistent beat in her gauzy flapper-style dress gave him an instant hard-on.

All he wanted to do was forget her. Instead she kept sucking up more and more of his brain space. He'd had her. So why did he still want her? Why wouldn't any other good lookin' woman in the club do? But his radio was tuned to her station and he couldn't change it. God knows he'd tried.

He cut through the crowd, taking a straight line toward his target. Guests in various states of inebriation gyrated around him. He'd been in places like this before, where you didn't need a partner to get on the floor and dance. Women outnumbered the men, and a guy could find himself in the middle of an adolescent fantasy—surrounded by willing women who wanted to party. Not his scene. But he knew plenty who practiced the more-the-merrier method of recreation.

Amelia had her back to him and didn't see him when he stopped behind her.

"This cat-and-mouse game is getting old, sugar." He struggled to keep the anger out of his voice. Her ditching him again had pissed him off that much. If not for the concierge, Toby wouldn't have known where to find her tonight.

She whirled around with a hand to her chest. She had on another one of those push-up bras that gave her the kind of cleavage he wanted to bury his face in.

"Toby. What are you doing here?"

"Looking for you."

The women she'd been dancing with opened their circle to include him, but Amelia planted herself between him and her companions. Hunger flickered in her eyes burning a trail over his black shirt and pants. She wanted him and she didn't want to share. The knowledge made his pulse beat as hard and fast as the bass drum throbbing from the speakers. But then she blinked and the reserved nurse returned.

He'd be damned if he could untangle her mixed signals. She alternated between burning his brain and freezing his johnson.

Someone jolted him from behind, knocking him off balance. He struggled to regain his equilibrium. Amelia's hands curled around his biceps and steadied him.

"Could we…?" She nodded toward a dark corner.

Screw that. He needed to get off this floor before he fell like a drunk and out of this noise before his head exploded.

He headed toward the nearest exit and found himself in an enclosed and mostly deserted courtyard overlooking the Mediterranean. The doors closed behind them, muffling the racket inside.

Amelia released his arm, took a deep breath and then blew it out again before meeting his gaze. "Toby, I thought this…thing between us would work. But it won't."

His eyebrows lowered like a slamming garage door. Green flag. Red flag. What was her deal? "We're good together, Amelia. Like it or not, I flip your toggle switch. And you sure as hell flip mine."

"But I don't think I can—"

Her protest lit the fire of anger and frustration that had been stewing since the phone call from Earl, his team manager.

"Don't give me any crap about your mother. She may have a short fuse, but she at least cared enough to stick around. Mine didn't. And if you've been trying to insult me by comparing me to your father, then you missed the mark. The man's a hero. Mine was a drunken, out-of-work bully. Yours had a job ninety-nine-point-nine percent of the population doesn't have the balls to do. He risked his life to save others. Mine—"

"You're wrong. My father was an adrenaline junkie who thought of nothing but getting his next fix. He never thought about his safety, his family. *Me*." Her eyes widened. She slapped her fingers over her mouth and then slowly lowered her hand. "I'm sorry. I don't know where that came from and I shouldn't have said it."

His anger deflated like a sliced tire. "Sounds like your mother's not the only one who can't forgive him for getting hurt."

"I'm not angry with him. *I'm not*." But she was. Toby understood. He'd been there before.

He stepped closer, close enough to catch a hint of her perfume on the cool night air. Close enough that the need to take her into his arms almost got the better of him. He settled for skimming his index finger down her stiff spine. She shivered. "It's okay to be angry, Amelia."

"No, it's not. Anger isn't productive or healthy. And it always leads to—" She shook her head and looked away.

"Am I gonna have to nail you to the bed again to get you to talk?"

Her gaze jerked to his and a shocked laugh burst from her lungs. "Leave it to you to make this about sex."

"Then make it about something else. Finish what you started."

"It's complicated."

Why did he care? He didn't need to be drawn into the drama of Amelia's life. He had enough drama in his own. Especially now. Maybe that was it—he wanted to think about someone else's problems for a change. "I had a concussion, not a lobotomy. My brain still works. And I'm not going anywhere until you explain."

She bit her bottom lip and then resignation settled over her face. "My mother and I have never been close, but before the accident my father and I were. I was his…princess, for lack of a better description."

"And you became his servant."

"It wasn't like that. I wanted to help. And my mother—"

"Your mother…?" he prompted when she clammed up again.

"My mother suffered from a severe case of caregiver depression. Some days she couldn't get out of bed, and when she did it was usually to lose her temper and shout obscenities at Dad. And he gave as good as he got. When they got going, they'd cause wounds they couldn't fix."

"Sounds like you had to become the adult in the family." Something they had in common. "How did you manage school?"

"I just did. It was kind of a refuge, you know? And it wasn't Mom's fault that she fell apart or that she and I didn't get along. I think she saw me as the reason none of her dreams came true. She was only seventeen when she accidentally became pregnant with me. She had to give up her plans for college and medical school. Her parents sent her to one of those homes for unwed mothers where they try to talk you into giving up your baby. She ran away to be with my father and refused to speak to her parents again."

"How did you manage financially if neither of your parents could work?"

"Dad had disability insurance from the fire department and another policy with the bank that paid off the mortgage if he couldn't work. It was enough for a while, but then he contracted pneumonia and spent a month in the hospital. The medical bills piled up. We couldn't cover them. When I was sixteen, the hospital's collection agency put a lien against our house.

"We were already dancing around social services intervening and putting me in foster care. I had to do something. I had never met my mother's parents before, but I found them and begged for help. I didn't know what else to do. They got Mom the psychiatric help she needed to get past the depression and helped with the bills. They paid for my education. Otherwise I never would have been able to afford college."

Amelia was a fighter. Another thing they had in common. The last thing he needed was something else to like about her.

"And you think sleeping with me will land you in the same boat as your mother?"

She nodded. "I don't want to get stuck with a guy who takes stupid chances. It turned her into a really ugly person."

Well, that was honest. Unpleasant. But honest.

"One, you won't get stuck with me. Two, I may not have a wife or kid depending on me, but Haynes Racing has four hundred employees who count on me to keep roofs over their heads and food in their family's stomachs. I have no intention of letting them down. That's why I *don't* take stupid chances.

"I'm betting your father didn't either. And it sounds like he did everything he could to look out for you financially in case something happened to him.

"Accidents happen, Amelia. Bad things happen to good people. Cheaters profit and innocent bystanders get hurt. Sometimes life sucks. The only thing you can control is the decisions you make."

The words sank in a half beat after he said them, and he realized they didn't only apply to Amelia. He'd been riddled with guilt over Vincent's accident even though a NASCAR investigation had cleared him and his crew of any wrongdoing. Toby had done everything within his power to make his pit as safe as possible. *Accidents happen. Innocent bystanders get hurt.* Vincent didn't blame him. Maybe it was time for Toby to quit blaming himself for Vincent's injuries and move forward. The weight on his shoulders eased.

He refocused on the woman beside him. "I doubt your father went into that fire hoping to come out paralyzed. Most men I know would rather die than become dependent on the ones relying on them."

He shoved his fists into his pockets and stared at the lights outlining the three jetties of Larvotto Beach below. "The last time most of my team saw me, I was unconscious and being airlifted from the infield. My team manager told me today that morale has hit rock-bottom at HRI. The team is falling apart and making stupid mistakes. Somebody's gonna get hurt. And I can't do a damned thing about it because I'm cornered here like a kid in time-out."

He huffed out a heavy breath and tried to rein in his frustration. His exile wasn't her fault, but his team was his responsibility. He had a job to do and he didn't know how he could do it from here. "They need to know I'm okay."

"You want to get back in your car," she said quietly.

"Hell, yes." He faced her and saw the worry pleating her forehead. She claimed she didn't care, but not even the dim lighting in the courtyard could hide the concern plain as day on her expressive face. He wasn't sure how he felt about that. Part of him liked it. Part of him wanted to run. "But I'm not ready. And, contrary to what you think, I don't have a death wish. I won't drive again until I'm cleared."

If he was ever cleared.

"Why don't you go home?"

"You're just trying to get rid of me because I make you hot."

A smile flickered across her mouth and her cheeks pinked in the milky moonlight. "Maybe."

"I'm supposed to be watching the wedding party. Even though we both know that's bull."

"Vincent asked Franco—Stacy's…um…boyfriend—to watch over us, too, so it's not like we wouldn't have someone to turn to if problems cropped up. You could go home for a few days, reassure your teammates and then come back. Vincent would never have to know."

The idea sounded plausible. Doable. "I don't lie to my friends. I'll run it by him. If he agrees, I'll go." He needed to go.

He curved his hands over her smooth shoulders, savoring the warm satin of her skin. "While I'm gone, do you think you can dig up some of your father's courage and find the guts to admit you want me instead of blowing hot and cold?"

She stiffened. "I don't want to want you. I'd give anything not to want you."

That hit hard and low. "A driver's not good enough for you?"

She winced at the harsh tone of his voice. "It's not you, Toby. It's me. I don't like who I am when I'm with you."

"A sex goddess who blows my—" he cocked an eyebrow "—mind?"

She blinked, blushed and then shook her head. "An impractical, impulsive, out-of-control stranger."

"We've covered that. I told you bed's the one place it's good to lose control. And I like losing it with you." He tucked a windblown strand of hair behind her ear and then cupped her cheek. The hitch in her breath sent him flashing back to the sounds she'd made hours ago when he'd been deep inside her, but something soft and warm in her expression warned him to paint the boundaries. "What's wrong with a little sex between friends?"

Her eyes widened. "Friends? Is that what we are?"

If not friends, then what? He had nothing more to offer. "I like you, Amelia. But neither one of us wants this to end at the altar. You in my bed in Monaco—that's what I want. What we both want. You're the one who laid those ground rules. And I guarantee you will not get stuck with me."

She tilted her head back and bit her lip. A string of emotions—caution, worry, desire—chased across her face before she blinked them away and met his gaze. "Okay. We'll have Monaco."

She needed an intervention, Amelia decided Sunday night. Because she'd lost her mind.

There was absolutely no other way to explain why she'd agreed to Toby's risky proposition.

As soon as she'd agreed to his terms Friday night, he'd whisked her back to the hotel and into his suite, where he'd made lo—*ahem*—had sex with her for hours. Amazing, lost-count-of-how-many-climaxes-she'd-had sex.

By the time she'd awoken Saturday morning, Toby had already left the hotel. She'd run her hand over his empty pillow and wished he didn't have a self-destructive streak a mile wide. Sure, he claimed he didn't take unnecessary chances and she'd seen a few hints of rational behavior. But she'd also seen the yearning in his eyes when he talked about getting back in his race car. And it had only been weeks since his last crash.

Amelia knew from experience that daredevils never changed their ways. She'd had too many run-ins with frequent flyers—the patients who swore they'd never repeat the risky feat that had landed them in the hospital only to have them return later. She didn't trust mere words. Seeing was believing.

The scary part was that for one foolish moment this morning she'd wanted to change Toby, to ask him to take up a safer occupation. But for years she'd watched her mother try—and fail—to change her father.

A relationship with a man like Toby was akin to walking a high wire without a net. Sooner or later she'd fall and the landing would be painful. Probably crippling.

Getting involved with him was complicated on so many levels. Besides her dysfunctional family, there was Neal. She'd already buried one man she loved. She couldn't handle burying another. She couldn't—wouldn't—let herself love Toby. She could be his "friend" for her remaining time in Monaco, but that was where she absolutely had to draw the line.

And since she couldn't count on Candace or Madeline to be voices of reason, she'd decided to launch her own intervention.

A tap on her bedroom door yielded Madeline. "Are you sure you don't want to go with Stacy and me to Le Texan? I've heard everybody who's anybody hits their Alamo Bar for margaritas."

The chance to do more celebrity watching tempted her, but Amelia had more important plans. One way or another she was going to cure herself of this ridiculous crush she had on Toby Haynes. *And a crush is all it is.*

"No, but thanks for asking. You two have fun. I'm going to kick back, watch some TV and catch up on sleep."

A valid excuse since they'd been keeping late hours and Toby had kept her awake most of Friday night.

Stacy joined Madeline and asked, "You're sure?"

"I'm good here. I might even try one of those decadent desserts the chef specializes in. Have fun."

"Okay, then. G'night."

Amelia wiped her damp palms on her jeans and reached for the remote. Assignment one: witness every hair-raising lap and crash of today's NASCAR race. Assignment two: bury herself in Internet research and bombard her brain with race wreck and fatality statistics. Assignment three: a clean, swift break.

It didn't take long to find an American sports network

broadcasting the race live. Her stomach knotted and her pulse quickened as she watched the pace car circle the Michigan race track.

Toby was there. Somewhere. In the crowd. He might not be driving one of those cars today, but he would be as soon as he could be.

And she was going to sit through this race if it killed her, because she needed to remind herself what he did for a living.

Toby Haynes risked his life for sport.

"Hey, buddy, switch?"

Amelia's heart and feet faltered at the sound of a familiar deep Southern drawl. She stepped on Prince Dominic's toes, winced an apology and jerked to a halt in the middle of La Salle Des Étoiles, the location of *Le Bal de L'Été*, a charity ball held in the Monte Carlo Sporting Club.

Toby, with Madeline as his partner, stood beside them. The other dancers flowed past their little quartet.

Dominic released Amelia and bowed. "Certainly. Thank you for the dance, Amelia."

"Um…you're welcome, Your Highness."

Madeline, looking none too happy over the exchange, paired up with Prince Dominic. The irony of the situation tweaked Amelia's funny bone. Madeline, the one who'd sworn just days ago that she wouldn't fall for the magic of Monaco, had discovered her vacation lover was an incognito prince. A *real* prince with a crown, a kingdom and the whole shebang.

With more than a little reluctance Amelia moved stiffly into Toby's arms. Anger simmered beneath the surface. She didn't want to dance with him and kept as wide a distance as possible between their bodies, but there was no denying the pulse-accelerating effect of his warm hands resting on her waist and enclosing her fingers. She numbly followed his lead.

His silvery-blue gaze rolled across her bare shoulders, down her yellow tulle dress and back up to her face and upswept hair. "You look good."

Amelia glared at him, but her body tingled as a result of his thorough scrutiny, and her breath caught at the hunger in his eyes when their gazes met. Worse, her own hormones kicked into action.

"Let me guess. This is a booty call?"

His eyes narrowed. "Come again?"

"You could have phoned." She instantly wanted the bitchy words back. She sounded like a nagging wife, and that was something she'd vowed to never become. But after his big show of "friendship," Toby hadn't called or e-mailed once in the seven days since he'd left.

Wasn't it adolescent of her to have hurt feelings?

For a moment Toby looked as if he had something serious to say and then the playboy facade dropped over him as clearly as the curtain had closed after the play she'd attended with her suitemates Thursday night.

That killer smile curved his lips. And there went her toes, dammit. "Miss me, sugar?"

Yes. Dammit squared. "Your ego astounds me."

"That's not the only thing." A naughty glint lit his eyes and her pulse took off for the races.

She was annoyed with him for not calling and even more irritated with herself for jumping each time the hotel phone rang or the message light flashed.

She hadn't known if or when he would return until she'd looked up ten minutes ago and spotted him at the entrance of the ballroom, standing beside Vincent Reynard, the groom-to-be. For someone who'd been eager to get rid of

Toby two weeks ago, Amelia had been alarmingly happy to see him tonight. And then a bevy of beautiful, fawning females had surrounded him—the same way they had on the race shows she'd watched. At least none of these elegantly gowned women had whipped out a Sharpie and asked him to autograph bare skin the way the race fans had.

She was jealous, she realized with jaw-dropping shock, of the groupies and the ball beauties. She didn't have the right and didn't want the right to object to the company Toby kept. No, sir. Uh-uh.

But the overly attentive women raised her hackles.

Clearly her intervention hadn't worked as well as she'd hoped.

"Excuse me." She tried to pull away, but his hold tightened. He yanked her against the hard, hot length of his body. The lapels of his tux jacket scraped against her sensitive breasts, making her gasp as sensation shot straight to her core, and every cell in her body shouted, *Welcome home!*

That wasn't good.

"What kind of hello is that for a man who's flown across an ocean to hold you?" he murmured against her temple.

Her breath hitched and a tingle raced through her. She wrenched free without thinking and then noticed her sudden movement hadn't left him unsteady. "Your equilibrium has improved. You'll be returning to the track soon."

"Hope so. Let's get out of here."

"What if I want to stay and dance?"

You're being contrary, Amelia.

He glanced over the crowd—many of whom were staring back at them since they stood in the middle of the dance floor.

"I can manage a few slow ones while you hunt for famous faces."

Her temper cooled enough for her to notice his pallor beneath his tan and the strain tightening his lips. "Toby, are you okay?"

He shrugged. "I've been poked and prodded, X-rayed and MRI'ed from one end to the other this week. I've put out fires, done interviews and personally reassured each HRI team member and every sponsor. Reynard Hotels is only one of dozens we use. What I really need is to get horizontal. Preferably with you beside me."

Anticipation fizzed over her in a wave of goose bumps. The scary thing was that beside him was exactly where she wanted to be.

That definitely was not good.

Nine

Amelia had never had a date fall asleep on her before. Should she be insulted?

But Toby wasn't exactly a date. He was her temporary lover and the last obstacle to overcome in getting her life back on the right track.

Although the hotel was barely a mile away, traffic moved at a crawl compliments of the vast number of people wanting to celebrate the opening of the Monte Carlo season. Toby hadn't lasted five minutes in the dark car before his big body tilted against hers.

She liked the warmth and solid weight of him against her side. Turning her head slightly, she buried her nose in his soft hair to inhale his scent. Desire curled deep in her abdomen. How could she want him this badly? Which twisted Fate had cursed her to finding sexual satisfaction with the one type of man she'd sworn to avoid?

But was Toby really an adrenaline junkie in the sense that she'd come to know and despise through her job?

She'd spent countless hours on the Internet over the past week, learning more about NASCAR than she'd ever wanted to know, and what she'd learned had surprised her. Safety was apparently a priority for the organization, and the rules and regulations intended to keep the drivers safe were overwhelming.

Car racing wasn't bungee jumping, but she'd always dumped them in the same category. Reckless. Pointless. Stupid.

The articles she'd read about Toby from *Business Week* to *ESPN* had all been complimentary. They'd praised his driving skill, his coolheadedness, his business acumen and his determination to make his organization one of the best. In fact, one of the magazines had proclaimed Haynes Racing Inc. a rising star among NASCAR's top dynasties.

Was she wrong about Toby? She suspected she might be. Without a doubt he had an ego, but it looked as though he'd earned the right to be proud. And maybe she had been prejudiced.

Was she also wrong about her father?

As a child, she'd only heard her mother's side of the story. The slurs had only increased in frequency and viciousness after her father's accident. These days Amelia tuned out the words when the tone turned ugly. But until Toby had pointed it out, she had never considered the financial side. Her father *had* planned ahead and he *had* provided for them. If not for his pneumonia and long hospital stay, they would have managed without her grandparents' assistance—not that she'd ever wish Gran and Pops out of her life. She adored them both, and if not for them holding the fort, Amelia couldn't be in Monaco.

People who lived for the moment didn't plan ahead. They acted impulsively, foolishly and without thought for others. Despite his risky job, her father didn't fit that description.

Neither did Toby.

Or was she just fooling herself? Had sexual attraction impaired her ability to think logically?

She studied Toby in the darkness of the limo. Each flicker of light from passing cars and buildings accentuated the tired lines on his face. He looked softer somehow and more boyish without the playboy facade or the competitive edge sharpening his square jaw and prominent cheekbones.

Struggling with the need to trace the shadowy smudges beneath his eyes, she tightened her fingers around his where he'd linked their hands and rested them on his thigh and shifted her gaze to the designer boutiques, sidewalk cafés and posh hotels outside the windows.

Of the trio of her, Candace and Madeline, Amelia had always considered herself the together one. She was the one who knew where she was going and had a plan to get there. Or so she'd thought. She had a job she loved, a comfortable home and great friends. Before Monaco, she'd been convinced the only thing keeping her life from being perfect was the right man to share it with.

How could she have been so wrong? A man wouldn't fix what ailed her. She needed to work on herself. And why had it taken Toby and a trip abroad to show her the error of her ways? She'd learned more about herself in the past two weeks than she had in the previous twenty-seven years.

She'd been sabotaging her search for Mr. Right, emulating her mother's martyrdom and harboring a secret resentment toward her father for an accident that probably hadn't been his fault. She was a psychiatrist's dream patient. He'd hear her pathetic tale and see the dollar signs years of therapy would generate.

The question was, where did she go from here?

Amelia didn't have the answer when the limo stopped at the hotel entrance. She braced herself for another dose of Toby's magnetism and then gently shook him. "Toby, we're here."

He jerked upright, blinked and then his eyes zeroed in on hers. How could he look alert so quickly? "Sorry. Too many twenty-hour days."

"That's not good for you—especially with a concussion."

"Did I ever tell you your nurse voice turns me on?"

Heat seeped through her veins like an IV narcotic, leaving her flushed and dizzy. Luckily Louis opened the door at that moment, giving her a few minutes to recover.

Toby helped her from the car. "Night, Louis."

"Good night, sir." He nodded. "Mademoiselle."

"Good night, Louis," she replied as Toby's arm looped around her waist. He led her into the hotel and straight to the elevator. For some foolish reason Amelia's muscles tightened with nervousness. "Should I congratulate you on your team's performance last weekend?"

He turned sharply. "You watched?"

"Yes. And the race shows afterward, too." Her stomach burned and churned. "I saw you on the pit box. You're quite popular with female fans."

The brass doors opened. The hand at her waist urged her into the cubicle. Toby leaned a shoulder against the wall and appraised her. "Jealous?"

Yes. She focused on the seam between the doors. "I would like to think for safety's sake that we are exclusive during this…affair."

He caught her chin and forced her to look at him. His

eyes were direct and sincere. "I barely slept while I was gone. When I did, I slept alone."

She shouldn't feel relieved and hated that she did. If he'd tomcatted around, she'd have the perfect excuse to end this before it was too late. "I couldn't blame you if you did. Those women are beautiful, built like Barbie dolls and—"

"Easy."

She frowned. "Are you saying I'm not? Because I fell into bed with you faster than I ever have with anyone before. Then and now."

He laughed. "Sugar, you wear me out with all the chasing. But that's okay. I like chasing you. Great view."

He accompanied his words by patting and then caressing her bottom. Her internal muscles squeezed. Backing her against the wall, he lowered his head. Shamelessly eager for his kiss, Amelia lifted her chin. His breath swept her lips and her knees weakened.

The elevator opened with a ding. Toby withdrew, leaving her unsatisfied. He linked his fingers through hers and towed her down the hall to his suite. There was no question where she'd spend the night and she didn't play coy. For better or worse, she wanted this, wanted him.

She stepped inside and stopped abruptly. Two lamps lit the sitting area and a torchière illuminated the space in front of the windows where the dining room table used to be. "What is that?"

He banded his arms around her from behind, sandwiching her between the warmth of his hands on her belly and the press of his lean body blanketing her back. His lips grazed her bare throat, making her hot and trembly. "Ping-Pong table."

"I can see that. But why do you have one in your suite?" She gasped as he nipped her earlobe. His hands rose at a snail's pace to finally cover her breasts. For a man whose claim to fame lay in speed, he could be incredibly, torturously slow at times.

"We're going into training tomorrow. But tonight we're gonna make up for lost time."

The latter statement made her heart stutter, but she focused on the former. "What kind of training?"

"Eye-hand. Reflexes. Reaction times. Endurance." He shifted his hips, and the hard length of his erection pressed the small of her back. "Ever play video games?"

"Um…no."

"I'll teach you. Loser plays naked."

"I don't think so."

He had no problem with eye-hand coordination, if the thumbs simultaneously circling her breasts were any indication. And endurance… Her train of thought jumped the track as he pinched and rolled her nipples through her gown. Oh, yeah. Endurance had never been an issue either.

Desire knotted inside her. It wasn't fair that Toby could make her ache when the two men she'd loved enough for intimacy hadn't even scratched the surface.

He nudged her forward with a bump of his hips. They crossed the room and stopped with the side of the green table pressing inches below her mound. Toby released her without stepping away. The air shifted as he moved behind her. Out of the corner of her eye she saw his tux jacket hit the floor. His shirt followed. And then he unzipped her dress. His warm, slightly rough hands brushed her shoulders, sweeping the spaghetti straps down her arms until the yellow fabric pooled on the table. The cut of the dress hadn't allowed for a bra.

He sucked a sharp breath and ran a finger under the elastic of her plain white cotton panties. "These are so damned sexy."

He had to be joking. She wanted to turn and look in his eyes, but Toby held her captive between his hips and the table. "Don't most men prefer Victoria's Secret thongs or something sheer?"

His bare chest scorched her back and his hands recaptured her breasts. He caressed, plucked the tight tips and licked, sucked and nibbled her neck for excruciating moments before answering, "I'm not most men. I like these—" he snapped the elastic, and the slight sting below her navel was about the most erotic thing Amelia had ever experienced "—because they're straitlaced. When I get you between the sheets, you're anything but. You burn me up."

Had it not been for the table digging into the tops of her thighs, she might have collapsed. Leaning forward, she flattened her palms on the cool table to keep herself upright.

"Got a problem with that?" He pushed her panties past her hips, bunching them with her gown at table height. Slipping his fingers into the cleft of her body, he found her wetness. His growl vibrated against her nape and down her spine.

"No," she whispered. Desire arrowed straight to her core as he caressed her. Her fingers and toes contracted. She was incredibly close to climax and he hadn't even kissed her mouth yet.

She tensed, trying to maintain control, and he bit her neck, not hard enough to leave a mark but enough to make her drop her guard.

"Let go for me, Amelia," he ordered.

One hand teased her breast. The other delved through her damp curls with devastating, unrelenting accuracy. His teeth grazed a trail along her neck and shoulder as he relentlessly rushed her over the edge. She shuddered in his arms as release racked her far too quickly.

She needed more. Needed him. Inside her. She pushed her bottom against his erection. "Toby, please."

He grasped her waist, spun her around and lifted her out of her dress to sit her on the table. A quick movement stripped her panties down her legs, but he left her stiletto sandals behind. He stepped between her thighs. Clamping his hand behind her neck, he yanked her forward for a slap of her breasts against his chest and a ravenous meeting of mouths. His tongue thrust deep, tangled, stroked. His hurried hands raked her back, her bottom, her legs.

Impatient, she tugged open his belt and pants and cupped his erection through his briefs. What had he done to her? When had she become a woman driven by her desires?

He swore when her fingers delved beneath fabric to surround him, shoved his hand into his pocket and retrieved a condom and then let his pants fall to his ankles. Amelia took the packet from him, ripped it open and rolled the latex down his steely shaft.

He gritted his teeth and inhaled deeply through his nose, and then his hands curled around her hips and pulled her forward. She guided him into her center, where he plunged deep in one sure stroke. His heart pounded hard and fast beneath her palm and his chest hair tickled her skin.

He speared his hands into her hair and then muttered against her lips as his hips pistoned. "Hair. Down."

She reached up and released the single clip. Her hair tumbled in a cool tangle against her shoulders. His fingers stabbed into the strands, dragging her back until her spine pressed against the cold table.

The table was hard. Toby was harder. Hotter. He pounded into her. She tangled her legs around his waist and arched to meet each hurried thrust. This wasn't like before. This need was stronger. Deeper. More intense. Her muscles quivered as passion built swiftly. The control she valued so highly was nowhere to be found. Seconds later, release rocketed through her.

Toby's groan mingled with her moan as he shuddered above her and then stilled. His labored breaths steamed her neck. His lips and hands soothed as if to make up for the frenzied lovemaking.

Slowly he eased upright, bracing his weight on one arm. His gaze met hers and his palm cradled her cheek. "For what it's worth, I missed you, too. Didn't want to. Didn't have time to." He shrugged. "But that's the way it is."

Her stomach swooped as if she'd plunged over the peak of the highest roller coaster. And there in the least romantic place in the entire world—flat on her back on top of a Ping-Pong table, for pity's sake—Amelia realized this wasn't a crush.

She'd done the unthinkable.

She'd fallen in love with Toby Haynes.

And there was no chance at all that he'd ever return her feelings. Or that she'd want him to.

Whoever had come up with the line "Out of sight, out of mind" was full of crap.

Toby stared at the ceiling, unable to sleep despite the fatigue chaining his body to the mattress. But instead of rising and dealing with the mountain of race weekend work waiting on his notebook computer, he stayed where he was with Amelia tucked against his side and her head on his shoulder. Warm. Soft. Asleep. Her sweet-smelling hair teased his chin and her soft puffs of breath stirred his chest hair. One silky leg snaked across his.

She'd been antsy as hell to leave after that embarrass-ingly fast encounter on the Ping-Pong table, but he'd bulldozed her into the shower and then back to bed for a slower round. He had to make it up to her for going off like an inexperienced kid beneath the high school bleachers.

What in the hell had happened tonight?

He'd been looking forward to surprising her at the ball, to telling her about his medical progress and his crazy week and hearing about hers. But the moment he'd spotted her in the prince's arms he'd wanted to kick some royal ass. Knowing the guy was her suitemate's lover hadn't made a bit of difference. Toby had wanted blue blood on his knuckles.

Because of his father, Toby didn't do violence. He let his driving do the talking instead of his fists.

And he didn't do jealousy. He had never made a fool of himself over any woman and never would. But he'd felt more than a twinge of possessiveness tonight. Amelia was his. For now. He'd worked damned hard to get her back in the sack.

It hadn't helped that he knew she deserved a man who could give her the royal treatment and fulfill all her silly romantic notions. God knows she had a surplus of those.

Despite having the Atlantic Ocean and a seven-hour time difference between them, she'd monopolized his thoughts all week. He'd driven himself to exhaustion day after day, but every night he'd fallen asleep thinking about her. She'd invaded his dreams and been his first waking thought each morning—a result of the morning boner those dreams had generated, he assured himself.

He'd wanted her no-nonsense opinion on this medical test or that one and he'd wondered what she'd think of the other drivers' wives. Some were in it for the money and attention, but there were a few stickers he thought she'd like.

Did Amelia have what it took to be a sticker? To stand by her man through good times and bad?

Probably. But it didn't matter. He didn't do long-term relationships.

He had to nip this thing he had for Amelia Lambert in the bud before he wasted any more time picturing her naked on the king-size bed of his motor coach.

He had two weeks left to get his fill of her, and the only way to do that was to saturate himself with her company and her body. Starting now, he'd stick to her as tight as the decals on his race car.

And then it would be over and he'd be free of this obsession that had haunted him for months.

"Where are you going?"

Amelia winced at the sound of Toby's sleep-roughened voice behind her. "To my room."

She gave up on the stubborn zipper and reached for the doorknob. She'd hoped to escape his suite without having to face him. The discovery of her feelings was too new and raw.

She heard him cross the room, and then his warm fingers brushed her spine as he finished zipping her dress. "Stay. I'll order breakfast."

Her nerve endings danced beneath a tent of goose bumps. She didn't want to turn around. Didn't want to look him in the eye. If he guessed her feelings, he might pity her, and she'd had a lifetime of pitying looks from the neighbors after each of her parents' shouting matches.

Or, worse, he might paste on that professional face he wore when approached by autograph-seeking fans. There was nothing wrong with that face if you didn't know him well enough to see the walls behind the smile. But she did.

That brash smile hid a really nice guy. One who was loyal to his friends and his employees. One who'd been abandoned by his mother and hurt by his father but had still managed to turn out all right. Better than all right. And it was those moments when she'd glimpsed past the cocky attitude that had landed her in this trouble.

"I need clothes. I can't wear my evening gown all day."

The pale yellow tulle showed signs of having spent the night on the floor. Last night the gown had made her feel like a wood nymph. Today it looked more like crumpled litter.

And she needed space. To think. To decide how to fix this mess she'd gotten into. *If* it was fixable.

"I'll lend you a shirt." His arms banded around her, pulling her stiff body against his. From the intensity of the heat, she guessed he'd climbed from the bed naked to come after her. "You'll look sexy as hell in my shirt."

"I don't want to miss Candace's morning meeting."

"Vincent hasn't seen her in weeks. He'll keep her occupied."

"You don't know that for sure."

"Yeah, I do. Last night he told me he planned to take her to his place and keep her in bed for a week." His bristly chin prickled deliciously against her jaw, and his hands stoked the fires that should have been extinguished last night. "Sounds like a good plan."

"Toby—" Her breath hitched as he cupped her mound through the wispy layers of fabric. "I can't find my panties. Last night's or the ones you stole the other day."

"I'm holding them for ransom." She felt his smile against her cheek and heard it in his voice.

His fingers worked magic, pooling heat beneath his palm. If she didn't get away soon, she'd cave. She twisted abruptly and pulled out of his arms. He looked sleep-rumpled and sexy with his hair standing in golden spikes and a morning erection that begged for attention. *Dangerous territory.*

She focused on the tiny scar on the bridge of his nose rather than his eyes or his gorgeous body. "I want my own clothes."

He swiped a hand across his chin. "Yeah. Okay. Bring a couple of days' worth while you're at it."

"Why?"

"You'll be spending your nights here."

Internal alarms clanged. "That's not a good idea."

"You like sneaking out every morning?"

Not really. "Sharing your room is too…domesticated."

"It's convenient."

She gathered her courage and met his gaze. Her resistance wavered, but she soldiered on. "Have you ever lived with a woman before?"

"No."

"And I've never lived with a man. I don't think we should be each other's firsts for something so important."

"It's only for two weeks."

"It would still feel like a commitment to me. And you said…you didn't want one of those." She hated the slight rise in her voice, as if she were asking instead of stating a fact.

His expression closed. "Monaco only. That's our deal."

Her heart sank a little. Yes, that was their deal. One she'd readily agreed to. How could she have known her feelings for Toby would change? But his hadn't. And just because she'd fallen for him didn't mean she could ever be comfortable with his hazardous career.

That being the case, she couldn't and wouldn't let herself get used to playing house with Toby. It would make ending this relationship even more difficult.

His eyebrows lowered. He looked ready to argue but shook his head as if deciding against it. "Today's race day. I want to show you what I do when I'm not in the car. One of my techies did some space-age stuff and rigged up my laptop so I can communicate with the team live. You can listen in on the radio."

His excitement was palpable and curiosity got the better of her. "Okay."

"We'll start after we work out. Bring clothes for today and tonight, too." He turned and strode back into the bedroom.

Amelia stared after him, both stunned and amused by his assumption that she'd comply without question. He'd soon see otherwise.

And as inevitable as sunrise, she'd soon see heartbreak.

Who was this impostor and what had he done with Toby Haynes? Amelia asked herself as she paced Toby's suite Sunday night.

The seductive playboy had vanished, and in his place sat a sharp, decisive, no-nonsense businessman. Even his body language had changed. Instead of a casual you-know-you-want-me-come-and-get-me posture, Toby looked commanding and every inch the multimillionaire force to be reckoned with the magazines declared him to be.

He communicated with his teams via a headset microphone and watched the race live through his laptop. Beyond the computer screen on the coffee table, a big flat-panel TV hanging on the far wall also played the race. Toby watched both with an eagle eye and juggled comments and responses to and from the three race teams he had running today as easily as he'd recite his alphabet.

Frankly Amelia found this new persona incredibly sexy. And she hadn't had many complaints with the previous one.

For the past two hours he'd analyzed and discussed how to run this race from thousands of miles away. When time permitted, he'd turn off the microphone and explain some of the goings on to her.

Amelia had expected to be bored. She wasn't. The difference between watching this race with Toby and watching last weekend's alone was like night and day. In fact, this behind-the-scenes view fascinated her and had taught her a very important lesson.

Racing wasn't about the wrecks. It was strategy. Like chess. Only faster. And with more at stake. Sure, most of the technical lingo streaming through the speakers zipped right over her head, but from what she gathered, rocket-science calculations influenced every decision, from when and how many tires to change to when to stop for gas and how much to put in the tank.

She'd had no idea driving in circles—or in this case, on an irregularly shaped road course—could be so complicated.

A string of curses erupted from the computer. She recognized Toby's substitute driver's voice. The young driver was a hothead. It wasn't the first time he'd gone off.

"What happened?" she asked as his car pulled out of line. Several vehicles passed him.

Toby silenced the mic. "He got hung out to dry." At her confused frown he explained, "The car behind Jay's bumped him out of place. He lost the draft. It slows him down and he falls back in the pack."

The driver made a few erratic moves on the track as if he wanted to sideswipe someone.

Toby said, "Jay, if you bend my car on purpose, you're out of a job. Shake it off. The best revenge is finishing ahead of the dickhead, and if you keep your cool, you can be a contender. We're not looking for a win. Just a top-ten finish."

Another surprise: winning wasn't everything. Consistency ruled. A bunch of top-ten finishes triumphed over a few number ones in the NASCAR scoring system.

"I'm going to take him out," the driver replied.

"If you try, you run the risk of cutting a tire, hitting the wall and taking yourself out. Play it safe. Be patient."

Play it safe. Be patient.

She never would have expected to hear those words from Toby's lips. She would have expected a risk-taking adrenaline junkie to encourage retribution. Instead Toby calmly talked his guy out of anger. Again.

Energy rolled off Toby in waves—waves that filled Amelia and made sitting still difficult. He'd been focused so intently that, other than talking to her, he hadn't taken a break since before the race began. His voice was beginning to get husky. She crossed to the minibar, poured him a glass of iced water and slipped in front of him.

He winked his thanks and her heart hiccuped. Two weeks. She had two weeks left and then he'd be gone. Back to his races. Back to his female fans.

Another pair of cars bumped. Smoke filled the air surrounding them and sparks arched off the pavement. "Caution flag's out, Jay. Settle down. Be ready to move on green."

Toby flipped up his microphone, caught her hand and pulled her into his lap. His thighs were hard beneath her bottom, his palm warm on her belly, her need instantaneous.

"Having fun yet?"

"Yes." And she meant it. She marveled at the change. In him. In her. Instead of viewing the race as forty-three men trying to kill themselves, she'd caught Toby's excitement.

Omigod. Surely with her aversion to dangerous sports she wasn't becoming a NASCAR fan?

He massaged her nape. "When we get back to the States, I want you to come to a race."

Amelia gasped in surprise and hope surged in her chest. Was he saying he wanted more than Monaco? And if so, could she live with knowing each day he went to work might be his last?

She didn't know. The only thing she knew for sure was that she didn't want to become a nag like her mother.

As if he'd read her mind he said, "Just one race before we say goodbye."

Her hopes plummeted. Apparently this race—her race to win Toby's heart—was all about the crash.

Ten

Some butts were made for bicycle shorts, Amelia decided Wednesday afternoon as she watched Toby climb from his bike at the top of the hill outside a village perched on the side of a mountain.

She'd enjoyed every bit of the scenery on today's ride from Monaco into France, including the jagged cliffs, olive groves and cypress, pine and mimosa trees. But she'd especially enjoyed following Toby's tush in skintight black Lycra.

The week while he'd been in the States had dragged, but the four days since his return had flown past. When Candace didn't have her working on the wedding, Toby had kept her occupied for the remainder of the days and nights. She hadn't had a moment to herself.

With his equilibrium returned, Toby had exercised and played at a furious pace, but always with the proper safety gear and always including her. If she'd ever doubted his safety-consciousness, then he'd shown her differently. He'd practically armored them both to go mountain biking today and Jet Skiing yesterday. He'd made her wear eye and hand protection and a mouth guard to play handball. A mouth guard, for pity's sake. That had to be the least sexy thing she'd ever worn in her life.

Boy, had she been wrong about him being reckless. That didn't help her situation. If he'd been careless just once, it would have made pulling back easier.

She dismounted and walked beside him. "So where are we and why are we here?"

"Roquebrune-Cap-Martin has a tenth-century castle. Since you're into that stuff, I thought you'd enjoy a tour."

She fell a little deeper in love with him in that instant, as she had done a half dozen other times this week. Like when he'd surprised her with a snow globe of the Monte Carlo Casino, her favorite building, or when he'd taken her to dinner and a couple of clubs where celebrities hung out and let her gawk her fill of famous faces. And now a castle tour.

"We'll leave the bikes here and climb." He gestured first to a modern bike rack and then to the historic-looking steep stone steps.

She pressed a hand to her heart while he secured the bikes. Would he go to this much trouble if he didn't care about her?

He shoved his sunglasses into his hair and pulled a bottle of water from his knapsack—a bag that included everything from sunscreen to a first-aid kit. She knew because she'd watched him pack it.

"Thanks." She twisted off the cap and sipped. The chilled water cooled her parched throat. A rivulet escaped her lips and ran down her chin.

Toby reached out and caught it with his thumb—a

thumb that caressed her jawline and eventually paused over her rapidly beating pulse. His silvery-blue gaze locked on hers and heated.

She gulped and offered him the bottle when what she needed to do was dump the cool liquid over her overheated body.

He raised the plastic to his lips. The simple act of drinking behind her seemed as intimate as a kiss, and it, combined with the promise in his eyes of passion to come later, stole her breath and dried her freshly moistened mouth. Sexual energy crackled between them.

Toby recapped the bottle, dropped it back in his pack and captured her hand. With each step she took into the past down medieval stone streets and steeple-covered alleyways Amelia became more determined to make her affair with Toby last as long as the ancient castle walls around them.

She couldn't be happy with just Monaco anymore. And maybe it was time she fought for what she wanted.

"I should have known men would bring sex toys and gag gifts to the shower," Amelia said to Candace Thursday night in the Hôtel de Paris's luxurious Churchill Suite.

Candace flashed a wicked grin. "And I hope you and Toby enjoy your party favor."

The bride-to-be had given each member of the wedding party a set of "lovers' dice." One die had a body part on each side. Face, lips, breast, genitals... The other had commands. Caress, touch, lick, bite... The players were supposed to roll the dice and do whatever the cubes commanded.

The hot look Toby had flashed Amelia when he'd opened his gift had nearly incinerated her on the spot. Without a doubt he was looking forward to using his new toy, but not because he needed help being creative in bed.

Amelia shook her head to clear the haze of arousal clouding her thinking. "Candace, you have to stop match-making."

"You must admit I did a stellar job this time. You guys are perfect together."

All Amelia had to do was convince Toby of that. And she intended to try.

A knock on the door yielded the porter towing a luggage trolley.

"Would you please load up the gifts and carry them to the limo waiting downstairs?" Amelia instructed.

He went to work and Amelia turned back to Candace. "I could wring your neck for lying to me—to all of us—about this pregnancy. Not only was it *not* a secret, you've been using your morning sickness like a get-out-of-jail-free card."

"Oops. Busted." Candace gave an unrepentant shrug. "Tonight was truly amazing. I can't thank you enough. You and Toby make a great team."

The Jack-and-Jill shower had been a success not only because the menu Amelia and Toby had chosen had been delicious and the setting spectacular but also because the naughty gifts and commentary provided by Vincent's friends had kept everyone entertained.

"And that video roast Toby put together for Vincent with the other NASCAR drivers was a hoot. I laughed so hard I almost wet myself. He's definitely a keeper, Amelia."

"Enough already. Message received."

The porter finished and headed for the door.

Candace kissed Amelia's cheek. "That's my cue. I'm going to take this loot to Vincent's place. If you see him before I do, tell him he owes me for skipping out early. I know he and Toby had to talk business, but this is a huge haul. I'll see you tomorrow."

Smiling at a job well done, Amelia shut the door behind her friend and scooped up the last of the wrapping paper. She stuffed it into a trash bag and glanced at her watch. Room service would be here with dinner in just over an hour. She scanned the suite one last time. Maid service would clean up tomorrow, but Amelia wanted to get the worst of it before Toby returned. He'd disappeared somewhere with Vincent about twenty minutes ago.

Early-evening sun streamed through the wall of windows at her back, casting a golden glow across the parallel white sofas. She tilted her head and considered the fireplace centered in the dark wainscoted wall. Was it too warm to have a fire? She'd never made love in front of a blaze. It would be a first, one of many she wanted to share with Toby.

When room service arrived, she'd ask them to light the logs. Happy with her decision, she set the trash bag by the door and headed for the bedroom.

Her blood raced in anticipation of the night ahead—one of only ten they had left in Monaco. Because he'd reserved the room for the entire day and night, Toby had suggested she pack a bag and plan to stay here tonight instead of returning to Hôtel Reynard.

All week Amelia had stubbornly refused to move into his room despite his repeated requests. Tonight she had a surprise for him. She'd not only packed, she had some sexy ammunition that she'd picked up when she'd bought Candace's negligee at the designer outlet. The teddy was easily the most decadent piece of lingerie Amelia had ever owned.

Convincing Toby he wanted to continue their relationship beyond Monaco wouldn't be easy, but she couldn't give up without a fight. She had every intention of using this sumptuous suite and luxurious bath to further her seduction. If she was lucky, he'd return in time to join her in the oversize tub.

She reached for the zipper at the back of her dress, but the sound of male voices coming from the balcony outside the bedroom stilled her hand. The door was partially open and the gauzy curtains undulated in a gentle breeze.

"I can't believe you did it."

She identified Vincent's voice and the smell of cigars and smiled at his compliment. He'd enjoyed the shower even though Candace said he'd protested that real men didn't attend bridal showers.

"You melted the icy nurse and got her into bed."

Amelia's blood ran cold. *Icy nurse?* Were they talking about her?

"It took you a year to do it," Vincent continued, "but you won the bet, man. I owe you a grand."

"You don't owe me anything," Toby replied.

"Yes, I do. None of the other guys will believe you succeeded. If I hadn't spotted Amelia coming out of your room this morning, I wouldn't believe it myself."

Amelia's pulse roared in her ears. Her knees weakened and her head swam. Cold formed inside her like an expanding snowball. Gasping, she leaned against the wall to keep from falling.

A bet. Toby had seduced her on a bet.

And she'd fallen in love with him.

Anger replaced humiliation. Outrage quickly followed suit. She wanted to throw something. To scream. To rant. To curse him. But she reined it in. She'd always had her mother's temper, she realized. The difference was Amelia knew how to control it.

She marched across the bedroom, shoved the sliding glass door wide open.

The men spun to face her.

"You jerk."

Toby dropped his cigar in the ashtray and slowly rose. "Amelia—"

"You used me."

Toby's jaw muscles bunched and his lips flatlined. "I didn't."

"How dare you make sport of my feelings? But then, you make sport of *your life*. I guess breaking my heart is no big deal." She held up a hand when he tried to speak. "I'm entertainment? A joke between you and your buddies?"

"It isn't like that."

"Did you or did you not make a bet to have sex with me?"

She saw the truth in the guilty flush on his face. She'd wanted him to deny it. Pain engulfed her like an avalanche. Cold. Hard. Fast. It pummeled her and left her dizzy.

"That was a long time ago." He strode toward her, reached for her.

She flinched out of reach. "Don't touch me."

"Sugar—"

"I'm not your sugar. I'm not your anything. All I am is another easy lay for NASCAR's poster boy."

"You're not easy. You're—"

"An idiot. An idiot who fell in love with the man I thought you were. Clearly I was deluded." Her eyes and throat burned. Terrified she'd break down and cry in front of him, she backed away. "And you're an even bigger idiot than I am, Toby Haynes. Because I loved you despite your enormous ego, your dangerous occupation and the fact that you're convinced every woman will leave you like your mother did."

She gulped a series of breaths and fought to regain her slipping control. "I would have stayed. No matter what."

He just stared. Silently. The man who talked all the time—even through sex—remained mute.

"You lose, Toby. We both do." A sob forced its way up her throat. She turned on her unsteady legs, snatched up her purse and overnight bag and ran from the suite like a coward.

This was one battle she wasn't strong enough to fight.

"That wasn't pretty," Vincent said.

"Shut up," Toby growled and tried to make sense of the sucking void opening inside him.

He ought to go after Amelia. But he didn't know what to say. He'd done the crime. He had no defense. Even if wanting her had stopped being about the bet a long time ago.

"I'm sorry she overheard. I thought she'd left with the rest of them."

Unable to untangle his thoughts or his tongue, Toby turned and looked at his friend.

Vincent's head snapped back as if Toby had punched him. "Shit. You fell for her."

"Of course not," Toby denied automatically. But he wasn't sure if the words were true. He wasn't sure of anything except that he'd hurt Amelia, and the pain in her eyes shredded him.

She'd said she loved him.

Past tense.

"You fell for her. And I screwed it up. Candace is going to kill me. She's been trying to get you guys together forever."

Vincent raked a hand down the unmarred side of his face, and for once Toby couldn't muster the guilt he felt every time he saw the scars caused by a freak accident behind his pit wall.

He couldn't feel anything. Numbness invaded him.

He'd made Amelia cry.

During the months he'd hounded her at the hospital he'd seen her lose patients and deal with hell on earth, which is

how he'd come to view the burn ward. But he'd never seen
Amelia cry. Until now.

He'd hurt her. And he had to fix it.

But he didn't know how.

Or why it mattered so much.

Thank God she'd caught them.

Amelia raced out of the hotel and right up to the limo as
the porter loaded the last of the shower gifts into the trunk.
She handed him her bag and joined Candace by the door.

Candace turned. "Did I forget something?"

"Get me out of here."

"What about your plans to spend the night? And why
are you crying?"

Amelia put a hand to her cheeks. Wet. She hadn't even
noticed the tears. "In the car. Please. Let's go. Hurry."

"Sure. Okay." Candace glanced back toward the entrance
and then followed Amelia into the plush interior. "Start
talking."

Amelia took a fortifying breath. "Toby slept with me on
a bet."

"Oh, please. He's crazy about you. And the way he looked
at you when he opened his dice…" She fanned her face. "I
almost had an orgasm for you."

"I heard him, Candace. I heard Vincent say it and
Toby didn't deny it." She accepted a tissue from Candace
and blotted her face. "I fell for him and all he wanted
was to score."

The teasing smile faded from Candace's face. "I'll
skewer his nuts and Vincent's, too, if he was in on this."

At the moment, her petite blond friend looked capable
of doing exactly that.

"Candace, I can't go back to Hôtel Reynard. I can't

look Toby in the eye and know I meant nothing to him. I just…I can't. I need time."

"Then you're really in love with him?"

Amelia's throat clogged, preventing speech. She nodded.

"Amelia, I've never seen you as happy as you've been this past week. Not even with Neal. Don't you want to give Toby a chance to explain?"

"I did. Please—help me find another place to stay or I'm going to have to go home."

"The man is an idiot. He doesn't deserve you."

As much as Toby had hurt her, Amelia's hackles rose at the insult. "He's not the idiot. I am. We agreed on a temporary affair. Monaco only. I'm the one who had a change of heart. You can't blame him for not loving me."

"Of course I can." Candace pulled out her cell phone. "I think I know of a place where you can stay. One he'd never think to search—assuming he has a conscience and decides to find you and apologize. If he does, you'd better make him grovel."

But Amelia knew that wasn't going to happen. She'd been nothing more than a game to Toby.

Game over.

The woman was like a ghost, Toby decided at the brunch he and Amelia were supposedly cohosting. One minute she was there and then, when he tried to reach her, she vanished.

On Friday she'd dodged him at the engagement party held on the world's largest privately owned yacht, which happened to be moored in Monaco's harbor. The yacht owners were friends of the Reynards and had expressed interest in sponsoring a race team. Toby hadn't managed to give a damn. He'd been too busy thinking a person could only run so far on a boat and yet Amelia had escaped him.

Saturday she'd avoided him at the cathedral when the wedding party had met with the officiant for an explanation about the differences between American and French ceremonies. The people of Monaco followed French law and that required a civil service. But Candace and Vincent wanted a religious blessing, too. That meant getting married twice. Toby couldn't imagine marrying once let alone repeating the mistake.

Talk about double jeopardy.

For an hour he'd sat two yards across the aisle from Amelia. He might as well have been on the other side of the Atlantic. She wouldn't look at him or speak to him.

When he'd tried to corner her after the preacher wrapped up his long-winded spiel, the bridesmaids had closed ranks and whisked Amelia away on some bridal errand.

The standbys he used with other women weren't working. He'd tried sending flowers, chocolate and jewelry, but each gift had been returned to his suite. He didn't know what else to do. He'd never had to work hard with women. Before Amelia, that is.

The schedule he'd copied from Candace's calendar weeks ago must have been scrapped, because Amelia hadn't been anywhere she was supposed to be.

The past two days, he'd taken to loitering in the lobby near the penthouse elevator, hoping to catch her when she stepped out, but this morning the concierge had informed him Amelia had moved out of the hotel. He couldn't say where she'd gone, and none of the bridal party or Vincent would talk.

Toby's only option was to ambush her at the brunch today, but so far his plans had been thwarted. He hadn't been able to get close enough to apologize. Amelia had managed to keep herself on the opposite side of the wide flagstone terrace earlier. And then, when they'd come inside to eat, she'd seated herself twelve feet away at the far end of the long dining room table.

He stared at her, willing her to look up, and ground his teeth in frustration. He could work his way through a pack of cars at almost two hundred miles an hour, but he couldn't get through two dozen guests.

But they were in a private villa, and he'd be damned if he'd let her escape again without talking to her.

Halfway through the meal, one of the servers stepped to Amelia's side and whispered something. Amelia nodded, rose and followed the woman out of the room. Toby saw his opening and headed after them. Out of the corner of his eye he saw Candace stand and Vincent pull her back down into her seat. He'd thank his buddy for that intervention later.

"Yes, that's fine. You can serve it with chocolate ganache and fresh raspberries instead of whipping cream," he heard Amelia say as he neared the kitchen, and then her heels clicked in his direction.

He ducked into an archway of the nearby study and then snagged her arm as she passed and reeled her into the room.

She squealed in surprise and then recognized him and jerked her arm free. "You scared me."

He shut the door. "I wouldn't have to sneak up on you if you'd quit avoiding me."

He missed her, dammit. Missed her sappy romantic notions. Missed her snappy set-downs when his ego got out of hand. Missed her touch. Her kisses. Her bony knees, for god's sake.

"I've been busy. What do you want? I have to get back."

He studied her pale face and the shadows beneath her hazel eyes that even heavier-than-usual makeup couldn't disguise. "I'm sorry."

Her chin lifted. "Sometimes sorry isn't enough."

"Dammit, Amelia—"

"What do you want from me, Toby?"

"I…don't know. But…not *this*."

She folded her arms across the top of a sleeveless lavender lace dress that outlined every single one of her delicate curves to mouthwatering perfection. "*This* is of your own making."

He didn't want to fight with her. He wanted her back in his bed wearing a sheen of sweat, a satisfied smile and nothing else.

But that wasn't what she wanted to hear right now.

"I won the bet when we slept together the first time."

"That makes me feel *so* much better." Her sarcasm cut deep.

"I won and I didn't tell anybody because I—" He scrubbed the back of his neck. "Because I didn't want them to know."

She studied him in silence. Waiting? For what? He didn't know. He inhaled, exhaled, searched in vain for the answer. "You were giving drivers frostbite left and right. Vincent was facing a setback. One of the grafts didn't take, and they'd just told him he might never regain use of his right hand. He was pretty torn up."

"I remember."

"I was trying to give him something to think about besides another round of debridement and more surgery. But one of the other guys overheard and news of the bet spread like stomach flu."

Her face softened. But he didn't see forgiveness. And that was what he wanted, he realized. He wanted her to forgive him. "I never intended to hurt you, Amelia."

"It was still a rotten thing to do."

"Yeah." He shoved a hand through his hair. "But we

would have ended up together sooner or later. This thing between us—"

"It's over, Toby."

He couldn't accept that. She reached for the doorknob, but he wasn't ready to let her go. He splayed his palm on the wooden panel, holding it closed.

"The neurologist I've been seeing over here has cleared me to drive." He'd found out this morning and he hadn't told anyone. Not Vincent or even his teammates, who had vested interests. But he'd wanted to tell Amelia.

"Congratulations," she replied in a flat tone.

"I'll be flying back home immediately after the wedding reception Saturday to try and make the race. I'd have to start in the back of the pack since I'll miss qualifying, but it'll be worth it to get behind the wheel again."

"Driving with jet lag would be stupid."

"You're the one who said jet lag kicks in later. It shouldn't hit me until after the race."

She looked ready to argue. Instead she bit her bottom lip and shrugged. "It's your life."

She tried to step around him.

He cupped her shoulders and felt the muscles bunch. "Amelia, I am sorry."

Her eyes, more green than gold at the moment, met his. The sadness in the depths hit him like a head-on collision. "So am I."

She ducked away and left him. And he didn't feel any better.

The most romantic wedding in the world was going to be absolute torture.

Amelia fidgeted with the silk wrap of her strapless dress, the flowers in her upswept hair and then her monochromatic bouquet. Multicolor bouquets were considered in poor taste in Monaco, so Candace had chosen all white flowers.

Madeline came up beside Amelia to study their reflections in the big gilt mirror, and the phrase "Misery loves company" sprang to mind.

"We're a pitiful pair, aren't we?" Madeline whispered.

They were dressed similarly but in different shades. Candace had been determined to squeeze color into the ceremony somewhere and she'd done so with the bridesmaids' gowns. Madeline's dress was the palest green, Amelia's a soft-blush pink.

Madeline shifted a long, dark curl. "What were we thinking?"

Amelia met her friend's gaze. Madeline's vacation affair with the prince had also blown up in her face. They'd commiserated last night over drinks after the rehearsal dinner. Amelia still felt a teensy bit hungover.

"We weren't thinking. That's the problem. And you were right—my taste in men sucks. I couldn't find true love with a map." Amelia glanced at Candace on the far side of the room with the photographer. Her friend's wedding gown—an exquisite creation of a hand-beaded bodice and a silk douppioni skirt that hid her pregnancy—made Amelia's heart sigh. "And Candace deserves better than two wet-blanket bridesmaids, so slap a smile on."

"I will if you will."

Both forced smiles at their reflections and then grimaced. Amelia shook her head. "Not very convincing."

Stacy glided up. Her gown was pale blue, her smile genuine and blindingly bright. "It's not over until you leave Monaco."

"It's over," Amelia and Madeline chorused simultaneously. Toby planned to leave Monaco immediately after the reception, which would end in—Amelia glanced at her watch—four hours tops. The difference was that she now trusted his judgment. If he said he was ready to drive, then he was. He wouldn't take unnecessary risks. But that didn't stop the apprehension from tensing her muscles. Just because they couldn't be a couple didn't mean she didn't want him to stay safe.

"You two shouldn't give up so easily. You still have a chance for your dreams to come true." Stacy's lover had proposed last night at the dinner after the civil ceremony, and the accountant's face glowed with as much happiness as the bride's.

Madeline's laugh held no humor. "And I thought Amelia was the romantic of the bunch."

Amelia shook her head. "Not me. As you pointed out, even though I didn't know it, my feet have always been firmly planted on the ground. And I plan to keep them there. The blinders are off. No more temporary men."

The music swelled outside the antechamber and someone tapped on the door. Candace snapped to attention. "That's our cue."

She gathered the folds of her gown and floated toward them in a cloud of rustling silk. "Before we go, I want to thank all of you for making this day—heck, this entire month—unforgettable."

"If you make me cry and ruin my makeup, I will never forgive you," Madeline said but blinked furiously.

Amelia laughed her first genuine laugh in a week. "Ditto. Let's go tie this knot before your groom realizes your bridesmaids intend to vacation at your villa in Monaco every year for the rest of their lives and changes his mind."

Candace grinned mischievously. "That's the beauty of the French system. We tied the knot with the civil ceremony last night. There's no stress of wondering if he'll change his mind and bolt today. It's too late. I've already hooked him."

She grabbed Amelia's and Madeline's hands. "Today is just for fun. So try to have some."

Not likely, Amelia thought as she followed Stacy and Madeline toward the nave. Stacy walked down the aisle first, followed by Madeline. Amelia took her place and looked up.

Mistake. Her gaze found Toby's. He wore a black tux, a stark white shirt and black tie. His golden hair gleamed in the candlelight, and he was so handsome he took her breath away.

Her heart pounded. Her knees locked. Her stomach knotted. This would be the only time she'd ever walk down the aisle toward this man, the man she loved.

"Go, sweetie," Candace's father prompted from behind her.

Amelia blinked, refocused on Vincent and headed toward the altar a few beats behind schedule.

Had someone leaded the soles of her designer sandals?

Vincent gazed beyond Amelia, his attention no doubt on his beautiful bride. The love in his eyes brought a lump to Amelia's throat. Would a man ever look at her that way?

Neal hadn't. No, the look in Neal's eyes had been more like…gratitude, she realized. He'd been thankful to have her, but he probably hadn't loved her. Why else would he have kept postponing their marriage?

And she hadn't loved him either. Not the way he truly deserved. Amelia missed a step at the discovery. She'd wanted to love Neal because he was perfect in every way—except for his terminal illness. Gentle. Reserved. Predictable. Despite that, she hadn't been able to make herself love him wholeheartedly or make herself desire him.

Desiring Toby had come all too easily, starting at that

first meeting. Loving him had sneaked up on her, and that unexpected blow had made it all the more powerful.

At the brunch he'd said he hadn't meant to hurt her, but that wasn't the same as loving her.

She reached the end of the aisle, took her place and lifted her eyes to find Toby's silvery-blue gaze focused with unwavering intent on her. She saw want and regret and frustration in his expression, but she didn't see love. And his love was the one thing she wanted more than anything else.

She blinked and turned away.

The service began. Amelia barely heard the words. And if a tear or two slipped down her cheek, she hoped everyone would attribute it to tears of happiness for her friend.

She wasn't going to sleep with another man unless he loved her. She deserved that, didn't she? And if that meant she either had to do without sex or had to buy herself a battery-operated boyfriend, then that's what she'd do.

From now on it was all or nothing. No more dead-end affairs. No more men who couldn't commit.

If she couldn't have the kind of love she saw shining on Candace's and Vincent's and Stacy's faces, then she'd rather be alone.

Alone. And empty.

Amelia followed the steward carrying her luggage off the yacht. The owners who'd hosted the engagement party had been kind enough to offer her refuge after she'd fled Hôtel Reynard.

The rest of the wedding party had already left Monaco. Vincent and Candace were on their honeymoon. Franco had taken Stacy to his French family estate. Even Madeline's prince had come through. He'd surprised them all with a proposal during the wedding reception yesterday and then he'd whisked Madeline off in the royal jet to his country in the South Pacific to meet his family.

Amelia was happy for her friends but a little saddened, too, that she hadn't found what they had.

A limo longer than any she'd ridden in during her stay in Monaco waited at the end of the jetty. This one would easily carry ten or more people. The driver climbed out and opened the rear door for her.

"Louis?" *Toby's Louis?* But Toby had flown out yesterday. Vincent had probably arranged for Toby's driver. He'd also arranged for Amelia's.

Coincidence. Get in the car, Amelia. It's time to go home.

"Good afternoon, Mademoiselle Lambert. I trust you enjoyed your stay in Monaco?"

"It is the most romantic country in the world," she dodged. There was no way to explain the range of emotions and personal discoveries she'd made here in the past month.

Louis smiled. "That it is."

"Could I have a minute?"

He nodded and then joined the steward to help him load her luggage in the trunk.

Amelia turned a full circle for one last look at the harbor, the Mediterranean and the jagged landscape. She'd teased Candace about coming back to visit every year, but Amelia wasn't sure she could handle the bittersweet memories. She'd have to if she wanted to stay in touch with her friends—and she did. Candace had said she and Amelia were almost family.

Louis returned to her side. "Mademoiselle?"

"I'm ready." She climbed inside the dim, cavernous interior and the door closed behind her. It took a second for her eyes to adjust. The first thing she saw was a bouquet of roses on the nearest seat. A dozen *red* roses.

A shuffle of sound drew her attention. She turned her head and saw Toby in the back. Her stomach tumbled to her toes. "You're supposed to be in Daytona."

"Next week will be soon enough to get back on the track." He wore a blue silk shirt the exact shade of his eyes, navy pants and sunglasses. Her own panicked face reflected back at her in the lenses. "Sit down, sugar."

She wasn't ready for a tête-à-tête with Toby, but the car started rolling before she could reach the door handle, and diving out…not a good plan. She scrambled for a seat, the farthest one from him, and buckled up.

Toby stayed where he was a good six feet away with his fingers laced in his lap. The pose looked casual until she noticed how tightly his fingers were knotted and searched his face.

"What's going on?"

"You were right," he said. "I use the bravado to keep people at a distance. That's because the last woman who saw the real Tobias Haynes didn't like him enough to stay. Plain ol' Toby, a serious kid who loved anything with an engine, wasn't good enough."

A kid? "Are you talking about your mother?"

"Yeah."

"Toby, she fled an abusive relationship. She did the right thing in getting out."

He hesitated and then said, "She should have taken me with her."

She couldn't imagine the heartache he must have felt. "Yes, she should have."

"The point is, I'm not always charming, witty or fun."

Where was he going with this? "This is news?"

He stiffened. "Hey—"

"Toby, *the point is,*" she repeated his words, "when you

cast off the playboy-jerk armor and quit trying to get into my pants you're a very likable guy."

"Yeah?" He sounded surprisingly unsure.

"Yes."

"You like it when I get in your pants."

She sighed. "Toby—"

"My father called me *To-buy-ass* instead of Tobias." Toby glanced out the window. His jaw looked rigid enough to snap. "He said I was a worthless piece of crap and once the Haynes charm and looks faded I'd have to buy my women like he did."

Amelia's heart squeezed at the pain he couldn't quite conceal beneath the clipped words, and anger stirred toward the man who'd hurt him. "I don't think I'd like your father much."

"Not many people did." He faced her again. "He kicked me out when I turned eighteen. I hitched a ride to Concord and begged until somebody let me push a broom in a race shop. I had a knack for engines, and that got a little attention. I worked my way up from there. It took years before I could convince somebody to let me get behind the wheel."

She'd read some of this online, but not the part about his father. Details of Toby's life before NASCAR had been impossible to find. She knew because she'd searched.

"Racing…what I've accomplished…it all proves my dad wrong."

"You should be proud. You worked hard and earned your success."

His jaw shifted. He sucked one deep breath and then another. "I'd give it up if you asked me to."

Shock rippled through her. "What? Why would you do that? Why would *I* do that?"

She hadn't even noticed the limo stopping, but Louis

opened the door, so it must have. Moments ago Amelia would have given anything to get out of this car. Now she wanted to stay and find out exactly what Toby was trying to say. "Toby—"

"Immigration is waiting." He came forward, climbed from the car and then offered her his hand.

"You can't drop a bomb like that and then walk away." And then she stopped and studied the unfamiliar surroundings. "This is not the Nice airport."

"No. It's a private strip. We're flying back on the HRI jet."

"But I have a ticket."

"It's been canceled." He hustled her into the small building and through the formalities.

Afterward, she looked up from tucking her passport back into her purse and found him holding a blue velvet box.

A jewelry box.

A *ring* box.

Her heart skidded to a halt and then pounded like a woodpecker on speed in her chest.

He'd removed his sunglasses, and for the first time today she could see his eyes. But she couldn't read them.

"For you. No matter what happens, this is yours to keep."

Don't get your hopes up. He's commitmentphobic.

Her hands shook so badly she could barely hold the box. She took a bracing breath and lifted the lid and saw a ring.

A key ring.

Disappointment weighted her shoulders.

What did you expect?

"What is this?"

"Keys to that little blue car you fell in love with. It should be waiting in your driveway when you get home."

Her mouth dropped open. "Toby, you shouldn't have. It's too much."

"You take care of everybody else. Somebody needs to spoil you."

"I—I don't know what to say."

"*Thanks* should do it. And maybe a kiss. Or two."

Did he expect her to resume the affair at home? "What do you want from me?"

He hooked his hand around her elbow and guided her toward the doors leading to the runway. "I've been giving some thought to that crazy idea of yours."

"What crazy idea?"

"The one about the dog, the kids and the white picket fence."

"There's nothing crazy about—" The glass doors slid open and the words died on her lips. Two parallel rows of white picket fencing created a four-foot-wide path across the asphalt. About thirty feet from the terminal the fencing took a right-angle turn behind a big metal storage box.

"Maybe it's not such a dumb idea after all," Toby said beside her.

Her feet moved numbly forward. This seemed a little *Wizard of Oz*-ish, like traveling the yellow brick road.

Toby pulled her to a stop before she could look around the corner. "Let me give 'em to you."

A mixture of emotions tumbled through her brain. Confusion. Hope. Caution. "What are you saying?"

His eyes warmed and her breath caught. She blinked, convinced that she was mistaken in what she thought she saw.

Toby cupped her cheek. "I'm saying that standing in that church I realized I wanted to hear you saying those words, making those promises to me. And I wanted to make them to you. I want forever with you, Amelia. The kids, the dog, the porch swing. The whole deal."

A tremor started in the pit of her stomach and worked

its way outward. Her lips quivered. Her throat closed up and her eyes burned. She closed her gaping mouth, opened it again, but no sound emerged.

Toby thumbed a tear from her cheek, one she hadn't even noticed escaping. His lips turned up in a clearly forced smile. "But not the cat. The cat's a deal breaker."

A laugh bubbled from her chest. She could tell the joke was a nervous one and part of the carefree facade he wore like protective armor. "Oh, Toby…"

He pressed a finger to her lips. "HRI is strong enough to survive whether or not I ever climb back in the car. I have to finish this season because I'm contracted to my sponsors, but after that I'll give up driving if you want me to. What matters is having you by my side."

He cupped her shoulders and turned her around. The picket fence path led to the stairs of a small white jet. *Marry me, Amelia* had been written in huge red script down the side of the plane. She could only gape. Happiness swelled within her. She tried to contain it. He hadn't said the most important words yet, and she refused to settle for less.

And yet he'd offered to give up driving for her. That had to mean something, didn't it?

"It'll take about a mile of this white stuff to circle my property. Lucky for you, I can afford it."

She faced him. He held another ring box, this one open to display a gorgeous heart-shaped diamond on a wide gold band. Her lungs failed. She pressed her fingers over her mouth.

"You're into the hearts and flowers and stuff, so…" He shrugged. "If you don't like it, we can get something else."

He tipped up her chin, forcing her to meet his gaze. The love she saw in his eyes, on his face, made her dizzy with joy, and no matter how many times she blinked, it didn't go away. She wheezed in a breath.

"I always swore I'd never let a woman get close enough to hurt me. I never guessed that letting the right one—*you*—go would hurt more. I know I acted like an ass. But if it's not too late, please give me a chance to earn your love again.

"I didn't tell the guys about our night together because I didn't want to share. It was special. At the time I didn't realize how special. And then you dumped me with that cold note and I knew I had to get you back. You started out as the one who got away. A challenge I had to win. But then you stole my heart and became the one I can't forget."

He dropped to one knee. "I love you, Amelia. Marry me. Please."

"You love driving."

"I love you more." He stated it simply and without hesitation.

She reached out a tentative hand and stroked his hair, his cheek. "I would never ask you to give up something that makes you so happy."

"Then don't make me give up you."

Those perfect words sent a shiver of delight through her. "It's not too late, Toby. I couldn't stop loving you that easily. Even though I did try.

"You've shown me time and time again you're not the daredevil adrenaline junkie I thought you were. I trust you to not take foolish risks. And I don't want you to give up driving until you're ready to quit.

"Yes. Yes, Toby Haynes, I'll marry you."

She bent and gently pressed her lips to his. He rose swiftly, crushing her into his arms, sweeping her off her feet and deepening the kiss.

She wound her arms around his neck and smiled against

his mouth. If anyone had told her a year ago that her knight in shining armor would ride in a race car instead of on a white stallion, she'd have told them to have their heads examined.

But this time she was more than happy to be wrong.

* * * * *

MILLS & BOON
Desire 2-in-1
On sale 18th July 2008

In Bed with the Devil *by Susan Mallery*

She'd been the shy, mousy girl he'd never looked at twice.
Now she was the only woman he wanted in his bed.

High-Society Mistress *by Katherine Garbera*

He will stop at nothing to take over his business rival's
company…including employing his enemy's daughter and
making her his mistress.

❧

A Convenient Proposition *by Cindy Gerard*

She was pregnant and alone. Then Mac McDonald demanded she
accept his marriage proposal. But would their in-name-only
marriage ever be real?

A Splendid Obsession *by Cathleen Galitz*

Novelist Dave Evans is stuck in his latest book until redheaded
tornado Kayanne Aldarmann provides him with a spark
of inspiration!

❧

Playboy's Ruthless Payback *by Laura Wright*

His plan for revenge meant seducing his rival's innocent daughter.
But *is* she the innocent pawn he thinks her?

Like Lightning *by Charlene Sands*

Trey Walker came from a long line of men who broke women's
hearts – and he was determined not to break sweet Maddie Brooks'.
But she was impossible to ignore.

Celebrate 100 years of pure reading pleasure with Mills & Boon®

To mark our centenary, each month we're publishing a special 100th Birthday Edition. These celebratory editions are packed with extra features and include a FREE bonus story.

Plus, you have the chance to enter a fabulous monthly prize draw. See 100th Birthday Edition books for details.

Now that's worth celebrating!

July 2008

**The Man Who Had Everything
by Christine Rimmer**
Includes FREE bonus story *Marrying Molly*

August 2008

Their Miracle Baby by Caroline Anderson
Includes FREE bonus story *Making Memories*

September 2008

Crazy About Her Spanish Boss by Rebecca Winters
Includes FREE bonus story
Rafael's Convenient Proposal

Look for Mills & Boon® 100th Birthday Editions at your favourite bookseller or visit
www.millsandboon.co.uk

2 FREE

BOOKS AND A SURPRISE GIFT!

We would like to take this opportunity to thank you for reading this Mills & Boon® book by offering you the chance to take TWO more specially selected titles from the Desire™ series absolutely FREE! We're also making this offer to introduce you to the benefits of the Mills & Boon® Reader Service™—

- ★ FREE home delivery
- ★ FREE gifts and competitions
- ★ FREE monthly Newsletter
- ★ Exclusive Reader Service offers
- ★ Books available before they're in the shops

Accepting these FREE books and gift places you under no obligation to buy, you may cancel at any time, even after receiving your free shipment. Simply complete your details below and return the entire page to the address below. You don't even need a stamp!

YES! Please send me 2 free Desire volumes and a surprise gift. I understand that unless you hear from me, I will receive 3 superb new titles every month for just £4.99 each, postage and packing free. I am under no obligation to purchase any books and may cancel my subscription at any time. The free books and gift will be mine to keep in any case.

D8ZED

Ms/Mrs/Miss/Mr ....Initials ....

BLOCK CAPITALS PLEASE

Surname ....

Address ....

....

....Postcode...............................

Send this whole page to:
UK: FREEPOST CN81, Croydon, CR9 3WZ